LEE COUNTY LIBRARY
107 HAWKINS AVE.
SANFORD, N. C. 27330

THE BLIND BEND

By the same author
CRUEL IN THE SHADOW

*To my father
in his Seventieth Year*

THE CHRONICLES OF INVERNEVIS

THE BLIND BEND

Lorn Macintyre

ST. MARTIN'S PRESS
NEW YORK

Copyright © 1981 by Lorn Macintyre
For information, write: St. Martin's Press,
175 Fifth Avenue, New York, N.Y. 10010
Manufactured in the United States of America

Library of Congress Cataloging in Publication Data

Macintyre, Lorn Macinnes.
  Blind bend.

  I. Title.
PR6063.A2422B5   1982   823'.914   81-14604
ISBN 0-312-08388-2   AACR2

THE BLIND BEND

BOOK ONE

CHAPTER 1

As the gig descended the steep hill that August evening in 1904 the 'Karelia Suite' by the Finn Sibelius, which the young woman had heard on honeymoon in Austria, was beginning again in her head, a haunting horn like the owl calling in that fading wood yonder, a humming of strings like the late midges swarming beyond her swaying veil. It was the music of menace as well as magic. She had heard it in the liner's propellers churning across the channel, in the train wheels hurrying her across bleak moors. But with the Highland landscape widening dramatically, the harmony with all things northern was swelling her breasts against whalebone, caressed strings speeding up into a climax. As darkening loch and twin-peaked mountain suddenly came into view from the airborne boat of the gig, the sun's burnished circle broke up and trumpets blared, ravishing. Her spine sagged against padded wood. Only music could do that for her, she now knew.

It looked as if there were four, not three standing stones on the summit to the right, above the Home Farm. But the additional shape turned suddenly, becoming a woman semaphoring with frantic arms against the spectacular backdrop of the sunset. Below, across the river, the Macdonald tartan bag in the piper's oxter was punched into sound, the ivory-lipped drones twisted into harmony. Simultaneously the nursed flame was thrust into brushwood piled in a ten foot wigwam. Men, women and children began to converge from the trees.

In the gig the young woman's breathing was making her veil move, her white glove compressing her husband's hand as the two blinkered horses broke into a high-stepping trot on the dusty road above the river, the black drum of the coachman's hat swaying, brass harness jingling. Hooves and wheels were now accompanying the joyful cadence in her head as it turned to follow the whitewashed mansion across the river, under the mountain. Some of the tall clustered chimneys were spurting smoke. She closed her eyes and was already sinking into a hot bath.

Her husband Niall, seventeenth laird of Invernevis, was looking the other way, up to the standing stones, where white-vested Druids had sacrificed virgins in time past. A woman was plunging down through the deep heather, but there was no sign of a pursuer. Damn it: despite his strict orders, the tinkers were probably camping up on the moor, though their drunken carelessness had fired it several summers before, destroying grouse prospects. It did not do to stay away too long, even for honeymoon.

'Look!'

His wife's white glove was rising to point out the climbing flames ahead, where the road veered for Wade's hump-backed bridge. When he heard the pipes skirling into 'The Macdonalds' Welcome to Invernevis' he groaned. Amplified by the mountain, the sound killed 'Karelia', but she was glad for her husband, who had grumbled that orchestras playing contemporary music held no charm for him. During the Finn's Suite in Vienna he had kept shifting his game leg, legacy from the recent South African war. Mahler he could not stomach. Now he was having a private serenade from the instrument of his ancestors, implement of war as well as peace. Hers too, but too harsh, confined by mountains.

Across the bridge the road forked for mansion and south. There, where lucid water moved sluggishly in the long hot spell, salmon fins showing, the locals had lashed saplings to lichened stone to erect an arch. The flowers and greenery from croft plot and big house walled garden, bound and twined in the sunset sky, symbolised the interdependence of mansion and hamlet, with the river beneath the three arches no division.

Since the wedding had taken place in Sutherland, they had gathered at Wade's Bridge to welcome home the honeymooners. The bone-dry branches for the bonfire had been gathered in armfuls inside the flaking white pillars and rusting horizontal gate which marked the beginning of the big house policies and privacy. Father Macdonald, the local priest and also a trustee of the estate, was in charge of the celebrations, and it was he who had stationed the woman up at the standing stones to watch for the gig coming from the evening train. On the evening the laird and his lady returned from their continental honeymoon, the villagers were on the wrong side of the river, with the priest's blessing, with whisky flowing and the pipes sounding, dead wood from the avenue crackling up into the discoloured sky as the sign of the cross brought the gig to an abrupt halt on humped stone. The tenants stood about, awkward in their sabbath clothes, black for the men, their boots sombre convex mirrors, the streak of silver across waistcoats, brass studs holding closed the cutting alien collars. The women wore nondescript long dresses, some bought unseen from Glasgow, others from the big house wardrobes, fought over at jumble sales. At some shoulders, the tattered wheels of parasols. Children in cut-down clothing were stood on the parapets, but always within reach.

The priest said a short prayer, beseeching health, prosperity and procreation for the two persons sitting above him, made one by God now, the crowd risking his anger by raising their heads and peering through their fingers during the unintelligible Latin, to see the lady's golden curls become part of the sunset. A little smudged-faced girl in a frilled frock with a bow and laced boots sucked her thumb and stared up apprehensively, her other hand clutching her mother's. Above, in the black lacquered gig with gold embellishment, her uncle's balding head was bent in prayer, though the lady had lifted her veil and was smiling. The child judged it safe to smile back.

After 'Amen', Father Macdonald handed up a black casket like a child's coffin in which a three foot high sterling silver epergne in the form of stag antlers was embedded in satin, with an engraved plate on the fluted throat:

FROM LOYAL TENANTS TO MAJOR AND MRS.
MACDONALD OF INVERNEVIS ON THE OCCASION
OF THEIR HOMECOMING AFTER THEIR MARRIAGE.
AUGUST 1904.

The laird knew the contributions that would have had to be levied from every croft to pay for such splendid silver, so when he gave brief thanks on behalf of both his voice was blurred with emotion. The expectant faces circling the gig beamed, not because of his obvious pleasure, which they took for granted, but because of the beauty the veil could not hide. But having smiled as her husband spoke, she had nothing to add except a 'thank you so much', which was lost by the pipes stirring again, more brushwood fed to the flames, the horses slapped forward, the tenants cheering, holding up the bumpers from the stone jars, glasses clashing in *'Slainte!'* as the horses hauled between the white pillars.

Mary Rose, née Mackay, of Kiltarlan, Sutherland, rode up the avenue of Invernevis House to become mistress of that mansion, the trunks containing her trousseau and plastered with the grand hotels of a two month honeymoon following on a second discreet gig. The epergne balanced on his lap, white straw hat with the black band over his shattered kneecap, her moustached husband looked once again at his bride as the big wheels running in ruts took them into silence and shade. Even after so much sun, Mary Rose's skin still had that pallor of fragility that had confined her to bed so often since childhood, until that dreaded word tuberculosis began to be used, but sparingly. But perhaps it was the shadow cast by the big wheel of the flower-encrusted straw hat which she wore towards the back of her head, the shapely brow behind the white veil bolstered by the golden curls which had first fired his love when he met her under the electric lighting of an Edinburgh hotel two years before. Fears for her health faded with the realisation that she was more beautiful than ever, with the last of the sun filtering through the trees ending its fire in her hair. His hand reached and their fingers touched. She smiled, and the springs beneath rocked him into recollection, the returned pigeons inflating their invisible throats. She reminded him of his sister Laura, dead three years, the only sunbeam in that gloomy mansion. He had tried to retrieve his happiness by marrying Mary Rose, and yet, as he rode up the avenue with his bride, he wondered if it was not in some way the betrayal of a dead girl who had had no one else. For the feelings, however strong, which he had sitting beside Mary Rose were not the same as when he had walked that way with his sister. It had something to do with purity and harmony, like the glimpse of the white patch at a pigeon's throat throbbing in song among burnished immobile leaves above. He found himself glancing back, as if someone was following, darting among the trees, but it was only wisping smoke from the welcome bonfire. No, it was wrong to compare sister and spouse. He loved both equally, and Mary Rose was living. The tree on which he had cut his own and his sister's initials on the day he had left for war reeled back and was gone.

The gig was approaching the blind bend, that place of sudden gloom and chill where the trees gave way to tightly packed rhododendrons of overpowering funereal odours, the pipes' welcome fading behind. As the gig lurched on the bend Mary Rose began to shake violently and fell against her husband, sending the black casket sliding from his knee, the catches springing, the epergne tumbling out, its gilt horns shedding rhododendron blossom before it was dented on stone. His straw hat was crushed under the big wheel.

Roddy the coachman pulled the horses to a halt and climbed down to retrieve the trophy which had rolled into the dark tunnel of the rhododendrons. But with her pallid face against his white linen sleeve producing no response to his entreaties, and her hand like ice, Invernevis shouted down to the coachman to 'leave the damn thing!' and get them up to the house as quickly as possible.

It meant using the whip on horses lulled by the halt at Wade's Bridge. With a stretched bull's penis snaking to their gleaming flanks, they lifted their hooves high, hurrying the four wheeled vehicle and its three occupants, one dead to the summer evening, past the walled garden where crab apples hung like small gnarled fists in the gloaming, and the bees swarmed mournfully back to their conical houses. The big back wheels sprayed gravel as they locked to halt outside the three storied whitewashed mansion of bulging bay windows, ivy encrusting the sandstone porch, screening the Invernevis coat of arms with its Gaelic boast: *Mairidh Sinn, We Shall Endure*.

The servants had been lined up on either side of the porch to welcome home the laird and his new lady. Taking as her signal the sound of the pipes from Wade's Bridge, stout Mrs Livingstone, cook and housekeeper had shuffled along the line, inspecting, her swollen ankles agonising on the treacherous gravel. Mr Symmers, the bald old butler with the shiny swallow tails and drink problem no peppermint could suppress, was ordered to straighten his tie, and did so meekly, with shaking fingers. Frank the footman, fair moustached and handsome in a predatory way in his tight-fitting uniform, with green piping down the trouser leg, smiled insolently at Mrs Livingstone because he knew she could find no fault with his appearance. But she told him to stand straight. Small, stocky and silent, Duncan the ghillie was wearing the only suit he possessed, of tweed plus-fours which no iron could press, but the cook smiled at an old and trusted friend. Ranald the gardener had exchanged his customary green for black and looked uncomfortable, but he too was passed without comment because of the bunch of roses which he had so carefully nurtured through a feverish summer for the homecoming bride and which he bore, awkwardly, in his arms.

The house-maids and table-maids had to be spoken to sharply, to stop their giggles and make them straighten the curves of lace above their brows. Then came Maggie, Duncan the ghillie's daughter and Mrs Livingstone's promising assistant in the kitchen; but no favouritism could be shown on this occasion, so Maggie was told to close the top button of her black dress, despite the heat.

But the speed with which the gig lurched into view broke up the line. Waving her hands as though the servants were hens, Mrs Livingstone shooed them through to the back of the house, but detained Maggie, her father and the gardener, whose flowers now lay forgotten on the iron seat which had been Laura's favourite.

In the strong but gentle arms of ghillie and gardener, the new lady of Invernevis was carried into the gloomy hall, where a hollowed-out tree from the estate waited to receive walking sticks, and where, high on the walls, a frieze of stags' heads was arranged, casting their fankled shadows on the floor, the brass plates screwed to their throats too high to tell that they were the trophies of the laird's late father.

Then up the wide staircase, dominated by a multi-coloured window of stained glass bonded with lead, depicting a life-sized Invernevis chieftain *circa* eighteen hundred in full regalia, the right hand upraising a basket-hilt sword, left hand holding a studded circular shield. Through the sombre picture-gallery, ancestors in oils of both sexes, all haughty, hemmed in by gilt, staring down from dramatic black backgrounds, hands at sword hilts or slender throats. Leading the way, Invernevis's shoulder knocked a frame, leaving it swinging behind.

The new lady of Invernevis was carried along to her bedroom which was connected to the laird's and which had been vacated by the laird's mother. Mary Rose lay on the canopied bed while Mrs Livingstone fussed around, arranging pillows and sending Maggie in search of smelling salts. Invernevis had gone back down to send Duncan the ghillie for Doctor MacNiven, despite Mary Rose's weak protests. She had tried to tell her husband what she had seen as the gig approached the blind bend. Something blocking the way; something too horrible and incomprehensible for words. It was like a giant black jellyfish, going in and out, as if it was breathing. No, more red than black. But before she could shout out the gig's wheels were sinking into it, and then came the terrible coldness, the feeling that her being was leaking away. Her husband would say that it had been tiredness after the train journey and the euphoria of the welcome home; that it had been a trick of the light breaking through the tightly packed rhododendrons; perhaps the shadows of the horses' black bellies. But she would swear to what she had seen. On her previous visits to Invernevis she had walked that bend with him, without seeing anything though there had been a sudden chill.

He was kind and considerate, and had had enough worry already. On honeymoon, while they relaxed in deck-chairs, watching the bathing boxes of royalty being hauled into the blue Mediterranean, he had tried to explain the history of his family, his face shaded by the wide-brimmed straw hat, but he had had difficulty in finding words. He was trying to give a diagnosis of his father's illness (which she had understood had been swamp fever) when the organ grinder on the promenade behind had begun to supply music for his grinning monkey to dance to, much to the delight of the crowd, and in particular the sailor-suited children. He had tried again to explain, in bed, in the ambivalent darkness, but she had put her hand over the silhouette of his moustache. She had lain back in the stifling Mediterranean night, listening to the sweep of the sea, the groan of a late lift, hoping it would be over soon as he shadowed her, the shattered kneecap of his left leg hurting her thigh, and brandy fumes mingled with cigar smoke. She had done her duty. There was bound to be a lot of children, if her body would allow, because he was a virile man and a Catholic, the only objection her mother had had to the marriage, insisting that her daughter was to have the first choice of religion for the issue. There had been a bitter row, and though she had not taken sides, she had been glad to see her mother's authority challenged.

But her growing doubts must not be allowed to find words because her mother had bred her to believe that women were for the service of men. Mary Rose had a voiceless admiration for Mrs Pankhurst and the others who had chained themselves to London railings in order to get votes and other equal rights. But what Mary Rose wanted to be liberated from was something these suffragettes did not oppose: domination by male limbs, the brutality of the act. Her interests lay in other things, the music of Sibelius, the paintings of Gauguin she had seen in Paris. Such tastes could not be satisfied at Invernevis, yet she had been willing to forego them for the sake of her husband. What had happened on the blind bend was a warning that time and tradition would oppose her. Or was it a warning about the future?

While Mary Rose was reviewing a marriage that was barely two months old, her husband was downstairs in the library, having scribbled the note to Doctor MacNiven and dispatched Duncan the ghillie by horse to deliver it. Invernevis was extremely worried by her fainting fit on the blind bend. He might have put it down to the long journey and the excitement affecting her weak constitution, but then he remembered that his dead sister Laura had reported what she had called 'funny feelings' on that bend.

Memory was prompted to release hazy childhood recollections of someone saying that there was something strange about that part of the avenue, though he had never experienced it himself. It couldn't have been his father, because he was sceptical about such things, scorning the idea of the dead returning. Nor his aunt Carlotta, because her Catholic hereafter was firmly divided between heaven and hell, with no prospect of escaping the eternal flames by returning to earth. Mama? It might have been Mama, because her mind had been befuddled by superstition. Might it have been Mrs Livingstone? But she had been a shy, silent cook in Invernevis's boyhood, though since then the tinkers had turned her mind. Or perhaps it had been said by any of them, Carlotta and Mama in particular, to stop a boy going down the avenue, and thence to the village, to mix with those sly indolent villagers his father had consorted with, drinking and playing quoits?

When he handed the ghillie the note to take to the doctor, Invernevis had wasted precious minutes by detaining him to ask, as casually as he could, if he had heard 'any stories' about the blind bend. The ghillie's look had forced further explanation, Invernevis using his hands more than words in his embarrassment.

'You know what I mean. Queer feelings. *Seen* anything strange?'

But the ghillie shook his head. His world was the reality of a fin showing, not a ripple caused by stone. As far as he was concerned, the blind bend was cold because of the tightly packed rhododendrons keeping out the sun.

'Maybe you should get Ranald to cut them back, sir.'

But Invernevis shook his head dismissively.

'Tiredness, sir, that's all it is. The Mistress will be all right after a rest. After all, sir, you've been round the world.'

Invernevis smiled at this exaggeration from a man who had never left the boundaries of the estate. He was fond of the ghillie. He was a loyal servant who had helped Mama to lift and wash his father when he was suppurating through syphilis; and Duncan had given his blessing for his son to go out to South Africa as Invernevis's orderly, only to lose him at the battle of Magersfontein, a loss never mentioned except with pride.

Yes, Duncan was probably right. Invernevis was making too much out of Mary Rose's turn on the blind bend because he himself was tired after the long journey home, the leg that the Boer bullet under Magersfontein Hill had left straight for life giving him a good deal of pain. His wife was tired too after the hot sun of the continent. Hadn't his mother-in-law and brother-in-law Jamie warned him that she wasn't strong?

It suddenly occurred to him that she might be pregnant, which caused him to pace the library excitedly, a male child taken for granted. That would be one up on Alexander, who only had a daughter. It meant too that the insult of only being the life-renter of the estate by the terms of his father's will would be erased, because his son would succeed in full. That would break the power of the trustees, in particular Father Macdonald. Better not to tempt fate, though. He didn't know much about women, but began to fear that it was far too early. Doctor MacNiven was the best judge, however, and so while he waited, he smoked and paced.

Duncan the ghillie, coming clattering down the avenue on a horse, made the celebrating crowd part, and though the priest had his hand raised to the bridle, the ghillie had no time to stop to announce something that the priest could not help with. The subdued crowd deserted the dying fires and empty stone jars as the ghillie galloped for the village, finding Doctor MacNiven at home in his surgery. He wouldn't join in such festivities in case he was called out, though he had a decent toddy every night. Despite the apparent urgency of the laird's scrawl, he would go on his own gig, at his own pace, because a flogged horse would affect his next call. Death, being democratic, drew no distinction between croft and mansion.

'All right, you can put your shirt on,' he advised the small, fair moustached man in the twine-lashed trousers lying on the leather couch in the corner. At his big desk the doctor crossed his legs and frowned as his steel nib scraped. The note he had just received from the big house had been set aside.

The patient swung his ploughman's boots down and began to button up.

'I knew I shouldn't have bothered you,' he said, hybrid accent slurred by whisky. 'It was only a turn, in the Arms. Too much scything, to get the corn cut in case the weather broke.'

The thread of the doctor's chair squeaked. 'Scything be damned,' he said angrily, scanning his patient over his small gold spectacles. 'Too much drink. I don't like the sound of that heart of yours. You're killing yourself, man, and you're not yet thirty. Think of Kate and the child.'

Alexander shrugged and stood up. 'There's nothing wrong with my heart. You're just saying that to frighten me off my dram. The same tactics as my brother uses. Here.' He put two fingers into his waistcoat pocket and produced a sovereign, slapping it on the edge of the desk.

The doctor pushed it away. 'If you're not going to accept the diagnosis, I'm not taking a fee. But remember: I did warn you.' He picked up the note. 'Now I've got to go up to the big house. Your sister-in-law's taken a turn. Do you want a lift home?'

'No. I've got somebody to see in the Arms,' Alexander said, leaving the sovereign. He stopped at the door. 'And don't you dare say anything to *anyone* about me having a weak heart, or I'll have you up for professional misconduct.'

The doctor sighed and crushed the note in his fist. 'I was just writing to a specialist in Glasgow, asking if he would have a look at your heart, but there's no point, when you're taking this attitude. See yourself out.'

At the big house Doctor MacNiven climbed the stairs to examine his new patient, pacing the pulse with a large gold watch, a present from the old laird, for half a century of the diagnosis of the ailments on both sides of the river. The doctor went down to the library, announcing that it was only exhaustion through travel and the excitement of the reception. He prescribed several days in bed, then diagnosed the look of disappointment on Invernevis's face with the remark: 'Not yet,' accompanied by a faint smile as he remembered how the laird's father had hated the confirmation of a swelling female.

'I wasn't thinking about that,' Invernevis denied. 'I don't think she's strong.'

The doctor was snapping shut his bag on the library desk,

and did not raise his eyes. 'She'll be fine. There's more sunlight here than in Sutherland. A very beautiful young woman. Not unlike your sister Laura in looks.' He then indicated that he would sit for several minutes, but he wouldn't take a dram, and he didn't want to hear about the honeymoon sights because an old woman was waiting for him in the village.

'It's your mother I'm worried about,' he said, when he had scooped up his shiny swallow tails to sit down. 'Mrs Livingstone sent for me a couple of times when you were away because she went back on the bottle and was getting out of hand, saying that people were climbing up the ivy to look in the window. Black people.' He did not smile. 'I know nursing your father was a strain on her, but he's been dead five years.' He sighed. 'I just don't know how she gets her supplies. Your aunt used to suspect Roddy, but I've had a talk with him, and I know he's telling the truth. If she keeps on like this, she's not only going to upset your good lady; she's going to kill herself. Don't forget the stroke she had a couple of years ago. The next one will finish her. The strange thing is: she stopped for quite a long time after your sister died, and your aunt went away.'

'I'll have to do something about it,' Invernevis said grimly, angry that his mother should have ruined their homecoming. He knew what the doctor was trying to say — that she had begun to drink again in his absence abroad, out of spite, because he had introduced a young mistress to Invernevis. Well, one thing was certain; Mama wasn't going to be allowed to interfere as Carlotta had done. Mary Rose was the mistress now, and the house would be arranged and run to her liking.

'Sending her away to a home isn't the answer,' Doctor MacNiven warned, easily reading his mind. 'Remember how much you were against that for Miss Laura. This is your mother's home. She had a hard time with your father, and she needs love and attention.'

'Can't you give her something?' Invernevis asked coldly, conscious of the criticism. His father hadn't been all that fond of Doctor MacNiven, who could take liberties because he was the cleverest man in the district.

Doctor MacNiven shook his head and put his hands on his knees, preparing to raise his bulk, his long sloping head gleaming in the last of the evening light.

'The cure for an alcoholic can't come from outside. It *must* come from here.' He tapped his heart. 'A person must really want to give it up and be determined to make the effort before anyone else can help. But you can make a start by getting her to leave her bed in the morning. Get her downstairs, with your wife. Make her feel wanted, part of the family. I'm sure she and your wife will get on well because your mother's a very warm-hearted person, though she's had more than her share of sorrow.'

Invernevis nodded curtly and followed him out, watching the springs tilt as the doctor climbed on to the gig, clapping on his tall black hat and plucking the whip from its socket.

'Now don't worry. Your good lady will be up and about in a couple of days!' he shouted, the whip flicking, the gig lurching forward.

Invernevis stood watching the black hat bobbing round the blind bend before going upstairs to see Mary Rose, taking the steps slowly and thoughtfully because he was irritated by what the doctor had implied about Mama. She certainly hadn't been neglected. In fact, her son had given her as much of his time as he could, and had excused so many of her binges because he knew what his father had been. But her being drunk on their return from honeymoon was unforgivable. It was bound to cause trouble with Mary Rose because her brother Jamie being an alcoholic had made her hate the stuff. As long as she didn't ask, he wasn't going to mention Mama that night, though she would discover soon enough.

Having found a bottle of smelling salts left by Miss Carlotta in the old Mistress's sitting-room, Maggie, Mrs Livingstone's assistant in the kitchen, had had to hold the bottle under the new Mistress's nostrils while Mrs Livingstone fussed with blankets and bottles.

Maggie's hand was still shaking from the confusion she had been thrown into through the speed of arrival of the Master and new Mistress off the late train. She had expected them to stay longer at the welcome home bonfire, dismounting to talk to the tenants. She certainly hadn't expected the new Mistress to arrive dead to the world on a galloping gig, having to be carried upstairs by her father the ghillie and the gardener.

But it wasn't only the way that Mrs Livingstone had sent her for smelling salts that had frightened Maggie, though she had watched her mother's last struggle for breath: it was the cook's quick whispered explanation that the new Mistress had 'seen something' on the blind bend. Maggie's mother had told frightening stories as she hunched over the peats on rare nights of recollection, when she wasn't too tired after the day's labour on the croft, hoeing and harvesting, milking and lugging peats because her husband was too occupied up at the big house. Her mother's back had been a giant claw on the wall as she recalled seeing lights like candles on the doorsteps of those about to die, and sometimes seeing the lights moving between croft and cemetery. On the night Miss Laura had died, Maggie herself had seen a light going down the avenue, and quite often, working at the kitchen table in sunlight, with the door open behind her, she had heard the Skye terriers growling as they had done when Miss Laura teased them. When the tinkers came down from their camp to get their smoke-blackened cans filled with hot sweet tea, the twisted skips of their caps shielding their eyes, the inverted stumps of clay pipes at the corners of their stubbled mouths, they talked about Miss Laura, whom they called 'the little Princess' in Gaelic, as though she was still living, as though they had just met her on the avenue.

But what *had* the new Mistress seen on the blind bend? She didn't seem to be able to get words out as she lay there, the colour of flour, her breasts heaving, fists gripping the fine silk of her dress. She was certainly beautiful, Maggie thought wistfully, sitting by the bed and watching a last ray of sun streaming through the window overlooking the river, its glory lost to the golden head. It was eerie, the darkening window, the fire on the pillow, the silence of evening broken only by the recumbent woman's heavy breathing, like sighs; and outside the scorn of an early owl. It reminded Maggie of the illustrated story of a princess which her mother had picked up for a few pence at a jumble sale, the only book Maggie had ever owned, apart from her Missal. It had been a sad story of a beauty who had slept for too long.

Maggie was frightened, wanting to go back down to the familiar kitchen with its cheerful grate, but Mrs Livingstone had ordered her to stay while she went down to fill stone bottles for the new Mistress's feet, which felt as if they had been wading in the river in winter. Even more frightening than the atmosphere: the new Mistress's eyes were turned on Maggie, watching without words, so sad, the way Miss Laura had looked when Miss Carlotta had scolded her, or worse.

Maggie sat, looking at her knees, praying that Mrs Livingstone would come to relieve her, not wanting the responsibility of sitting with the sick, a role her mother had performed many times in the village. Maggie was nearly nineteen, though her small round face with its pale flawless complexion seemed to contradict the fact. Dark hair parted in the middle was at her shoulders, and would eventually reach her waist. By inclination as well as order the drab dress hid her jutting maturity. She had come to Invernevis House from the family croft on her fourteenth birthday to become scullery-maid, standing at a chipped stone sink from dawn till dusk and often into darkness, six days a week for ten pounds per year, live in, uniform but not footwear provided, with attendance at chapel compulsory on Sunday mornings. That was in the days when Miss Carlotta ruled servants and family, manifesting herself in severe black silk gowns, in kitchen and servants' hall, with bunches of keys on the belt at her thin waist, so that she became known as 'the holy ghost'.

Maggie should have been alerted when the pale lady with

the lovely red hair came twice to Invernevis; and when the engagement ring was taken from one of the glass cases in the drawing-room, she had run upstairs. But Mrs Livingstone, having satisfied herself that the red eyes of her assistant did not signify the same as in the days of the old laird, had sat her down at the white scrubbed table, transferring the cracked brown teapot from its customary place on the corner of the stove to between them, and spooning out plenty of sugar. She explained to Maggie that if the Master didn't marry and produce bairns, then Invernevis couldn't go on and there would be no need for a new cook. Lairds sometimes got servant girls into trouble but they never married them, and no one expected them to.

'You're old enough for me to be telling you these things, and that's what your mother would have wanted, God rest her soul.' The teapot tilted again. 'No, girl, a new Mistress here will make all the difference, because the old lady's getting too much of a handful, though she's had her sorrows, God knows. And you'll see a difference in the laird because he misses his sister a lot more than he shows. Master Alexander hasn't been any help to him. He needs someone, and she's a very nice lady, though I don't think she's all that strong, so the fewer upsets the better. I doubt if my feet will see me through another year, so they'll be looking for a cook. You've a lot to learn, but if you stick in like your mother did, I can put in a good word for you. And you're well in with the old lady, though if she thinks she's pinching you for her personal maid she's got another thought coming. Anyway, let's forget all this nonsense and get the dinner ready. You do the sweet, show them what you're capable of, so they'll know they won't have to look far for a new cook when my feet give out.'

Maggie was recalling that conversation with Mrs Livingstone as she sat by the new Mistress's bed in the deepening dusk, the golden hair dull now. They had been on honeymoon, and though Maggie had no experience, she could imagine. The sudden image of his moustached mouth sent a thrill through her in that big bedroom chilled by evening. She felt, not jealousy, but pity for the young lady stretched on the bed. Maggie shut her eyes and prayed that things would work out for the new Mistress in that house haunted by Miss Laura's skipping spirit, and Miss Carlotta's tall stern figure in black, metal jangling at her waist. Maggie was going to try very hard to please them both. When Doctor MacNiven came in, she went down to the kitchen. Her father had hooked the last salmon of the season in *Linne Bhuidhe*, the Yellow Pool, easily reeling in a twenty pounder exhausted by the sun on slow reduced water, where the shade of boulders offered no respite. It wasn't sport, but Mrs Livingstone had wanted a salmon, to show the new Mistress the culinary possibilities at the bottom of her lawn.

Mrs Livingstone had seen to the boiling herself, and when it had cooled in the big slatted larder at the back door, told Maggie to give it a tasteful foliage of lettuce and whatever else the walled garden would yield. She had flushed the caterpillars from the crisp green leaves Ranald the gardener had brought to her, wrapping them round to protect the pink flesh from the sun streaming through the back door, the old Mistress's two Skye terriers slumped on the step, sounding like bellows. The glistening tomatoes from the hot-house had to be pricked round with the point of a knife, serrated and split into two crowns to be placed at head and tail on the Spode ashet. The cucumber was sliced thin, into almost transparent wheels, placed and moved till colours matched.

The arrangement had demanded all Maggie's concentration and artistic sense, for, as Mrs Livingstone had warned, the first meal in her new home for a bride made an impression that went beyond the palate. But when she came downstairs, after sitting with the new Mistress, Maggie saw the adorned salmon lying intact on the ashet on the white table, and almost cried over the wasted effort.

Mrs Livingstone saw the look and said sharply: 'Now don't start feeling sorry for yourself because you went to a lot of trouble. It's happened to me hundreds of times, and it'll happen to you, if you're cook after me. It's their privilege to take it or not, and she's not having any of it tonight because she's unwell, not because she doesn't like the way it's done. But it'll keep till tomorrow, and besides, the Master will take some tonight because he's very fond of salmon. So let's get it through to the dining-room.'

But when the ashet came back, there was only a small breach in the pink flesh.

CHAPTER 2

As Doctor MacNiven had predicted, Mary Rose was up and about in a few days, still looking pale but assuring her husband that she was feeling fine, though she didn't want to go down the avenue again, which meant she couldn't get up to the village.

Her decision alarmed Invernevis. If the people came to hear of the cause, they would think her peculiar; and if they didn't hear, they would think her uninterested, even hostile, as Miss Carlotta had been.

'I've asked the servants, but there aren't any stories about the bend,' he assured her. 'If there had been, I'd have heard long ago.' Then, still seeing her dubious: 'I'll tell you what I'll do. I'll ask Father Macdonald to come up and say a prayer there, if that will put your mind at rest, though I don't think there's anything there. It's probably because the place never gets the sun because of the bushes, and besides, the road dips there, so a gig tilts, giving you a queer feeling.' He didn't tell her that Laura had had queer feelings while on foot.

'I don't believe in that sort of thing,' she said, and he sensed that she was irritated because he had preferred an exorcist of his own faith. Before he could put it right she had gone off to find Mrs Livingstone for a conducted tour of her new home.

The house had been built to replace the original one demolished stone by stone by Duke Cumberland's dragoons in the Forty-Five, because the Invernevis chieftain had been 'out' with the Young Pretender. The portraits and heirlooms had been looted, most of them never to be recovered. The bulging bay windows were intended to attract more light from the north for the scholarly successor, but the mountain above shadowed them. The large public rooms were on the ground floor, facing the river, except for the library which looked up the avenue and which was the traditional retreat of the laird's, allowing him to escape from his family to drink, dress flies, or scrutinise the dozens of illustrated fishing books on the floor-to-ceiling shelves. Above were the bedrooms for family and guests, the latter rare after the late laird's contagious illness, and on the top floor, under the slates, the cramped sleeping quarters of the servants.

'How many rooms are there?' the new Mistress asked Mrs Livingstone.

'You know, I've never counted,' the cook said, struck by the question. 'I suppose there'll be over twenty. But there's so many big cupboards and long passages. Not an easy house to run. It's certainly done for my ankles, Ma'm.'

They began in the drawing-room, entered by double doors and dominated by the oak-encased organ that Miss Carlotta had installed, gilt pipes making a grid on the faded Indian carpet.

'It's an ugly thing, Ma'm,' Mrs Livingstone said, fists on her hips, swollen feet planted wide as she surveyed the organ. 'And so loud you could hear it at the top of the house. The Master's thinking of selling it. He says he would get a good price for it from a cathedral.'

'I don't know if I can allow that,' Mary Rose said, only half laughing when she added: 'I rather like its grandeur. I might even play it. Happy tunes, for a change.'

Mrs Livingstone could see no humour in the reply. 'Well, Miss Carlotta almost put the Master's father off his head, playing it night and day, and nothing but church music. It wasn't very cheery.'

'What exactly *did* he die of?' Mary Rose asked, scrutinising the high gilded ceiling discoloured by oil-lamps. Even with a big fire on, the room would never be warm. Were those cobwebs at the corners?

'Something he picked up in the swamps of India, Ma'm, when he was out there with the army,' the cook said, rearranging a cushion. 'It fair knocked the strength out of the Mistress, having to nurse him. He was a fine big strong gentleman; awful good on a horse, but he went to nothing, and wasn't able to lift a finger for himself. That's him, there.'

Mary Rose picked up the silver-framed photograph from the cloth-draped circular table Mama had cluttered with family photographs in emulation of her beloved Victoria. The new Mistress saw a bearded face with piercing, almost lecherous eyes, brutal thighs forced into riding breeches, the boots to the knees.

'And who's this beside him?' she asked, touching the smaller photograph showing a fair-haired boy looking uncomfortable in a kilt.

'That's Master Alexander, Ma'm. He was a lovely little boy.'

Mary Rose felt that the affection in Mrs Livingstone's tone might be a slight on the laird, but waited for the cook to continue. Mrs Livingstone, however, wasn't prepared to go further without prompting.

'I've never met him,' Mary Rose said.

Mrs Livingstone looked perplexed, not knowing what she was supposed to say to the statement, so she said nothing.

'He married a local girl, I believe.'

'Yes, Ma'm, the daughter of MacPherson, up at the Home Farm. That's their house, there, down by the river,' Mrs Livingstone said, moving into the bay window. 'They have a wee girl, the spitting image of the old Mistress, they say.'

'And I presume this is Miss Laura,' Mary Rose went on, picking up the next photograph, a girl in a lilac dress, hitched to reveal black button boots, and with a silly smile as her fingers locked.

'That's the poor wee mite,' Mrs Livingstone confirmed, returning. 'Not long before she was taken away from us.'

'What kind of girl was she?' Mary Rose asked, chilling at Mrs Livingstone's phrase.

'The happiest wee girl in the world, so long as the Master was about. But when Miss Carlotta had her to herself things were very different. Always hitting her, she was, and for nothing. That's what finished her, I always say, though at the time I should have spoken up. But you didn't want to make it worse than it was already. It was the Master going off to the war that did it, you see, because Miss Carlotta got her claws into Miss Laura, and the Mistress was too busy with the old Master. Not that I'm saying the Master was to blame. He had a duty to his country, and his father wanted him to go. But it broke the Master's heart, though he doesn't show it. Oh aye, we *all* loved Miss Laura. Such a cheery wee mite to have about the place, always coming into the kitchen, wanting to lick the bowl for the chocolate cake, always getting in everyone's way, but you didn't mind that. And the way she used to set the dogs off.' She smiled, shaking her grey head incredulously.

'What age was she when she died?' her sister-in-law asked, still holding the photograph in its ordinary frame.

'I'd have to work it out, Ma'm, but around sixteen, I expect. The Mistress had her late, and it wasn't easy.'

'And she was still licking bowls at sixteen?' Mary Rose said, trying not to make too much of a question out of it.

'Well, not quite, Ma'm, because she got very quiet and stayed in her bed towards the end, though Miss Carlotta said it was only laziness. The last time we saw Miss Laura really lively was at the Hogmanay dance the Master holds for the tenants. I think she took too much out of herself.'

'What was wrong with Miss Laura?' Mary Rose asked, keeping her eyes on the photograph.

But Mrs Livingstone had been too long in service with a temperamental family, too well trained by Miss Carlotta. Gossip got distorted and soon reached the village, giving some a reason for gloating.

'It's not my place to say, Ma'm. It's not anyone's place,

really, because it was God's will, though the tinkers are always saying that she was the wisest of us. No, you'd best ask the Master, but if you want the advice of someone who's been about here for a long time and knows his ways, best to let him try and forget. After all, he's got you, now, Ma'm, and he'll want to forget.'

There was no reply to that, so Mary Rose asked: 'Which is Miss Carlotta?' as she surveyed the array of photographs.

'You'll not find her there, or anywhere in the house, Ma'm. She didn't like having her photograph taken. Because she was so thin, I expect. No, there's nothing left of her in this house, but that organ, and maybe a feeling — Anyway, enough said. Now these covers' — she was smoothing the frayed floral sofa — 'the Master was going to get new ones, but left it for you to decide. There's a lady comes round who makes them up.'

Mary Rose nodded abstractly as she surveyed the large room. It certainly needed a lot doing to it to make it a pleasant place to sit in. The green silk draping the walls was faded by the sun and peppered with moth holes, and the ceiling needed decorating, which would require scaffolding. Then the room was so cluttered with furniture, three sofas, all different, the springs dubious, and one leaking at an arm. Assorted chairs, mostly for stiff spines, some with embroidered backs, a pair featuring the Invernevis arms picked out in various silk threads by spinsterish needles of the previous century. These and the glass cases ranged along the walls made it look like a museum. Mary Rose's dress whispered over bare boards, and she was looking down on spurs and medals resting on green baize, some with labels attached, the blue ink badly faded. Pieces of jewellery glittered among porcelain snuff boxes. She tried to raise the lid.

'Locked, Ma'm,' Mrs Livingstone said from the other side of the room. 'After pieces started to go missing when he was away at the war, the Master had new locks fitted. There's only one key, and he keeps it on himself all the time. He says some of these heirlooms are very valuable. *I'm* not even allowed to clean them.'

'What a beautiful set!' Mary Rose was staring down entranced by a heart-shaped hand mirror and two matching brushes backed in silver, with a monogram within a shield. But the poor light prevented her from deciphering. 'They must be *very* old.'

Mrs Livingstone had shuffled across to see what had taken her fancy. 'Oh no, Ma'm, not old. The Master gave them to Miss Laura for her last Christmas. The poor wee mite didn't get much use out of them, but she thought the world of them.'

'I see,' Mary Rose said quietly, turning to the room again, going up to the mantelpiece to examine the porcelain clock on which an arch of glazed naked nymphs guarded the passage of the hours.

'Miss Carlotta found it in a cupboard and cleaned it up with cotton wool, herself,' Mrs. Livingstone volunteered. 'It's French, but I can't remember which century.'

But Mary Rose was now trailing her fingers over side tables scattered with silver trinkets, a scaled fish, more snuff boxes, the sterling metal gleaming. She picked up a big book lying on the used blotter of a desk. Written in Italian, it was illustrated by photographs of naked women — girls mostly — in various poses.

'This is surely not the Master's!' she protested.

'Oh no, Ma'm. It belonged to Miss Carlotta. She was a great one for Italy and its works of art. She took the other books away with her, but I found that one under a cushion while I was doing the cleaning. She was a right clever lady, Ma'm. She used to sit day after day at that desk, writing books about what a bad thing drink was. She gave me a copy, Ma'm, but I'm not very good at the reading. Still, Father Macdonald said it was a very useful book.'

'Burn it,' Mary Rose said, handing her the art book.

Mrs Livingstone was taken aback. 'Oh I don't think we should do that, Ma'm. It'll be a very expensive book. We could post it on to Miss Carlotta, if we could get her address from Father Macdonald.'

'Burn it, it's indecent,' Mary Rose said angrily, thrusting the book at her.

'Indecent, Ma'm?' the cook echoed, utterly bewildered. 'But it's a book about art – Italian art. Miss Carlotta was always showing the maids her art books, to improve their minds.'

'I want to hear no more of this,' Mary Rose ordered. 'Put it in the stove. Now let's see if the other rooms are any better.'

Clutching the book, Mrs Livingstone led her new Mistress into the dining room. It was dominated by a long extending mahogany table, a black pool in which were mirrored the dented horns of the epergne wedding present from the tenants, retrieved from the rhododendrons at the blind bend. Behind the mahogany sideboard a long mirror failed to attract light from the window, whose rotting brocade curtains were held back by faded gold cords. Family portraits and landscapes not significant enough for the gallery upstairs had been relegated to the dining-room walls, hanging by chains from brass claws gripping the wooden cornice, and below them, additional Chippendale chairs for when additional leaves were inserted in the table.

'It's the ceiling again,' Mary Rose sighed. 'So high and dark. And look at the grime on the walls.'

'I don't remember the place being decorated, and I've been here over thirty years, since they came home from India,' Mrs Livingstone admitted. 'It's the cost, I suppose.'

'Well, it'll have to be found somewhere,' the new Mistress said decisively. 'What on earth's that?' She drew back in alarm from the sideboard.

It was a very large ram's head, black-faced, with curling horns and cairngorms for eyes, giving it a malevolent appearance, a thin devilish mask. The horns were capped with silver circles which could be lifted off for snuff, and a cavity had been made in the skull to keep cigars humid. A silver shield between the eyes bore the inscription: 'For Auld Lang Syne.'

'Oh – *that?*' Mrs Livingstone said, laughing. 'We call it

Auld Nick. The Master's father was presented with it by the officers of his regiment when he left India. Miss Carlotta wanted it burned, but the butler hid it in a box.'

'Get it out of here!' Mary Rose said, going pale. It was almost as obscene and mocking as Carlotta's art book.

'I'll tell Symmers to take it out, Ma'm,' Mrs Livingstone said quietly, leading the way upstairs to the bedrooms, through the hall of horns, past the stained glass window on the landing.

'This is the only one that's been done up lately, the one you slept in when you came here before,' Mrs Livingstone announced, opening the door of the Blue Room.

Mary Rose stood on the threshold, struck by the recollection of massive inlaid mahogany that had reflected light, little sacks of lavender in the drawers, a pile of snowy towels folded over the gleaming brass bars on either side of the wash-stand. Now the room reeked of dampness and disuse, the mahogany dull, and at the foot of the bed, on the writing desk where she had sat, putting the promise of Invernevis down on paper for her mother, a vase of dried-up flowers.

'Of course we haven't had guests for a long time, what with the old Master being laid up,' Mrs Livingstone was saying, 'and then only Colonel Hooker. He was a friend of Miss Carlotta's, but they quarrelled about drinking and he stopped coming. Or rather, was stopped. The Master tells me he's a trustee.'

Mary Rose's face showed that she wasn't interested in estate affairs. They toured the other bedrooms, large cold rooms with masses of mahogany, china on marble, and frayed carpets on stained boards. They made Mary Rose shiver, and close doors behind her.

'This was Miss Laura's room,' Mrs Livingstone announced, letting out dampness. Mary Rose stepped in to look. The bed had been stripped down to the blotched horse-hair mattress, and the wardrobe gaped, the vacant hangers, four in number, on the corroded brass rail. A cracked ewer and basin stood on the mottled marble wash-stand, a cake of carbolic congealed in a dish beside. The plain wallpaper was peeling above the empty fireplace.

Mary Rose moved to the window overlooking the lawn and touched the head of the rocking horse with the long black mane and steel stirrups. It creaked, nodding in the poor light.

'It's really the nursery, Ma'm,' Mrs Livingstone said from the doorway. 'But Miss Carlotta kept Miss Laura in it. It's a very cold room, even if you've got a fire in it.' And, seeing her new Mistress touching the wall: 'The house needs a lot doing to it. Once the dampness gets a grip, you'll never get rid of it, unless you strip the plaster. I just can't keep a sack of salt downstairs now. It's up here, in the linen cupboard, would you believe.'

'I think I'd believe anything about this house,' Mary Rose muttered. As she closed the door she noticed a black-haired doll lolling on a chair by the bed, arms dangling, head tilted idiotically.

Mrs. Livingstone was making for the front stairs, but Mary Rose pointed to the door at the end of the passage and called. 'We haven't seen in there.'

'It used to be Miss Carlotta's room, Ma'm, but the old Mistress is in it now,' Mrs. Livingstone said, without coming back.

'I'd like to see it.'

'But she's in bed, Ma'm.'

'I haven't seen her since we came home.'

Mrs Livingstone came back to turn the key and hold the door open slightly, avoiding her new Mistress's face.

The room stank of stale drink and sweat, and clothing was strewn on the floor, for the previous night Mama had got a fresh supply smuggled upstairs by the footman, for which he received the last silver trinket from her dressing-table. Her teeth lying on the bedside cabinet, Mama sprawled, sparse whitening hair wisping her face, mouth wide, nostrils sounding.

From where she stood, appalled by her mother-in-law's condition, Mary Rose could see the gleam of glass under the bed, and, in the bay window, the open lid of a commode.

'Shut the door,' she said breathlessly, leaning against the wall.

Fearing another turn, Mrs Livingstone was fussing. 'It's not like you think, Ma'm. She's only tired, not drunk. She had such a time nursing the old Master, and it went for her nerves.'

'But don't the maids clean the room? It's disgusting!'

Mrs Livingstone saw that in trying to smooth over the situation, she had put her professional position at risk. 'Oh, they go in regularly to clean the room, Ma'm, but she won't get up, and as soon as their backs are turned, she messes it up again. I'm very fond of her, but she's a stubborn lady, and if you try and force her, there's a big row. I shouldn't be telling you all this, Ma'm, but it's just to let you see that it's not easy.'

'And why shouldn't you be telling me?' Mary Rose said reproachfully. 'I would hope that you wouldn't hide anything from me that goes on in this house. You can begin by telling me how my mother-in-law gets drink.'

'If I knew that, Ma'm, she wouldn't be lying in that state in there,' the cook said mournfully. 'I've tried every way of finding out. I've kept as good a watch as I could, with work to do in the kitchen, and a big staff. Miss Carlotta used to think it was the butler or the coachman, but it's definitely not them. I know them too well.'

'But you *must* have some suspicions,' Mary Rose said, watching her.

The cook's eyes went to her swollen feet. 'Suspicion isn't proof, Ma'm, and we had too much suspicion with Miss Carlotta. One thing I'm quite sure of, though: it's being brought up from the village, and she must be giving something to get it. I've searched the room, but she hasn't any money. Anyway, Ma'm, I'm keeping a good watch, and I'll catch whoever it is. The minute I do, they're in front of the Master.'

'No, don't worry him with it,' Mary Rose said in a tone that was an order. 'Bring the person to me. I'll deal with it.'

'Well, as long as you make it right with the Master,' Mrs Livingstone said dubiously. 'He likes things to be kept right. Anyway, you've seen all the rooms up here, except the servants, and I don't expect you're interested in these, so if you'll excuse me I'll go and get on in the kitchen.'

'No, I want to see the servants' quarters,' Mary Rose surprised her by saying. 'They're just as important as these rooms, because if you don't have a contented staff —'

She followed the cook up the narrow twisting stairs of bare boards to the rooms under the slates, the grey plaster flaking from the walls, and in some places gashed, where the old Master had struggled with a reluctant maid.

'They're all the same, Ma'm,' Mrs Livingstone said, almost apologetically, twisting a rattling handle.

The coomed ceiling was inset with a cobweb-curtained skylight filled with grey mountain slope, the floorboards bare. There was a black iron framed single bed, a dresser with some of the knobs missing, and a small wardrobe, the silvering of its mirror speckled with black.

'It was Miss Carlotta who arranged these rooms, Ma'm,' the cook explained. 'She didn't believe in comforts for servants, said it made them lazy. If you're moving about, see and don't give your head a crack.'

But Mary Rose wasn't listening. The pieces of a photograph lay on top of the wash-stand, badly stuck together, but clear enough for her to see her husband standing at the front porch in military uniform, his out-of-alignment face shaded by a feathered bonnet.

'Whose room is this?' Mary Rose asked, turning away as if she hadn't seen the jigsaw of the photograph.

'It's Maggie's, who helps me in the kitchen, the girl who sat with you when you were poorly the other evening.'

Mrs Livingstone had not noticed the photograph, and continued: 'This room's tidier than most of them, but young servants are all the same, nowadays. It gets a bit cold here in the winter, but very stuffy in the summer, because we're right under the roof. We've no water-closet on this floor, which can be a bit of a nuisance.'

'I'll speak to my husband,' Mary Rose said vaguely, brushing past Mrs. Livingstone. 'He'll explain about things.'

'Will we go down and look at the kitchen, Ma'm?'

'No, I've seen enough for today, thank you,' she said, treading fallen plaster and pondering as she went downstairs. There were far too many secrets, beginning with Carlotta's so-called art book. Mary Rose considered herself to be enlightened; had inspected naked stone and canvas in Venice, Rome, and Paris, but that book was obscene, young girls sitting or standing splayed. And Mama; obviously she was an alcoholic, lying like an animal in her own mess. Laura: why hadn't he explained that there was something wrong with her? Oh, he had tried on honeymoon, but even if he had, it was too late. He should have given her a full and honest account *before* the marriage, so that she could have decided for herself. Then things might have turned out very different. But what on earth was a kitchen-maid doing with a torn photograph of him? Had she taken it from a wastepaper basket, or was there something more sinister? Could it be that he had inherited some of the habits of his father, which she could guess at, judging by his photograph in the drawing-room, and the mysterious disease.

One thing was certain: there wasn't any way out. If she went running back to her mother, she would get an angry reception and be sent back again to make a go of it. Her mother was an expert at putting up a front. Women who separated from their husbands for however good a reason always had the finger pointed at them and became social outcasts. It was different for men. Look what King Edward had got away with when Prince of Wales, and was probably still getting away with.

And her brother Jamie: he drank heavily, had lost a fortune at cards, yet nobody seemed to mind. One day her sex would get the same status as men: the Women's Social and Political Union, growing daily under Mrs Pankhurst, would see to that.

Well, if she was going to have to stick it out in this awful house, there was going to have to be big changes. It needed redecoration from top to bottom, the dampness stopped, water-closets put in. Obviously it would cost a good deal of money, but surely her husband could find it by selling some land, if he hadn't got it already? He seemed to have plenty on honeymoon, with his cigars and brandy. After all, what was the point of having an estate if the house was falling down?

'Will that be all, Ma'm?' Mrs Livingstone asked anxiously, seeing they had reached ground level again.

'Please send through some coffee to the drawing-room,' Mary Rose ordered. 'I want to think about what needs doing.'

She stood in the sunlight, in the bay window, looking up the river, shielding her eyes to see Alexander's house. Now *that* was a much more sensible size, and in such a nice place. She had never met him, but he looked pleasant enough in the boyhood photograph on the table behind her. She wondered what the real truth was behind his removal from the big house. What did it matter if he had put a farmer's daughter in the family way, so long as he was happy and loyal?

But how had *his* photograph got into the kitchen-maid's bedroom? It certainly didn't look innocent, and Mrs Livingstone had pretended she hadn't noticed. There was a kind of conspiracy in the house, and she didn't like it at all. They knew well that something awful had happened on the blind bend in the past, but they weren't going to say. Surely her own husband wouldn't side with servants against her? But maybe she was making too much out of it. After all, he had told the truth about Carlotta, who was obviously more than a tyrant, to judge from the Italian art book. He probably hadn't told her the rest because he was ashamed of his family, which was understandable. And judging by the silver dressing table set in the glass case, which she went to have another look at, he had been very fond of his sister.

It made her feel she wasn't going to measure up. It was a household of strong personalities, and she was going to be swamped. The best thing was to keep to herself, make her own life. Was that a summer house down by the river? Of course it was; she remembered from her first visit, when he had shown it to her so proudly, saying that he had had it rebuilt in memory of Laura. She could sit there, out of the way, sewing and reading, on good days. And there was the walled garden, which she would take a special interest in. If she brought flowers into the house, that would help to brighten it. But she couldn't withdraw entirely. She had spoken her vows, and he was entitled to his conjugal rights. She didn't care for that side of marriage, but you had to consider his need for an heir. No, it was a silly attitude to take. Isolation wasn't the answer. If she had had the spirit to oppose her mother, her brother Jamie wouldn't be in such a pitiful state. Somehow she had to find the faith and energy to triumph at Invernevis.

It was Maggie the kitchen-maid who brought in the coffee tray, and as she set it down, making silver and Spode collide, Mary Rose studied her. Yes, there was no doubt that she was attractive, with that healthy colour Highland girls had, presumably because of the wholesome food and fresh air. Her long black hair was neatly kept, and her nails clean. But Mary Rose felt that there was a furtiveness about the girl's eyes. No doubt she wasn't as innocent as she looked. The pieced-together photograph she had seen on the servant's wash-stand rankled, but she decided to say nothing for the moment. What was the point, when the girl would only lie? No, she would take her coffee quietly, then go into the library, to see her husband about repairs and improvements.

Invernevis was occupied with the pile of mail on his desk after his two months' absence. The dozens of rolled-up copies of *The Times* could go unopened into the wastepaper basket, because he had read most of them abroad, and anyway, the end of the South African war had made him lose interest in what was happening in the wide world. But he could not afford to ignore a series of letters from his Edinburgh lawyers. They dealt with pressing estate problems, the most urgent being the future of the granite quarry across the loch. The two hundred Irish navvies hacking at granite and huddled in shacks, crossed by open boat on Saturday night to get drunk and disorderly in the Invernevis Arms in the village, some of them missing the last ferry home. Senseless with drink, they sprawled in the dust, cradling stone jars like Pictish warriors in burial mounds, blocking the track to the chapel, built by Carlotta and in which Father Macdonald conducted Mass, insisting that all the village, including infants, be present. The Irishmen had shouted obscene suggestions at village women, and a backward girl who had had a baby was supposed to have been mounted by one of them.

Invernevis had been warned about an impending tragedy in anonymous letters from the village, but had been indecisive in deciding the future of the quarry because it brought in much needed money to the estate, the farm and croft rents being so low, having been fixed by a father more benevolent to his tenants than to his family. But under pressure from MacPherson of the Home Farm and from Father Macdonald, acting as priest and trustee, Invernevis had decided that the quarry had to be closed. He had written to his Edinburgh lawyers before going on honeymoon, and now had their reply, nearly two months out of date. In the new century the typewriter had replaced a clerk's copperplate, and in large blue type Richardson the lawyer reminded Invernevis that he was only the life-renter of the estate; therefore the powers of decision on all matters pertaining to the estate rested with the trustees, of which Richardson was one, along with Father Macdonald, the trinity completed by Colonel Thomas Godfrey Hooker, impecunious old soak, former drinking crony and fellow lecher of the old laird's, and latterly, suitor of Carlotta, because of her investments. Hooker was in hiding from his creditors, but Richardson and the priest had exchanged letters on the future of the quarry. The priest concurred with Invernevis with regard to closure, but Richardson was bound to point out as the most experienced trustee, with thirty years of looking after all aspects of the estate because of the old laird's lack of interest, that the revenue lost in closure would have to be found elsewhere, meaning raising the rents. Since Richardson and Father Macdonald were divided, they had agreed to give the decision to Invernevis.

He immediately saw what was behind this unusual complaisance. Because he was seeking election to his client's exclusive Edinburgh club, the socially ambitious lawyer had no wish to quarrel with Invernevis. And though Carlotta was pushing him to get the quarry closed down, Father Macdonald was unwilling to give his blessing to the alternative of higher rents because that would set local opinion against him.

Opening the next letter from the lawyers, Invernevis saw his predicament made even more difficult, for the directors of the quarry company had replied to the threat of closure with an offer to pay double the rent on an extended lease. Glasgow was desperate for granite paving slabs as the city expanded and modernised to meet the challenge of twentieth century industry. In time, the directors promised, they would reduce the unruly Irish labour force by introducing more crushing and cutting machinery.

It was an intolerable position to be put into, when he didn't even have the authority to make such a decision. It wasn't the lawyer and the priest who were to blame; it went back to his father's spiteful act in tying his hands with trustees because he, Niall, was the elder son and not Alexander. His father's spite went beyond the son, to the son's heir, because the will stipulated that in the event of Niall not having a male heir to succeed outright to the estate, it passed to Alexander and his heirs. Yet here were the trustees asking him to take a decision which not only affected his status as laird, but also the financial stability of the estate.

As well as all these things, he had to think of Mary Rose. She hadn't brought a big dowry, despite the extent of the family's Sutherland estates, because most of the money had had to go to her brother Jamie, the reluctant heir to the baronetcy whose carelessness with cards in the Mess and subsequent bouts of drinking in Edinburgh had cost many thousands. Before marriage Invernevis had thought of Mary Rose as being a shy provident girl dominated by her formidable mother in the bleak fastnesses of the north, but she had surprised him on honeymoon by buying several very expensive silk dresses in Paris, and had taken full advantage of the *coiffeur* and other facilities offered by the huge Mediterranean hotels where they had stayed, in suites with period furniture and marble bathrooms. Not only that: he had had to pay for prime seats in the great concert halls of Europe, listening to interminable grating music, his game leg aching. In Paris he had had to stop her paying God knows how many francs for an unintelligible canvas by someone called Renoir.

But he couldn't blame her entirely, because he had never discussed money. He had wanted to, once or twice on honeymoon, but knew that that sort of thing just wasn't done. Besides, to have asked her to economise would have spoilt her pleasure, and he had wanted her to enjoy herself before they returned to the austerity of Invernevis, with Edinburgh and its gown shops over a hundred miles away. Now they were home, however, they would have to watch their expenditure carefully, and break the habit of wine with every meal. Through the army years of solitude and frustration, he had developed an addiction to cigars, and appreciated brandy, but would have to cut down on both.

He himself had very little money. It had been impossible to accumulate capital in the army, on a Captain's pay, and that only latterly. Alexander had inherited the bulk of their father's money, symbolically in brewery shares, though he was only the second son, and Mama had poured capital down her throat during the heir's absence in South Africa. When Richardson the lawyer had eventually stopped her signing cheques, she had resorted to selling heirlooms to hawkers, and had let their only Raeburn go for fifty pounds. He had been promised Aunt Carlotta's money, mostly invested in gold shares, climbing now with the peace, but they had quarrelled and she had gone. No doubt Elsie the kitchen-maid, whom she had taken with her to shape into a companion, would be the sole beneficiary.

He wouldn't benefit from the doubling of the quarry rent, because the revenue would go to the estate. He might persuade the trustees to spend some money on the roof of Invernevis House, which was in a precarious state. His father hadn't so much as replaced a slate, but of course he needed all his money to repair the damage he had done to the maids. He knew he was being measured against his father, but he was different. The old laird had gone up to the village, to share stone jars and play quoits with them, showing the strength that had overcome maids on the back stairs by lifting a plough with one arm. The son kept his distance, though he was always pleased to receive them at the big house if they had genuine grievances. So they were bound to be more suspicious of the son, which didn't make the decision about the quarry any easier. It was a problem to give a great deal of thought to, though in yet another letter Richardson warned that the decision couldn't be too long delayed, otherwise the offer of a double rent would be withdrawn.

There was a pile of household accounts, but Invernevis left them, to go over them later with Mrs Livingstone. Time to take some fresh air. Crossing the hall, with its stag heads and shot-holed standards, relics of Culloden, he stopped to scrutinise the salmon suspended behind curved glass on the wall, fifty six pounds of sagging flesh firmed for time, the record landed by his father from *Linne na Craoibh Daraich*, the Oak Tree Pool, after years of persistence, the fly that had tricked it temptingly dangled in front of its glazed eyes, the pincered jaws sulking at the permanency of deception. His ambition was to beat the record, not only for the satisfaction of supplanting his father, but to prove him posthumously wrong in preferring Alexander. Now that he was settled, he would devote time to the quest, but without neglecting his wife.

Where the lawn began sloping, a granite pillar with a hole stood, quarried in an age of the most rudimentary tools, stone attacking stone. Though its date of shaping could not be set, it had stood there since the first Invernevis settlement after Flodden. Men going off to war, in clan battles or the Peninsula, had linked hands through the holed stone and had one wish under a new moon, the wish void if spoken.

Invernevis stood, a hand resting on warm granite, the other hand with a cigarette, staring down at the stepping stones of the seventy yard wide Summer House Pool, the river reduced in the continuing drought. He was remembering the day he had left for South Africa and war, when Laura in her habitual black button boots had wobbled across insubstantial stone to the meadow beyond, the dark sockets of her damp boots turned to the sun as he promised to return. He had come home eventually, with a kneecap shattered by a Boer bullet, and a doll with real hair. But it had been too late. That already confused head of gold ringlets could no longer take the blows administered by Carlotta for small grammatical errors and exuberance, or was the cause the syphilis transmitted by his blind father? Whatever the reason, Laura had died, blind, and he had married Mary Rose.

But his relationship with Laura had been different because she was his sister, with no one else to protect her from Aunt Carlotta and an incomprehensible world in which the bee that gave sweetness also stung. On honeymoon he had explored those physical pleasures which shyness and the discipline of army life had denied him, and by which his father had set such great store, but it had been disappointing. Perhaps long abstinence had made him uninterested, or perhaps it was just too embarrassing, since he had been bred to formality. But it had to be done because he needed an heir, to discharge his first obligation to his ancestry, who had fought so long and so fiercely to retain these acres on both sides of the river.

As he saw the sun firing the peaks of the standing stones on the hill above the Home Farm, he felt trapped by his heritage, run into a trap by time, like a salmon into the stone chamber that jutted into the Cruive Pool several hundred yards upriver. His tradition was like the sparkling water that lay beyond his brogues where the lawn sloped; turbulent in stretches, almost stagnant in others, encompassing good and bad, big leaper and spent fish, idiot and intellectual, carrier of crosses and destroyer of churches. He had always spurned the strict Catholicism of his race, and in particular Carlotta's because it had not been tempered with mercy, but as he surveyed the almost menacing silence of the summer countryside, a buzzard drifting, the corn sheaves in the Home Farm fields bound together like hostages, he wondered if his disappointment over the physical promise of marriage hadn't something to do with a Catholicism that was as much a part of him as the peremptory mouth, the sweep of the forehead. It was as if the thin spinster Carlotta had left a growing legacy in the shadow of the mountain.

There was Alexander's house on the bank of *Poll Dubh*, the Black Pool. He had sought to defeat a heritage of gentility by laying his drunken shadow on a tenant's daughter. His house was shadowed by Wade's Bridge which shadowed the Yellow Pool, where Laura had wrestled with life one summer afternoon, wading to lift the drought-stunned salmon into a new element. That evening he had sailed for war. Time's current, which made no distinction between the two sides of the river, had carried her away, to end up where other stone arched at the river mouth. It was a landscape of death as well as life, of small things clawed crying from the stubble of the ripe cut corn.

Mary Rose touching his sleeve disturbed his depressing reverie.

'I've been round the house with Mrs Livingstone, and it needs a great deal done to it.'

Hearing the criticism in her voice, he kept his eyes on the river as he nodded.

'My father should have attended to it when he came home from India, because my uncle had let it go. He was a bachelor, a recluse, you see. It's the roof, mainly. When it rains, there have to be buckets everywhere.'

'I don't know about the roof, but I *do* know it wants redecorating from top to bottom. New bathrooms put in, and one for the servants as well. It's shocking, the conditions they have to live in.'

'Was Mrs Livingstone complaining?'

'No, I am. I think I have the right to. I've made out a list and left it on your desk.'

The time had come to talk about money.

'It's simply not possible, my dear. It would cost thousands. I haven't got that kind of money. Nor do the trustees.'

'It's not a woman's place to know about estate matters, and even if you tried to explain, I wouldn't understand. Mother didn't tell me anything about our own place, probably because Jamie was making such a mess. I don't even know what being under trustees means, but I did see the letters from the lawyers on your desk. Obviously you could get a lot of money by allowing the quarry to continue.'

He was angry at her for having read his correspondence, just like Carlotta, but knew they were on the threshold of their first row. Other things were bound to come out.

'I might get the trustees to spend some money on the house,' he began cautiously, 'but the quarry going on isn't in the best interests of the tenants.'

'And what about *our* best interests?' she asked angrily. 'They can't expect us to live in a damp, dingy house without proper sanitation.'

He was sad and shocked to hear a younger version of Carlotta. Any reply would anger her further, so he struck fire from the wishing stone for his cigarette.

She wasn't to be put off by silence. 'And another thing: why didn't you tell me that your mother was a drunkard?'

'I tried to, on honeymoon, but you wouldn't let me. Before God, I tried.'

'You left it a bit late, didn't you?' she said bitterly. 'All those family secrets kept from me.' She caught his sleeve and turned him round to face her. 'What did your father die of?'

He tried to keep his face bland as he said: 'A disease he picked up in the swamps of India.'

'What was it called?'

'Doctor MacNiven never put a name to it.'

'All right, so I can ask him. Now: why is it I've never met your brother Alexander?'

'I can answer that easily enough. I don't allow Alexander to come up to the house because of what happened with MacPherson's daughter. And Alexander doesn't want to come. In other words, we don't get on. I didn't want you to meet him because I don't consider him to be a suitable type of person for a lady like you.'

'But that's outrageous,' she said, having watched his face to make sure he wasn't mocking her. 'Your own brother. Jamie isn't a very suitable type of person for a lady like me, but I still go on seeing him. And your sister Laura? What was wrong with *her*?'

He turned to look up at the standing stones beyond the conical roof of the summer house he had had rebuilt in her memory. More than the sun made him narrow his eyes, as he said, after a long time: 'She was mentally retarded. If she wasn't damaged at birth, my Aunt Carlotta did it, with her hand.'

She saw she had gone too far, and she tried to save the situation by clutching at his arm, crying: 'I didn't mean to be so horrible! It's just that the state of the house made me so depressed. Not only the condition; the atmosphere. It frightens me, like what happened on the blind bend. If it was done up, it wouldn't be so gloomy, and I'm sure I could be happy here. I *want* us to be happy. You've had such sadness with your sister, and I with my brother, so we need each other.'

They linked arms as they went indoors.

CHAPTER 3

In ploughman's gear, trousers lashed with twine at the shins, collarless shirt above open waistcoat, Alexander was in his habitual seat in the corner of the Invernevis Arms with his cronies, old crofters in shapeless tweeds, studs shining at sagging throats. Carmichael, licensee and ex-policeman presided, massive in a butcher's striped apron, forearms exposed, eyes elsewhere as he pulled pints. He was on his last warning from the trustees for keeping a riotous house, and only wanted another year to make enough to retire to his native Glasgow. But this depended on the continuing presence of the Irish navvies boosting his takings with their Saturday night sovereigns, since the locals only dealt in sixpences. All Carmichael had to do in return was to tilt out double measures of Power's best Irish and keep control. His tongue usually saved him from having to vault the counter, though there had been several bad brawls, with breakages in more than glass.

The furnishings and decor of the small, dark, low-ceilinged room were spartan, a bare floor, benches and scarred circular tables, but as a concession to crofters coming in from the cold a sluggish fire, and above it a gilded mirror, the roaring stag advertising MOUNTAIN MONARCH. A crack ran across the raised throat from a brawl between Irishmen and locals which Father Macdonald had had to leave his warm bed to stop, thrusting a large silver crucifix (last present from the departed Miss Carlotta) through a shattered pane, then discovering Alexander unconscious under a table. Naturally the priest had complained to his patroness the next morning.

Alexander came in punctually at seven each evening, to sit at the same table with the same crofters. By custom the predominant language of the pub was Gaelic, to prevent Carmichael from overhearing and to give them scope to complain about him, but out of deference to Alexander, because he was the laird's brother, the crofters conversed in English. The topic was usually farming, with Alexander expounding the theories he had picked up from his father-in-law at the Home Farm, the crofters keeping their pipes in their mouths but their eyes mobile as they listened respectfully. They pulled his leg gently, implying that MacPherson might not be the farmer he thought he was, but Alexander resumed his animated monologue, demonstrating milking methods by tugging imaginary teats until the crofters' laughter exploded in smoke. Beaming, Alexander would dip into his waistcoat pocket, further depleting the kitty of two sovereigns which his wife Kate gave him each evening, without comment because her father insisted that the man was master of his own money, and that more was due to Alexander from across the river, which MacPherson would help him to collect. It was Alexander who always paid for the laden trays of large whiskies that Carmichael brought over at the snapping of fingers, when any other customer who tried to attract his attention in that way would receive the force of his fist. Protesting that Alexander shouldn't, the crofters murmured '*Slainte*' and inverted the generous measures daintily, between thumb and forefinger, no change on their expressions as they swallowed.

It was the Saturday night after the laird's return with his bride. The pub was crowded with Irishmen in reeking moleskins jostling for counter space, slapping down their sovereigns, watching Carmichael turning to the measure at the gantry, his wrist flicking like a conjurer, his thumb inside the brass. The navvies downed the doubles, which looked like thimblefuls in their fists, and wiping their mouths appreciatively, shouted that they wanted the same again, right away. In a dim corner a group of tinkers in assorted waistcoats and garish flannel from the attics of the big houses of several shires brooded over pints, still smarting at the firing of their tents by the Irishry several summers before. Clay pipes clamped inverted in the corners of their stubbled mouths, gold glittering at ear lobes, their wrinkled faces of indeterminable age and suggestion of supernatural influence watching from under the misshapen caps.

'So the laird's home, a married man at last,' one of the crofters in Alexander's company was shouting above the din aggravated by the metronomic click of dominoes. 'I didn't get down to the bonfire myself, because I had the beasts to feed, but the wife tells me she's a beautiful lady. Hair like the sunset, she said. But it sounds much better in Gaelic.'

'MacPherson thinks I'm coming on fine at the language,' Alexander announced proudly.

'I've no doubt you'll pick it up quick, Sandy, because if there's anything good about MacPherson, it's his Gaelic. Mind you, being able to speak it isn't everything.'

'I don't follow you,' Alexander said.

'I'm not rightly sure what I mean myself, Sandy, but it's got something to do with *feeling* it, in here.' He touched his heart.

But seeing how dejected Alexander had become, another was quick to say: 'Never mind, Sandy. You'll soon be speaking Gaelic as well as if not better than anyone in the village, and that goes for MacPherson himself. That won't please him.'

'But to get back to this business of the laird,' the first crofter said. 'Have you met the lady in question, Sandy?'

He shook his head.

'Och, he'll be getting invited up for a big dinner, and then he won't be wanting to come up to the Arms to talk to the likes of us,' another said.

'I won't be going up,' Alexander said angrily.

'Not that we're wanting rid of you, Sandy, you understand? You put us too much in mind of your father for that. Aye, one of the best. I never saw a man with such a steady eye for quoits. He could wrap the horseshoe round the peg first go.'

'And my God, could he hold his whisky,' someone else reminisced affectionately, in words that were not to be questioned. 'I once saw him drink a whole stone jar without drawing a breath, for a bet, it was. And when he was finished he was as steady on his legs as if it had been water. There'll never be another like him — meaning no disrespect to yourself, Sandy,' he added hastily.

'Sandy could show us a thing or two,' another said, closing an eye and nodding knowingly. 'He's nobody's fool.'

There was an interruption while Alexander snapped his fingers for another tray, the second sovereign clattering on tin, being hushed by Carmichael's massive palm. He put down a new clay pipe in front of Alexander. The crofters called Alexander's health in Gaelic, inverted glass, and pondered a new subject for conversation.

'There's talk of the quarry being closed down. Have *you* heard that, Sandy?'

He nodded as he tamped tobacco into fragile clay with a grimy finger.

'Of course you would, MacPherson's so much against it. And naturally, you'll be the same.'

Alexander startled, letting the match burn down to his nail. '*I* don't want it closed down. It'll put all those men out of a job, with no other scheme to go to.'

'But look at the fights they've caused in here,' a crofter said, surprised.

'That's only because someone — Carmichael usually — said something to rile them. If they're left in peace, like just now, they're decent men who only want a dram at the end of a hard week. Like yourselves.'

The crofters surveyed the moleskinned mass at the counter, but nobody would comment.

'Well, do *you* want it closed?' Alexander challenged. 'Because if it does it'll mean bigger rents.'

They looked at each other, then left the right of reply to the eldest. Even then, he puffed for a minute or so.

'Well, no, Sandy, we don't want it to close — but not for our own sakes, you understand. We agree with you that it would be a shame to put so many men out of work just because there's been a wee bit trouble in here. As for raising the rents, we just couldn't pay, because there's nothing in crofting but backbreak. But of course it's not for us to say what will happen to the quarry. That's for the laird and the trustees to decide. As you know from the night he came in here to stop the fight, Father Macdonald's dead against the quarry. He'll close it, if he can.'

'He's the one who's causing all the trouble,' Alexander said angrily. 'Just because he's getting a back-hander from my aunt.'

'Well, *we* don't know anything about family affairs, Sandy,' one said, looking significantly at his friends. 'But it's certainly true that the priest has got a big say in the running of the estate.'

'He's only a hypocrite,' Alexander said contemptuously. 'He says he hates drinking, and yet he'll take as much as any man, but only when the blinds of his house are down.'

The crofters were looking around to make sure that no one else was hearing.

'I wouldn't go so far as to call Father Macdonald a hypocrite, Sandy,' one cautioned, 'though maybe he's a wee bit too strict about the drink. But this business about the quarry: by wanting it kept open you're going against your father-in-law.'

'MacPherson doesn't bloody well own me,' Alexander said defiantly. 'I'm married to his daughter, that's all.'

'Aye, we all know you've got a mind of your own, Sandy, but MacPherson's a wild man if he's roused. And he's got the laird on his side, for once. It's your brother who wants it closed, isn't it, and he'll have the final say.'

'Oh he'll want it closed because of the red face he gets in front of his society friends when there's trouble on his estate. He knows he won't lose out by closing it because the trustees will just raise the rents. So in wanting it closed MacPherson's going against his own interests.'

'Have you told him this?'

'Who, my brother?' Alexander asked.

'No, no, MacPherson.'

'I tried to, but he doesn't believe they *can* raise his rent. He says he had some arrangement with my father.'

'Trust him,' one muttered, then aloud, leaning over: 'If MacPherson won't have to pay, we will. And with the laird having a wife now, a lot of money will be needed. Now listen Sandy: we would go up to see the laird about this business, but we're not very good at expressing ourselves. If he was like your father, and came down to the village, that would be a different matter. Maybe you'll go up to the big house for us, tell the laird that the crofters can't afford any more rent. In fact, tell him it's *less* rent we need, not more. Will you do that for us?'

Alexander looked from one expectant face to another, then shrugged. 'I suppose so, if it'll help. But I can't guarantee that he'll see me.'

'Aye, *he'll* see you, Sandy. Blood's thicker than water. Your father never turned anyone away from the big house, not even the tinkers, until he had to take to his bed, and your aunt took charge. Good man. I knew you were like your father. Now we're going to drink to this, and this time you're *not* going to pay. We'll all put something down.' He groped in his waistcoat, making metal click, then laid a shilling on the stained boards. Other coins came slowly, sixpences mostly, after careful scrutiny under the table. The crofter who had started the collection snapped his fingers and called to Carmichael: 'It's for the laird's brother!'

Carmichael brought across a tray of doubles, scooping the coins into his palm and counting carefully. There was a shortfall of two shillings.

'It was singles we wanted, not doubles,' the crofter who had summoned Carmichael said.

'It's always doubles for the laird's brother's table because he's always the one who pays,' the inn keeper said angrily. 'Now hurry up and get the rest out so that I can get back to the counter.'

He stood there, tapping the tin tray against his knee while the crofters looked at each other, searching waistcoat pockets and only coming up with pennies.

'It's the bloody prices you charge,' one said angrily.

'If you can't pay you shouldn't come in,' Carmichael said impassively. 'Unless of course you're always sure of being treated.'

'Meaning what?' a crofter wanted to know.

But Carmichael turned aside contemptuously, spitting. 'I could carry you to the door with one arm.'

Alexander slipped a florin across the table, saying: 'It's all right.'

'It's *not* right,' Carmichael said, picking up the coin and going away.

'Well, *Slainte*,' they said, subdued, lifting the glasses. 'Here's to a successful meeting with the laird.'

Alexander passed his clay pipe, and they all took several puffs.

'I was just thinking,' the eldest crofter said, rubbing his chin, as if it had been a great effort. 'It sounds selfish us sending you up to the big house to plead for us, Sandy. It's like you putting the drinks up every night, though we're aye offering. It's not us who'll be worst affected by the quarry getting closed, because you can't take blood out of a stone. It's these poor Irish buggers, as you were saying earlier. That's who you should be speaking up for. As you said yourself, Sandy: there's nowhere else for them to go, and no work back home. But of course, when you've spoken up for them, you can put in a word for us.'

Alexander nodded gravely, and accepted the clay pipe, which had come full circle.

The mahogany-cased clock on the wall pushed towards time, the Irishmen pounding wood with their fists for last orders, Carmichael with a towel over his shoulder, back turned as he tipped the measure, then tossed the sovereign into a drawer. It had scarcely come to rest before the doubles for which it had paid had hit Irish stomachs. The atmosphere was polluted by clay pipes and rancid moleskins, glass on the gantry protesting as studded boots stamped in support of 'Danny Boy', rendered by a massive Irishman with a livid scar on his cheek from flying granite, and a tear in his eye for the country from which he had been forced to roam in search of bread.

At ten Carmichael roared time, warning that the law would be in if they didn't shift. The pockets of moleskins were turned out into a kitty to buy bottles for the walk to the ferry and the chilly crossing, Carmichael not quibbling at several farthings' short-fall.

Alexander was hoisted to his feet by the crofters and steered towards the counter where a rare smiling Carmichael had his half-bottle carry-out ready for him, helping to install it safely in the inside pocket of the voluminous jacket handed down from MacPherson. Alexander was groping in his waistcoat pocket to give his last coins in settlement, but Carmichael leaned across the counter and pulled him close, whispering in his ear: 'That one's on the house tonight. I heard what you said about going to see your brother the laird about getting the quarry kept open. You'll not be the loser,' he said, winking.

Before Alexander could find words to protest his wish to pay, the crofters had pushed him out into the night.

'You should keep the bottle as a souvenir. You're the only man ever to get something from Carmichael for nothing. Even at new year there's nothing on the house.'

The Irishmen went singing and cursing into the warm night, the quiet countryside amplifying their guttural desires for gratification shouted at small lighted windows in Gaelic that was all too plain, urine soaking moleskin and emptied bottles exploding against rock as they went downhill towards the loch where the ferryman rested on his oars for the appalling pull.

Alexander and his crofting cronies lingered behind, crooning sad Gaelic songs to the brilliant stars, the half-bottle passed from hand to hand without wiping. Alexander insisted on linking arms and joining in the singing, ruining with his rudimentary Gaelic, the pronunciation distorted by the accent of the big house he hadn't been able to erase entirely. Where the road branched the Irishmen stumbled down to the ferry, but the crofters saw Alexander safely along the dusty road above the river, querulous in the continuing drought, the big house lights on one side, Home Farm on the other. Before parting with handshakes at the gate of the new house on the bank of *Poll Dubh*, the crofters reminded Alexander of the pledge made earlier that evening over whisky and wisping clay.

'Mind and speak to the laird about this business of closing the quarry, Sandy. See and put in a good word for the Irishmen.'

They retraced their steps, laughing under the stars while Alexander steadied himself, his new gate squeaking. As always, Kate was waiting up for him by spent coals, in her nightdress, her black hair coiled round her throat, her plain face showing tired resignation.

'Well, what's new in the Arms tonight?' she asked wearily as he barged against stubborn furniture on his way to the fire. 'I suppose the Irishmen were fighting again. Come over here till I see if you've got any bruises.'

'There wasn't a fight,' he said, slumping opposite her in scarred leather, groping in his pocket, cursing at finding the slender clay snapped.

'Well, it's a wonder.' She shook her head. 'I'll never

understand why you have to go up to the Arms every night. If you have to drink, we could get it in from the store. It'd be a damned sight cheaper. That's what my father does.'

'It's the company,' Alexander said. 'Drinking on your own isn't any good. Look what it's done to Mama.'

'You're a one to talk. If you could only see yourself, sitting there.' She sighed. 'It beats me what you see in them. Two sovereigns a night just to hear them talk; it's a big price to pay. You don't seem to realise that they're getting the best of the bargain because it doesn't cost *them* a penny. It can't, because you've got next to nothing in your pocket when you come home. Not even enough for the collection plate, *if* you were a church-goer. All they want is to be able to have their fill of drink for nothing every night and be able to boast that they were drinking with the laird's brother. Oh, it'll be *slainte* to your face, but behind your back —'

'We've had all this out before,' he said wearily, trying to light the broken stump of the pipe, the way the tinkers did.

'Yes, many times, with no effect, because you refuse to face up to the truth.' There was only pity in her voice as she said. 'Look at you, in these ploughman's clothes, full to the eyes, sucking on that silly pipe. That doesn't make you one of *them*. I'm one of them, but I'm certainly not proud of it because they're so damned cunning, so friendly to your face. I hope I'm not like that, but no doubt they think I'm one of them because you're supposed to have been such a good catch, and I'm supposed to have trapped you between my legs. I've told you a hundred times before, and I'll keep on saying it in case it finally gets through: you belong on the other side of the river. For God's sake go back before it's too late.' She raised her voice and appealed with her eyes. 'I mean that, Sandy, because sometimes I get this feeling that something *awful's* going to happen. Don't ask me to explain what I mean; I just *know*.'

'You've been talking to the tinkers again,' he said dismissively. 'I don't mind them coming here for tea, as long as they don't try to scare you.'

'They don't come here because they say there's something eerie about *Poll Dubh*.'

'You don't have to have the second-sight to know that,' he said contemptuously. 'Everyone knows my uncle drowned himself down there. That's why my father got the place.'

'At least *he* didn't sit drinking with his tenants in the Arms. He might have gone up to play quoits and have a dram with them, but he always went back to the big house in the daylight. That's what you should do: for good. We'll sell this house, and I can move back up to the Home Farm. I'll keep the wee girl, but you can see her anytime you like.'

'Don't talk so silly. Do you think I could walk away from the two of you, just like that? I don't belong up there. I hated that whole way of life, so bloody false, having to watch everything you did or said, in case the servants were spying and would carry it up to the village. It suits my brother.'

'At least he faces up to his responsibilities,' she said, 'and he's got himself the right sort of wife. I saw her at the welcome home bonfire. She's a beautiful lady.'

'So are you.'

'Oh Sandy, even if you *are* sincere, you're the silly one now. She was born to that sort of life; she fits in naturally, and no one will ever point the finger at her. Look at these hands. They tell my whole life story.' She held them to the fading peats. 'Not that I'm complaining. It's what I was born to, and I was quite content till you crossed the river. I don't mean that in a nasty way; it's just that I don't belong anywhere now.' She hesitated. 'They tell me your sister-in-law took a turn going up the avenue after the welcome home. At the blind bend. I never liked that place. Anyway, she's better now.'

'It won't take very long for that house to ruin her, like it did Mama. *And* Laura.'

'*You* didn't see very much of your sister.'

'Niall was her favourite. I stayed out of the way. Besides, Carlotta hated me. Anyway, that's all finished.'

'Oh no, it's not,' Kate said vehemently. 'You're going to have to do the right thing for once and go up to the house and meet your new sister-in-law. After all, even the crofters take off their caps.'

'I don't have the time for social calls,' he said harshly. 'I'm up with your father at the farm, trying to learn about it.'

'Oh yes, you're up there all right. You say you're so keen on farming, yet you won't ask your brother for one of the farms. My father's right behind you because he thinks you're such a great catch – for me.' She laughed bitterly. 'I'd have been happier with one of the village boys, living in a croft.'

'I do plan to go up to the big house,' he announced.

'Thank God you're seeing sense at last.' She crossed to kneel beside him, putting her cheek against his knee, her hands folded on his thigh. 'I didn't mean what I said about marrying a village boy, Sandy. It was just that I'm so worried about you. Let's go to bed.'

But he made no move. 'I'm not going up to see my sister-in-law. My brother. To ask him to keep the quarry open.'

Her head jerked up. 'But you're *mad*. Nobody wants that. These Irish animals are going to kill someone if they're allowed to stay.'

'You're wrong about them being animals, and people *do* want it to stay open. They know there's no other work for the Irishmen.'

'Now I know there *is* something wrong with your head,' she said, drawing back to watch him with alarmed eyes. 'It's your drinking cronies who have put you up to this because they're frightened of their rents being raised. They don't give a damn about the Irishmen, or you. Well, be warned: if you try to get the quarry kept open, the villagers who are your dear friends will turn against you. And so will my father. You know fine he wants the quarry closed down, and he's talking sense — for once. He's been all for you up until now but if you go against him in this you'll see a different side to him - one you won't like at all.'

'He'll come round to my way of thinking, because if the quarry closes his rent will go up. He thinks he's safe because he had a gentleman's agreement with my father, but there's nothing on paper, and my brother won't honour it because I married into your family. No, I must go up: tomorrow.'

'But it's the sabbath,' she cried. 'You don't disturb people with such things on a Sunday. Even the tinkers stay in their tents.'

'Monday may be too late. Anyway, my brother isn't very religious. Carlotta sickened him, like she did me.' He got unsteadily to his feet.

'I'll sleep in with the wee girl tonight,' Kate said in a harsh voice. 'And don't disturb us in the morning. You'll just frighten her because she hardly knows you, you're at home so little, and when you do come, it's with drink in you. I'm not going to have *my* child exposed to that.'

Making no concession to the sabbath in his dress, and still slightly unsteady through drink, Alexander took the short cut across the stepping stones and presented himself at the back door of Invernevis House at ten the following morning. Mrs Livingstone was shocked into speechlessness, but affection made her usher him in, Mama's Skye terriers making a great fuss of him, pawing at his lashed trousers and whining.

'I want to see my brother.'

'Well, I'll go through and ask, but I can't promise anything,' the cook warned him. 'Anyway, you wait here. Maggie, pour Master Alexander a cup of tea. Aye, I still keep the pot going, like in the old days,' she sighed.

Her face crimson, Maggie crossed to the cracked brown teapot on the corner of the stove, but Alexander raised a hand and shook his head.

'Not unless you've got a drop whisky to put into it,' he said, only half laughing.

'It's all through in the dining-room,' Maggie managed to say.

'I knew your brother,' Alexander said. 'He often worked beside me at the Home Farm. I was very sorry about what happened in South Africa.'

She bit her lip and nodded, then went back to bury her fingers in the flour in the bowl on the big white table. He had already defected when she had first come to work at the big house, and she had only seen him at a distance across the river, swinging a scythe or switching home the cattle at evening milking, his whistling carrying. As her fingers fumbled, blending dust and fat, she stole a glance and thought him rather handsome, with his fair moustache. He was shorter than his brother. There had been a lot of jealousy in the village when Kate MacPherson had got her claws into him. Maggie's brother had always had a good word for him, though her mother thought him a waster. There was something pathetic about him, the way he stood, twisting the skip of his cap in his fists. He didn't suit the clothes. They made you want to cry more than laugh. And his face was so white, like the stuff in her fingers.

Mrs Livingstone came back to say that the Master would see him, her eyes warning that he wasn't pleased about the visit. 'You know your own way through,' she said quietly, and as he passed she squeezed his arm and said something in Gaelic.

Alexander knocked on the library door and was shouted in angrily, his brother standing behind his desk.

'This is outrageous. And coming on a Sunday. If I'd been sure there wouldn't be a scene, I would have got Mrs Livingstone to turn you away. I suppose this is another attempt to embarrass me, only this time you know I've got a wife.'

'I didn't come to make trouble,' Alexander said, standing in front of the desk. 'I wouldn't have come if it wasn't urgent.'

'Don't tell me you've got *another* woman in the family way.'

But Alexander ignored this harsh reminder of their last row. 'No, nothing to do with me. I can look after my own affairs. It's about the quarry. I hear you're going to close it.'

'So you *do* take an interest in what goes on up here,' Invernevis said sarcastically. He lowered himself to the swivel chair, but keeping his eyes on his brother. 'Who was your informant, may I ask?'

'That doesn't matter. Is it true?'

'That is none of your business, now that you are away from here. It was *your* choosing, remember.'

'So it *is* true. I thought so. I'm here to ask you not to close it.'

Invernevis sat staring uncomprehendingly at Alexander. 'This is absurd. Your father-in-law wants the place closed – he told me in no uncertain terms on the night of the heather fire, you'll remember – and as far as I can see you always do as he says. Am I to take it that you've fallen out, and have come here to make things up?'

'It's got nothing to do with MacPherson. I'm here to speak up for the Irishmen. If the quarry closes down, they've got nowhere else to go, and big families back home to support.'

Invernevis's eyes were widening with every word. Then, seeing how serious Alexander was, he burst out laughing. 'You're quite mad. I know what happened: you were with them in the Arms last night, and they filled you up with drink and got you to promise to put in a word for them with me. What a bloody fool you are.'

'I wasn't even speaking to them last night,' Alexander said hotly.

'But you were speaking to someone.' He pondered, pursing his lips as he tapped a cigarette on a silver case, then struck a match on ridged glass. 'Oh, I see. Carmichael's offered you a case of whisky to get the quarry kept open, otherwise his profits will go to nothing. Your loyalty lies in a strange place. It's another way of getting at me.' He waved a hand dismissively. 'Oh, don't start denying it. You've made your attitude to me pretty plain in your conduct.' He got up and began to walk around, taking deep draws at his cigarette, and, without turning: 'It may surprise you to know that I've just been writing a letter to the lawyers, telling them I want the quarry to stay open.' He faced Alexander suddenly. 'But not for the reason you give. It's because the alternative to closure is raising the rents, and I don't want to do that. There's a condition, however, and that is that when they cross over to here on a Saturday night, foremen come too to keep good order.'

'The reason doesn't matter,' Alexander said. 'Just as long as it's not closing. Well, I'll be going now.'

'Having got what you came for. That was always your way,' his brother said bitterly. He wagged a finger. 'Well, don't imagine that this has given you a victory over me. I made the decision before you were out of your bed this morning. Hasn't it occurred to you that the money you got from father could have been put to the good of the estate instead of being poured down your throat - *and* others - in the Arms? If father had done the right thing by me, there wouldn't be any need to risk life and limb by keeping the quarry open.'

'The money isn't being poured away in the Arms,' Alexander said angrily. 'What do you think I built the house with? And there's plenty left. MacPherson invested it for me.'

'I know where that rogue will have invested it,' his brother said, laughing bitterly, 'and I'm sure he'll learn to live with the quarry, if it means his rent staying the same. Anyway, you've got what you wanted, as usual, leaving me with all the worries. I asked you before to help me by becoming the factor, but you refused, no doubt because you didn't want to be seen working for me. Yet you're quite happy to work for MacPherson. That's what I call loyalty.'

'Look: let's stop all this arguing. It's not too late to make things up,' Alexander pleaded, extending his hand.

But his brother turned his back, to stand staring up the avenue to the blind bend. 'It was too late even before I set out for South Africa. You could have stayed here to look after Mama and Laura, but you had to have your pleasure at the Home Farm. You're as much to blame as *him* for Mama turning into an alcoholic, and for Carlotta killing Laura. No, you're your father's son, all right, nothing but a waster, and you're best to take yourself away from this house for good. If *he* had done that, there wouldn't have been such tragedy. You wanted so much to belong on the other side of the river, so stay there. For good!'

Alexander shrugged, and turned to the door. As he crossed the hall, making for the passage leading to the back door and liberty, Mary Rose was coming down the stairs. She stopped half way, hand on the banister, struck into recognition by the boyhood photograph she had seen in the drawing-room, and by the facial resemblance to her husband. She descended quickly, smiling, hand outstretched, sweeping towards him in a swirl of silk, and he saw there was no escape.

'You're Alexander,' she said sweetly. 'How nice to meet you at last.'

He held up his hand to show how grimy it was, but she insisted on taking it.

'Honest toil's never unclean, and I see you've been working this morning. I'm so glad you came. Have you been seeing Niall?'

He nodded.

'Good. Now I'll go and arrange some coffee, and we can have a chat. There's such a lot I want to ask you about.'

'No coffee, thank you; I must go,' he said, casting a nervous glance over his shoulder at the library door, wishing she would keep her voice down.

Her face registered genuine disappointment. 'Well, when you've got more time. You must bring your wife up to dinner. I'm so looking forward to meeting her.'

'It's not easy, with the child,' he protested.

'Then bring the little girl with you,' she beamed, as if nothing could be simpler.

'Yes, well, I must be going,' he said, moving.

'Of course. You've got work to do. But I'll send a note down next week. Goodbye.'

She went into the library, to find her husband lost in thought at the window.

'I've just met your brother,' she said triumphantly. 'Very pleasant and good looking, too.'

He wheeled, dropping cigarette ash, but she kept on talking, as if she hadn't noticed. 'Was it just a social call?'

'No, business,' Invernevis said abruptly. 'Something he heard in the village.'

'So good of him to come and tell you. Well, I've got some news too: I've invited him and his wife to dinner. Let's say next Saturday.'

'You shouldn't have done that without consulting me,' he rebuked her.

Mary Rose flushed. 'I'm the mistress here now, and dinner parties are for *me* to arrange. Why shouldn't I invite them? They're our closest relatives.'

'Because we don't get on, and it wouldn't be fair to us or her to invite his wife up here. She's a tenant's daughter.'

She stared at him, shocked. 'But he's your brother, and you should love him, whatever he's done. Jamie's made a far bigger mess of his life than Alexander, but I wouldn't turn him or any wife he took away from my door. It's not just family ties; it's simple courtesy.'

'You don't understand,' her husband said. 'It was my brother who chose not to belong to this family by crossing the river to the Home Farm, and that's the way he wants it to stay. He wasn't doing me any favour coming up here this morning. He was looking to his own interests, as usual.'

'What did he want?' she asked, exasperated.

'Estate business, which I don't want to bother you with.' He saw how confused she was and came round the desk, putting his arm round her shoulder. 'My dear, let's not quarrel over Alexander. He's simply not worth it. Mama broke her heart over him, and even Carlotta did her best for him. Trust me. If it's dinner parties you want, there are far more suitable people in the county who have not shamed their families. But first we'll have to get the house in order. I've just written to the lawyers, telling them that I want the quarry kept open, because I don't want the rents to rise, and because we need some of the money to do work on this house. Now I'm going to ring for Mrs Livingstone to send through some coffee, and I'll join you in the drawing-room when I've sealed this letter.'

Mary Rose allowed herself to be steered out of the library, but stood dubiously in the hall. There was more to the Alexander business than he was telling her, yet another secret of that house she was coming to dislike. Whatever her husband said, she had liked Alexander. There was a lot of Jamie in him. And Alexander would have told her over dinner if there were any stories connected with the blind bend.

After Alexander had hurried through the kitchen on his way out, muttering 'cheerio' over his shoulder, Mrs Livingstone had to sit at the table with her small brown teapot.

'What a traffic for a Sunday,' she sighed. 'Did you see his face? I don't think we'll see him up here again, poor soul.'

'Why don't they get on?' Maggie asked, spreading lettuce under sparkling water.

'I don't think they know themselves,' the cook said. 'It goes back a long time, to when they were boys here together, and the father still living. He made too much of Master Alexander, likely because Miss Carlotta made so much of Master Niall. It's her I blame for most of the things that have happened in this house,' she said with sudden heat. 'Oh aye, it was Master Alexander the old laird was always taking on his horse, or up the mountain to shoot. Poor Master Niall was hardly ever allowed into the library. You would have thought that Master Alexander was the heir. And the Master blames his brother for not making enough of Miss Laura, I'm quite sure of that. You see, with Master Niall away at the war, and Master Alexander at the Home Farm, Miss Carlotta had Miss Laura where she wanted her, and we both know what happened. But it's not our place to know the reasons why, girl. We're only here to serve, so anything I say to you doesn't go out of this kitchen; do you understand? I always knew I was safe with your mother.'

The bell clanging on the board above the dresser almost made the cook spill her stewed tea. 'Merciful heavens, is there to be no rest on a Sunday, and my ankles wice what they should be. Well, all the maids are at the chapel, so you'll have to go through and see what they want, Maggie. It's the library, so watch yourself because he's probably in a temper after Master Alexander. The poor soul, sometimes I think he's the best of them.'

CHAPTER 4

Confidently expecting Richardson the lawyer to agree to the expenditure of part of the proceeds of the increased revenue from the quarry on modernising the house, Invernevis sent for Morrison, the architect responsible for building Alexander's house, the only architect within a radius of fifty miles.

The caped and artistically moustached architect stood in the library, hearing about his new commission.

'My wife wants certain improvements put in hand,' Invernevis explained from the other side of the desk. 'Go round with her to see what she has in mind, then come back here and give me a rough idea of the cost.' He crossed to crank the bell handle by the fire.

Morrison shed his cape and deerstalker in the hall and went through the house with the new Mistress, talking and gesticulating, sometimes shaking his head and sighing, sometimes laughing, jotting in a little black notebook. He saw the public rooms and kitchen, the guest bedrooms and servants' quarters, but went alone up the rickety ladder into the attic, carrying a lantern. Muffled knocking could be heard. Half an hour later he emerged with dirt under his nails and cobwebs clinging to his close fitting tweeds. There was a further consultation with the new Mistress before he went down to the library.

'Well, is the place about to fall down?' Invernevis asked breezily, amused by the serious, smudged face.

'Not exactly, but there's a lot that needs doing. Your good lady certainly has artistic taste, but that costs money. I'm talking about redecoration, good wallpaper, and scaffolding to get at the ceilings. It's not just a question of whitewashing them; the gilding will have to be restored, and that's a very slow and skilled job.'

'So how much do you estimate?'

'I haven't finished. In fact, I've hardly started. Do you mind?' he asked, showing Invernevis his cigarette case, and when he had his assent, lit up slowly. 'I'm an architect, and though I'm very interested in interior decoration, my main concern is with structure. What's the point of spending a lot of money doing up the interior of a house if it's going to be ruined in a few years? I'm talking about your roof. I've given it a good going over, and I'm afraid that it's in a very bad state. I warned your father a few years ago, but he did nothing, so now it needs a major overhaul. That means stripping the slates and replacing the sarking. And maybe some of the rafters, because there's worm in them. I'm sorry to seem so pessimistic, but it's a pretty serious situation. You can already see what's happening in some of the bedrooms. A really heavy spell of rain, and you could have water running down the stairs, and ceilings falling.'

'What's all this going to cost?' Invernevis asked hoarsely.

'At the moment I can't give you a precise figure, because I would need to go over the roof again and take measurements. But I don't see you getting much change out of a thousand pounds.'

'A thousand?'

'It sounds high, but so is the roof. You'll need a lot of scaffolding, and the men will have to be paid danger money.'

'I see. And the rest of the work my wife wants done?'

'This is slightly embarrassing for me, sir,' the architect said, lighting a fresh cigarette before the other one was finished. 'You see, I don't know how much money is available. Your good lady doesn't only want the place decorated. She wants certain structural alterations, like the kitchen gutted and modernised, and dormer windows for the servants' quarters, to give them more space and light. In fact, she wants to bring in another architect. Robert Lorimer.'

'I don't understand,' Invernevis said helplessly. 'Who is this Lorimer?'

'An architect who's making a name for himself. Family have Kellie Castle. He's building a mansion in Ayrshire, which I hear is very – advanced.'

Has he had any dealings with Campbell at Branglin?' Invernevis asked suspiciously. The proprietor of the abutting estate was his sworn enemy. The brute had purchased the place with East Indies money, made from slaves, most likely. When Invernevis was in South Africa Campbell had tried to buy a pool from poor drunken Mama at a knockdown price. 'I think his house is appalling.'

'No, Campbell employs an Edinburgh architect noted for good traditional Scottish Baronial. As far as I know, Lorimer hasn't worked in this part of the country. What your good lady has in mind is to get Lorimer to remove and rebuild the top floor.'

'But that would destroy the historical character of the house,' Invernevis said in horror. 'After all, it's classic eighteenth century.'

'I agree with you, sir, but your good lady sees it differently. She feels that comfort should come before tradition. Anyway, at a very rough calculation, if you do the roof, bring in Lorimer and then do all the interior decoration your good lady wants done, five thousand pounds. It's a very rough estimate, because I don't know what Lorimer's fees are, but he's becoming fashionable, and I should imagine you'll have to pay a lot for his services.'

Invernevis was now lighting a cigarette. There was no possibility of the trustees agreeing to even half that sum, and he had no capital to make a contribution. Nor had Mary Rose. He felt irritated with her, for putting him in such an embarrassing position with the architect, who was watching his prospective client's face closely, looking for domestic discord perhaps.

'Are you quite sure that the roof's as bad as you say?' Invernevis asked, to give him time to think.

'Yes, it's bad, but if your father had only spent a few hundred ten years ago, there would be no need for a major overhaul. I'll be able to give you a precise figure when I go over it again.'

'And if the Lorimer idea were dropped?'

'That would bring it down a great deal. Two thousand? It depends on what your good lady's plans are. She says she wants William Morris wallpaper and curtains, and new furniture by that chap Rennie Mackintosh who did Miss Cranston's tea-rooms in Glasgow. Have you been in any of them?'

Invernevis shook his head. It was growing more confusing by the minute.

'I have, but I can't say I like his designs. Too garish, not in keeping with the character of a house such as this. Maybe more suitable for your brother's house. Anyway, the final cost depends on your good lady's tastes.'

'I'm grateful to you for explaining all this to me,' Invernevis muttered. 'At the minute I can't say how much money will be available, but there will be *some*. Obviously the roof's the most important part, so I suggest you do a thorough survey and produce a firm estimate as soon as possible. Then we can see where we go from there.'

'I'll start tomorrow,' Morrison said. 'But there's one problem we haven't discussed: weather. The roof should really be done before the winter sets in, in case it's a bad one. I'll need time to get tradesmen organised - assuming you accept the estimate, that is.'

'I've no intention of calling in another architect,' Invernevis said coldly. 'Once I see your estimate I can instruct you.'

After the architect had gone, Mary Rose came in, flushed with excitement over her plans. She went round the desk, sat on her husband's lap and put her arms round his neck.

'Well?'

Embarrassed by her show of affection, Invernevis gently raised her to her feet and led her through to the drawing-room, where they could relax on the deep sofas. He sat opposite her, and before he spoke, lit a cigarette.

'It's very clever of you, my dear. Morrison was certainly impressed. But there are some problems. He says that the roof is the first priority - that if we don't repair it, we'll have flooding and ceilings down.'

'But the roof will have to be lifted off anyway, if the attic rooms are to be made bigger,' she interrupted. 'So you can do two jobs for the price of one.'

'Not quite,' he cautioned. 'In the first instance, all the sarking and a good many of the slates will have to be renewed. I'm talking about doing up the roof, as it stands. But if the attic rooms are to be altered, the rafters will have to come away, and the roof made bigger. That'll mean more timber and slates, not to mention the new windows, so it would be much more expensive.' Seeing her face, he tried to find a gentler way. 'But there's another aspect that worries me. By altering the roof you alter the whole character of the house, and I very much doubt if the trustees would agree to this. Don't forget that it's technically not *our* house; it's held in trust for any son we might have.'

'That's absurd!' she protested. 'Surely the character of the house doesn't come before the people who have to live in it. I'm talking about the servants as well. They're living practically under the slates, hardly able to stand up straight in these tiny little rooms, with hardly any light coming in, and no water-closet, never mind a bath. It's primitive, that's what it is. You can't expect to have a happy, loyal staff if they have to live in such conditions.'

'I've never had a complaint,' Invernevis said testily, uneasy at hearing her brother Jamie's revolutionary ideas of equality echoed. Hadn't Jamie championed the Boers, though they had ruined his arm? Such ideas simply wouldn't do at Invernevis. The servants were happy with their lot. They were fed and clothed and given shelter, and often they had to be buried at the estate's expense. It was a closed, contented self-sufficient world, and stirring things up could only cause trouble, as Carlotta had shown. But he couldn't believe that she was serious about the servants; it was just an excuse to get the fancy new architect Lorimer or whatever he was called brought in. He was going to have to be firm, but mustn't forget that she wasn't strong.

'Your concern for the comfort of the servants is admirable, my dear, but it isn't realistic. The trustees will never agree to spending all that money on this house, far less to major structural alterations. There will be a certain amount available, and it's got to be spent wisely, the roof first, then the rooms you use most, this room, the dining-room, your bedroom.'

'But that's only a small part of the house. What about the kitchen? It belongs in the middle ages. Mrs Livingstone might as well be cooking in the open.'

'I think you'll find that Mrs Livingstone is quite satisfied with what she's got. My father put in a new stove when he came home from India.'

'That was thirty years ago,' she answered scornfully. 'The world's moved on since then, though this place hasn't changed. There's electric light now, you know, which the architect tells me Colonel Campbell has at Branglin.'

'Because he diverted the river to make a dam, which he had no right to do,' Invernevis said. 'He's just an upstart, and his house is a monstrosity. We've managed for centuries with candles and then lamps. I don't want ugly fittings hanging from the ceilings.'

In the ensuing stalemate of silence she took up a piece of embroidery and went to sit by the window, driving the needle into the thick material. He crossed to join her, put a consoling hand on her silk knee.

'Let's not quarrel about this, my dear. I'm not denying you the improvements; in fact, Morrison will be back tomorrow to make up proper estimates. It's just that we have to be cautious, to do things in stages. I don't want to get on the wrong side of the trustees by asking for too much at once, before the extra income from the quarry has come in. We'll do a bit at a time, over the next few years, and you and Morrison can arrange it together, with you having the final say. Does that sound reasonable?'

While he was speaking the needle became a static spark between her fingers, and she stared up the river. 'How I envy Alexander,' she said with a sigh. 'Such an uncomplicated life. A manageable house, a family, able to do what he likes.'

'I doubt if he's as happy as he makes out,' her husband warned, angry that Alexander had upset the Sunday household. 'Evading one's responsibilities isn't the answer.'

'But facing up to them can be very tiring,' she said. 'I'm beginning to understand Jamie better now, even sympathise with him. I had a long and very melancholy letter from him yesterday, full of complaints about mother, saying she's a tyrant because she wouldn't give him the money to stand as a Liberal. And also a letter from mother, saying how heavily he's drinking. I wonder if I should go north and try and make peace between them.'

'I won't allow it,' Invernevis said firmly. 'They'll have to sort out their own problems from now on. It's quite unfair of them, when they know you don't keep well.'

'Yes, you need broad shoulders for this life,' she said wistfully. 'You know, I've got this awful premonition that Jamie's going to come to a bad end.'

'Like my brother,' he said, staring down at the small house on the bank of *Poll Dubh*. 'The only difference is that Alexander knew I was there to take over the responsibilities of the place while he sought his pleasures across the river. But Jamie doesn't have anyone else to take over the responsibilities. You certainly couldn't do it, and I wouldn't allow it, even though there wasn't a male entail.'

'Maybe he needs our help.'

'No, he's like Mama. As Doctor MacNiven says, the effort has got to come from within herself.' Since it was a morning for confronting problems, he had deliberately made the comparison. 'I've been thinking of putting Mama into a nursing home in Edinburgh. Things obviously aren't going to get any better here, and she's just going to distress you.'

'But that would be cruel!' she cried. 'Don't use me as an excuse. You're not the only one who's been thinking about her. The first thing we have to do to help her is to get her a personal maid, who'll keep her clean.'

'It's very thoughtful of you,' he said. Then, shaking his head: 'But she won't change. After Laura died she got a fright and pulled herself together for a while, but as soon as my back was turned, she was back on the bottle worse than ever. No, Mama's a hopeless alcoholic, and a nursing home's the best place for her. It'll be expensive, but she's got an annuity from the estate, and I'll make up the difference.'

'I won't allow it,' Mary Rose said angrily, turning to accuse him. 'That's not solving a problem; it's evading it, the very thing you blame Alexander for. It should be easy enough to discover who's fetching the supplies for your mother, and then we dismiss him – or her.'

'It's certainly not one of the maids,' he said, surprised.

'How do you know?' she asked coolly.

'Because I know them all well, and they wouldn't be disloyal like that.'

'I don't know, it might be that girl in the kitchen,' Mary Rose said, steady eyes on her husband. 'I notice that she never looks you straight in the face. And she does spend a good deal of time with your mother, doesn't she?'

'Good heavens, Maggie isn't disloyal,' he said, sensing that the remark meant more, but not able to work out another meaning. 'I can vouch for her, because her father's been ghillie here since I was a boy, and he did much more for my father than standing beside him at the river. I've never heard anyone speak ill of Duncan. And the mother was in the kitchen before she got married, so there's been a long family connection. I take a special interest in Maggie because I took her brother out to South Africa as my orderly and he got killed at Magersfontein. Jamie knew him. Maggie's young, but she's known a lot of sorrow, her mother dying of cancer, her brother buried so far away. And my aunt took a terrible spite to her and made her life hell. So I feel we owe her something extra. She's very good to Mama, goes up and sits with her, listening to her ramblings when I couldn't. I just hope she'll stay here so that she can become cook when Mrs Livingstone retires, because she's shaping up very well in the kitchen.'

'You seem to have more concern for the kitchen-maid than for your own mother,' Mary Rose said coldly.

It now occurred to Invernevis that some malicious person had told Mary Rose about the photograph which Maggie had once asked for instead of the usual Christmas present. Whoever had told his wife of it must have put the wrong construction on it. But who could it have been? Certainly not Mrs Livingstone, and not Maggie herself. Frank the footman? Invernevis had never liked his smooth city ways, and suspected him of being the carrier of Mama's supplies, though he had never been caught. What was he going to say to his wife, to allay any suspicions she might have? Wasn't it dangerous to raise the subject of the photograph, which she might not know anything about? She might have taken an irrational spite to Maggie, as Carlotta had done, but for a different reason, because Maggie was obviously close to Mama.

Mary Rose saved him from having to furnish an explanation. She had no intention of prompting him by referring to the pasted-together photograph she had seen on the kitchen-maid's wash-stand. It was his place to come clean, because marriage meant complete honesty from both partners. She turned to her husband: 'From now on *I'm* going to keep a watch, and I'm going to find out who's supplying your mother. As soon as I discover, it's instant dismissal, no matter who it is.'

He nodded, but he wasn't pleased with the arrangement. If the servants thought they were being spied on, it would only cause trouble, and they would come to dislike their new

Mistress as they had done Carlotta. Mrs Livingstone was perfectly capable of managing the servants, and knew their ways. Suppose Mary Rose picked the wrong person? Better to steer clear of that topic.

'Well, if you think Mama could be looked after here, I'll put an advertisement in *The Scotsman* for a nurse. I think it's better to get someone from away,' he added. 'Don't you?'

'I've got someone in mind. My old nanny. She's just the very one to handle your mother.'

He was surprised again, but didn't say anything. Was she looking for a friend from outside Invernevis already?

'That's settled then,' she said, her needle trailing blue thread again. 'I'll write to mother about sending Nanny Gunn, and you can arrange for the repairs and redecoration.'

'I was going to sell the organ,' he said, for something to say. 'I believe I could get five hundred pounds for it, which would pay for doing up this room. It's very drab.'

'Oh *no*. I've sent away for organ music.'

So there was to be no respite from the ugly brute that symbolised Carlotta and her Catholicism, its gilt pipes rising like a restraining palm in the room in which his sister Laura had whirled at the Hogmanay dance, cuffed out of life by a cruel hand.

Morrison the architect spent two days going over the house with a measuring tape, putting his young assistant out on to the roof through a skylight to probe where slates had been stripped by forgotten storms. He closeted himself in his office for a day with ready reckoner and trade catalogues, producing five close pages of longhand which he delivered personally to Invernevis. He went straight to the last page, to the final total of two thousand seven hundred and forty six pounds three shillings.

'What does this cover?' he asked uneasily.

'Overhauling the roof, putting in a bathroom on the first floor, redecorating the public rooms and principal bedrooms, work on the kitchen.'

'It's much more than I expected.'

'Well, the bulk of the expenditure's inside the house, not on the roof, because your good lady wants quality fittings and wallpapers. It doesn't cover curtains because that's not my department.' Then, seeing his client's face: 'I could cut it down, but quality would have to go.'

'No, there's no use getting a shoddy job that won't last,' Invernevis said, biting his fist as he studied the lined papers.

'It's high, I know, but it would have been three times that if I'd costed for bringing in Lorimer to raise the roof and create dormers, and Mackintosh from Glasgow to design furniture,' the architect offered in consolation.

'No, that's out of the question. Tell me: when could you make a start on the roof?'

The architect pursed his lips dubiously. 'That's proving a difficult one. There aren't any local joiners or slaters available, and it would cost far too much to take a squad from the south.'

'No locals available?' Invernevis said incredulously. 'But that's not possible. There were some working down at my brother's house before I went on honeymoon, doing the outhouses, and before that they rebuilt the summer house for me. You know that; you were the architect in both instances.'

'Yes, but I had a devil of a job getting them, and as soon as they were finished at your brother's they went back up to Colonel Campbell's. As far as I can see, building never stops at Branglin. Now it's a garage for a third car. The man has more money than sense.'

'He's nothing but a speculator who's profited at the expense of poor black people!' Invernevis shouted, losing his temper. 'That's not a house he's building; it's a monstrosity, towers and battlements stuck anywhere. He's trying to be the great laird but he's only a jumped-up merchant with no breeding. Now listen!' He leaned across the desk, wagging a finger. 'You get up to Branglin and tell the local tradesmen that there's urgent work to be done on the roof of Invernevis House. Remind them that they're *my* tenants, and that they therefore owe their loyalty to me. If that doesn't work, offer them more money to come down here to do the roof.'

'I've not much time for Colonel Campbell, and not only because he employs an Edinburgh architect,' Morrison said, shaking his head, 'but I'm sorry, sir, you're asking me to breach professional ethics by persuading tradesmen to leave one job for another.'

'Then if *you* won't, I'll get another architect,' Invernevis said decisively. 'You have two minutes to decide.'

Morrison didn't need that long. For financial as well as social reasons he couldn't afford to lose his most prestigious client. He had made a good job of Master Alexander's house, and there could be other commissions - a new chapel? - coming his way. He picked up his hat and sighed. 'All right, sir, I'll go up now, but Campbell might set his dogs on me.'

'Don't let him see you approaching the men. So that's the problem solved. How soon can they start?'

'Well, the joiners can start putting up the scaffolding at the beginning of next week, provided that I can get enough wood. There are sleepers down by the station that would be a big help.'

'Nothing simpler. Telegraph the head office and say they're for my use. After all, I let the railway company trespass. You get things moving, and I'll send this estimate on to my lawyers. And don't worry about Campbell; that swine hasn't the guts to do anything to you.'

The reaction of the trustees worried Invernevis. They were bound to raise objections to such a big sum, but after all, the mansion was the heart of the estate. Without its vital action the estate would die. But there was an even bigger problem - explaining the cut-back in plans to Mary Rose. There could be no Lorimer, no improvements to the servants' quarters, and the quality of the wallpaper was in doubt. As to the William Morris curtains and Mackintosh furniture, they came last on the list. But he wasn't going to say anything to her until the work was under way.

At the beginning of the following week, scaffolding began to gird Invernevis House, stout sleepers for the tradesmen to walk on. Within two days the structure rooted on the gravel at the front of the house had reared beyond the bay window where Mama lay behind drawn curtains, yelling because she thought the sounds and shadows outside were Indians swarming, to ravish as they had done in the Mutiny. She called on Sandy, but he didn't come, and then she remembered that he was on manoeuvres, miles away in the hills. She was going to have to write to him again that night, telling him that another woman, face muffled in a *sari*, had come to the door, complaining that her ten year old daughter had been molested by the Major on a rush mat, the big eyed undernourished child with her, already pendulous breasted, ready to tell her story to Colonel Gordon. But this one didn't want money. Instead, she pointed to the *Mem-sahib*'s pearls, which were an heirloom, worth hundreds of pounds, but they had to be lifted off and handed over before Carlotta heard. Which she did, because she came out just as the woman and child fled for the hills again, a small black fist clasping the milky seeds.

Carlotta made a terrible scene in front of the servants, shouting that the stories were true, and that the man was a pervert who ought to be deprived of the apparatus of assault. Of course she had to stand there and take it all from Carlotta because it had been Carlotta who had provided the money on the two previous occasions to buy the silence of the Indian mothers. But she was quite sure that all Sandy needed to do was to get leave from the manoeuvres and come back to Kamptree to prove his innocence, simply by being seen about. It couldn't be true. He was too handsome, too strong a man to stoop to that sort of thing. She would never forget the first time she had set eyes on him, dancing over crossed swords at Colonel Gordon's Cremorne on the circular floor of the Soldiers' Garden, the heap in the groin of his tight blue trousers moving as he rotated, hands high, to the pipes, with the deadly lethargy of a cobra, his eyes drilling. Not that she had been able to meet his nightly demands in the stinking sweltering barracks, but it would all come right when they got back to England, with Carlotta left behind in India. She would write again that night, telling him about the other Indian woman, imploring him to write to his elder brother at Invernevis, asking if he would abdicate. But before she wrote she would have to get somebody to clear away the Indians swarming up the outside of the house, making such a noise, after money, most likely. You couldn't be too careful about them, because look what they had done to the white women and children in the Mutiny. Carlotta handed out plain wooden rosaries she had sent by the dozen from England, but they would always be savages.

'Clear off or I'll get my husband and his soldiers to you!' Mama yelled, and the Invernevis men on the scaffolding outside the window looked at each other and tapped their temples.

'Coming back to defend her, eh? He was too busy using his weapon elsewhere.'

They laughed and resumed erecting the scaffolding, their hammers echoed by the mountain, cancelling Mama's ravings.

Richardson the lawyer replied that week, pointing out that his satisfaction over the renewal of the quarry company lease on a greatly increased rental was somewhat diminished by the idea of the revenue being spent in advance on the mansion house.

> Whereas myself and the other trustees recognise that essential repairs must be put in hand for the future benefit of the estate, with the roof having the first priority, it would appear that the redecoration of so many rooms, and the planned improvements are somewhat ambitious, if not extravagant. Of course we appreciate that with your marriage, a domestic situation that served well enough in the past will have to be altered, but we would ask you to keep such expenditure to an absolute minimum.
>
> It is our duty as trustees to point out that the increased revenue from the new quarry lease was primarily intended to effect much

needed improvements and repairs to the estate. For instance, Mr MacPherson at the Home Farm is pressing us very hard to repair his barn, and threatens to take us to court unless we honour the terms of his lease. And of course the majority of the estate crofts require improvements such as piped water.

In conclusion, we would warn you that the finances of the estate are by no means healthy, and that unless expenditure is confined to essentials, either the rents will have to be raised, or land sold. Both these courses we wish to avoid, but as trustees we must first and foremost have the best interests of the estate at heart. Under the terms of your father's will, we serve the future heir, and not yourself as life-renter, though we will endeavour to render you all reasonable assistance.

We understand that Colonel Hooker threatens to go to Leamington, which is worrying your aunt. It is proving increasingly difficult to get coherent decisions from the Colonel as a trustee, though he is continually writing to claim expenses.

Our regards to your good lady, and to your mother, whom we hope is in better health.

The lawyer's letter both worried and angered Invernevis. What did Richardson mean by keeping expenditure on the house down to an 'absolute minimum'? He must have received the architect's estimate of two thousand seven hundred pounds. Why then had he not set a limit? If the roof was to have the 'first priority', did that mean that the other improvements would have to be abandoned? If he wrote for clarification, Richardson would fix a figure which would probably only cover the roof. Damn the trustees: once again they were putting the onus of decision on him, yet he didn't have the authority. Then they would blame him for overspending. It was his father's fault in binding his hands with trustees, mocking his manhood by allowing others to pull the strings. And why should the Home Farm have priority over the big house when MacPherson was on a ridiculously low rent? There was no end to the greed of the man who had caused all the trouble with Alexander by tempting him across the river, using his daughter as bait. In final insult, the brute was administering Alexander's legacy, which should have been the elder brother's by right.

Then there were the snide asides in Richardson's letter, the criticism for not keeping in touch with his aunt, the reference to Mama's drunkenness. He wasn't going to take that from a man who was only a servant of the estate, albeit sitting in striped trousers in an Edinburgh office. And he certainly wasn't going to give rumour the opportunity to spread by ordering the architect to cut back on the improvement plans. The work would go ahead, and it was up to the trustees to object when the bills started to go in. Besides, if he showed the letter to Mary Rose, she would think they were bankrupt.

The scaffolding now reached to the roof, with slates being prised off to expose the rotten sarking, rafters peppered with worm, the hammers increasing conversations in the house to shouting, Gaelic songs heard from above between blows, the workmen at meal breaks sitting on sleepers, swinging their legs and surveying the Invernevis lands as they munched big slices of bread packed with local cheese. And work had begun below also. The silk came away with a snarling sound from the drawing-room walls as Mary Rose sat in the bay window with the architect, leafing through a tome of wallpapers. Eventually she decided on a heavy paper embossed with roses, and he went down to the village to telegraph to Glasgow for twenty rolls to be put on the morning train, leaving her to choose the papers for the other rooms.

There was much excitement among the servants about the renovations, particularly among the house-maids, for it meant less cleaning. Mrs Livingstone warned them to make the most of it, for there would be some mess to clean up when it was all finished. She was frightened that the new Mistress was going to include the kitchen in her schemes, and she confided in Maggie as flour was rubbed through a sieve in sunlight, the dogs shifting and sighing on the step as hammers intruded.

'It's an old type of stove, but you'll never get a better one for baking. If I put my hand into the oven I know if it's ready for the baking or roasting. And the cupboards: they might be all over the place, but at least you know where to put your hand on things. I'm not saying these things don't need doing, but it would have been better to make the changes gradually. And I don't like to think what it's going to cost, with all these tradesmen. She must have brought a lot of money with her, because Miss Carlotta was always moaning about how poor they were. I should know: when she was giving you out curry powder, you would think it was gold. No, the Master hasn't much money; the old lady seen to that when he was away at the war, and they say Master Alexander got the father's, which wasn't right, though he *is* a poor soul. None of this better get out of this kitchen, girl. Your mother was the only one I could say things to. What was I saying? Oh yes, about the tradesmen. Such a noise they're making, it goes right into your head. Well, they'll have to get tea, because there's always a cup of tea going here, be it a tinker or duke.' She peered. 'Now where's the young Mistress making for? I hope not down the avenue, after what happened at the bend. Oh aye, you can say what you like, but there's something not right there. The Master asked me, but I didn't want to worry him any more. She seems to be making for the avenue, and with a parasol, if you please. It puts you in mind of Miss Carlotta. Well, if I lose this stove, I'll be lost.'

Silk to her ankles against the last wasps of summer, white parasol sloped against her shoulder, Mary Rose wobbled over the gravel. All the wallpapers had been chosen, and she could leave their application to Morrison the architect, whom she found too ingratiating, anyway. Besides, the sound of the tearing silk got on her nerves, as if the old house was snarling at her for disturbing it after so long, and the hammers above had tortured her head.

The going became easier on compacted dust, until she turned off on to the silent upholstery of moss leading to the walled garden, its eight foot wall unstable where fruit tree roots sought freedom. The big iron gate with the lock made a mournful sound as she entered the complex of paths bordered by knee-high hedges. It was a garden serving both aesthetics and appetite, providing flowers and vegetables for the big house tables, supervised with jealous pride by Ranald, who had succeeded his father, and who knew the potential of every inch of soil. It was a struggle because it lay in the mountain's shadow.

He was knocking down crab apples with a pole as she approached, parasol wheeling, stopping in mute admiration to watch the green knuckled fruits thudding into the grass, stooping to retrieve one, polishing it on silk, sinking her teeth in with a crunching sound.

The pole stopped and his cap was plucked off as he noticed her.

'They're for stewing, not really for eating, Ma'm,' he warned. 'They'll give you a pain.'

'Hm, they *are* bitter,' she murmured, making a face but still nibbling. 'I was going to ask you to take me around the garden but seeing you're busy —'

'No trouble at all,' he said, leaning the pole against the wall, where ivy like gnarled fingers went over. 'But it's past its best.'

'It's still beautiful, though,' she said, surveying, looking at the sky, letting the parasol down.

He led the way between the narrow hedges, past flowerbeds already dying back. She stooped to lift the blotched pitted rose, pressing it appreciatively against her mouth, touching the declining Michaelmas daisy. Chrysanthemums lifted their brazen faces to the gloomy sky. Bees stumbled, too tired to transport pollen to the conical hives on the other side, Mama's sweet tooth having exhausted production, the bloated Queen dying, the successor already groomed.

They turned into the greenhouse, where a stove fed large cast-iron pipes, but the peach tree had yielded its fragile crop, and the grape vine, led in through a hole in the brickwork, was stripped, a discoloured cable.

'I sent them up to the house when you were abroad, because they were ready,' he said, as if he would have liked to perpetuate them for her return.

'Never mind, next year. Would you mind awfully if I came down from time to time to watch and learn? I do so miss the garden at home.'

He nodded, but knew she was already knowledgeable, and though a kindred spirit should have pleased him, he turned away, irritated. Old Mrs Macdonald had been content not to interfere, simply to eat the fruit and arrange the flowers he sent up in wicker. And the new laird never came about the place. It was his domain, as the kitchen was Mrs Livingstone's. He sent up selected plums and she stewed them into jam in a system that had been working smoothly for years. But from what he was hearing at meal times in the servants' hall, there was now interference, talk of a new stove, as well as a new roof and redecoration. He would resist the garden being re-organised, and if she overruled him, would hand in his notice. Campbell would give him a job up at Branglin.

They were outside again, stopping at the hives where the sterile workers crawled, mourning their coming death but still serving.

'I wish I had their energy,' she sighed, and he saw how pale she was under the wheel of the parasol.

'Except that what they gather we devour,' he said philosophically. 'Still, they would make it even if we weren't here.'

'And they would make it in the wild, in freedom,' she said. 'No one would take their sweetness away. Anyway, could you send up a basket of flowers so that I can make up a few vases?'

'There isn't much,' he warned her, 'and they won't last.' He was angry at having to yield up flawed things.

'Even a few days of colour and scent will work wonders for me,' she said, her nostrils taking in the final fragrances in the thunderous silence before the fall of the pitted fruit.

That night at dinner Invernevis had intended to warn her that there could be no Lorimer, but she was preoccupied with more pressing business, her eyes shining in the candelabrum light as she spooned carrageen with silver.

'Something else for Morrison to put on his list,' she began.

Groaning inwardly, Invernevis tried to look indulgent.

'I don't take enough exercise.'

'No you don't, my dear.' Was she going to propose an excursion, which meant that she had lost her fear of the blind bend? As long as it was not to Edinburgh, to spend money.

'I would like a tennis court.'

His spoon was audible against china. He had never played, but knew it was fashionable, expensive.

'I'm afraid there's no suitable site for a court,' he said evenly.

'Oh yes there is,' she said eagerly. 'Out there.' She was pointing to the lawn below the wishing stone.

'But we can't dig that up,' he said, horrified.

'It doesn't need to be dug up,' she explained. 'All that's needed is for the gardener to get rid of the bumps, and put up a couple of posts for the net.'

If it wasn't for her expression, he would have thought it was a joke in poor taste. Apart from creating noise, it would completely ruin the view down to the river. The landscape was already blighted by Alexander's house. But there was another consideration that might not have occurred to her.

'Who are you going to play with? I can't, with this leg.'

'I realise that,' she said, reaching over the mahogany to cover his hand. 'I was thinking of inviting Alexander's wife up.' She saw his look and went to stand behind his chair, putting her hands on his shoulders. 'What harm would there be in that? Doctor MacNiven told me I needed to take more exercise. And I also need a friend. Someone of my own age.' Her arms were round his neck, her head on his shoulder now. 'Please say yes,' she said dreamily.

But he was speechless.

CHAPTER 5

A few days later Nanny Gunn from Sutherland descended from the late train, the gig collecting her and her small strapped trunk, black initials at the reinforced corner, steel pins transfixing her severe black hat, mouth moving as if occupied with an everlasting sweet as the pebble lenses of her steel rimmed spectacles repulsed the setting sun. She said not a word to Roddy on the way, her spine perpendicular in the rough dark tunnel of the avenue, changing neither posture nor expression as the blind bend was rounded. Mary Rose was waiting for her in the dark porch, leading her into the drawing-room for the confidential reunion. Then, having taken a mutton chop without trimmings on a tray in her bedroom (Laura's old one), she went down in a grey belted tunic of serge to supervise the boiling of as many big kettles as the stove could accommodate, Mrs Livingstone swallowing stewed tea in mute rage at the table. The maids were mustered from the servants' hall, the two table-maids lugging the big kettles up the back stairs, the two house-maids sent up to the linen cupboard. Maggie was delegated to carry a tin bath to the old Mistress's bedroom. While she rolled up her sleeves, Nanny Gunn pushed the bath into position beside the bed with her boot. She leaned over, gripping the bedclothes which small mottled fists were clutching, a whimpering sound coming from the mound. When the fists wouldn't yield, they were prised open, and the clothes came away. Then a snarling as rotten silk was torn from Mama. She curled up in the depression of horse-hair, hiding her face with her arm, but Nanny Gunn slapped the jutting rump. With Maggie at the shoulders, Mama was rolled down to steaming tin, to settle, splashing, yelling. Wielding bristle lathered with carbolic, a tight-mouthed Nanny Gunn scrubbed the sweat of months while one house-maid kept priming with a kettle, the other stripping the bed, exposing the stains on striped flannel, bundling up the stinking sheets and blankets. Her face scarlet, Mama protested that all this hustling at the hands of an unknown assailant would precipitate another stroke, but Nanny Gunn's mouth moved silently, continuing to scrub even when blood was drawn on the arched back of that grotesque caricature, large grey stranded head and bunched neck sitting, or rather, lolling, on a body scaled down to girlhood again by alcoholic abuse, and a stroke that had disowned her left hand. The good hand tried to pull her clear of scalding tin, but Nanny Gunn jerked down her shoulders, and the rump cleaved, splashing.

Though she was sorry for the old lady who had been so nice to her, and though she was terrified of Nanny Gunn, Maggie wanted to burst out laughing, and got encouragement from the face the maid with the kettle was making behind Mama's conqueror. The old lady looked so comical, with her big mottled bum and bemused expression, swiping at the bristles as they came round and down to her still dark extensive triangulation.

When Nanny Gunn was satisfied that the carbolic had got to all crevices, Mama was hoisted dripping from her own dirt and swaddled in a huge towel, Nanny Gunn rubbing with her knuckles, going down on her knees to dry between the chilblained toes. Then, circling with the bottle of *eau de toilette* taken from the bedside table, Nanny Gunn shook until the bottle was empty, rubbing into the rough steaming skin.

'That's you clean now, my girl,' were the first words she spoke.

The house-maid was told to hurry up with the bed, and Maggie was sent to search the drawers for a nightdress. She found a silk one, fragrant in tissue, in a bottom drawer, but when Nanny Gunn tried to pull it over Mama's head, it ripped.

'That's the nightdress I wore on my honeymoon,' Mama moaned.

Nanny Gunn threw it into a corner and waited impatiently while Maggie produced a bigger one, of cotton. But there was a delay because Mama refused to allow it to pass over her arms, till Nanny Gunn took a hand.

'Now my girl, you'll get into that bed. I'll bring you some medicine to clean out your insides, and I'll be in this room at eight tomorrow morning, to get you up and dressed, even if you only sit at the window. No more drinking or lying in bed.'

A mute Mama rolled between starched white sheets, while Nanny Gunn went for the medicine. She returned with a green bottle and bone spoon, pouring till it brimmed. But Mama kept her jaws clamped and shook her head vigorously.

'All right, girl, we'll have to force your mouth open, the way they do to a horse.'

'What is it?' Mama moaned.

'Something to flush you out. Now open up.'

Mama did so, but closing her eyes, and the castor-oil was tipped in. She tried to spit it out, but Nanny Gunn muffled the mouth with her palm till it had to be swallowed.

'Instead of standing gaping, go and clean these,' Nanny Gunn ordered, thrusting the tumbler containing Mama's teeth at Maggie. 'And you others get this stuff out of here,' she added, making tin ring with her toe. 'Leave the sheets and blankets on the landing. They'll have to be boiled for hours.'

At last Mama was left in peace to consider the enormity of the invasion. She had been snatched from a dream of sweltering Kamptree, precipitated into scalding tin, imagining she was joining Sandy in the afterlife. Who on earth *was* that awful woman? Surely not someone Niall had imported. No, he wouldn't do that to his old mother. The daughter-in-law, most likely, because she was making so many changes, the hammers above keeping you from sleeping, the noise below. She hoped the girl wasn't going to turn out a tyrant like Carlotta, though one thing you *could* say for Carlotta: she didn't drag you from your bed. And Maggie, the kitchen-maid she had befriended, had stood by, doing nothing. What a place, when you couldn't get some rest after three children, the girl a breech birth, almost killing her. Just like the old days with Sandy. You went up for your afternoon nap, had barely settled on the top of the bed when you heard the rasp of his spurs along the passage, and that meant no rest, though you knew he had been at the maids again. She would rather Sandy's weight on her than having that awful woman hauling, then hurting tender places with the bristles, places you weren't meant to scrub because, as Sandy said, soap was no substitute. But where on earth were they getting all the money for the improvements, she wanted to know. The girl must have brought a big dowry. Well, it was better putting it into something old and solid than little Indian girls. What Alexander had got was only a tenth of what there had been, and a good part of it hers. Of course Carlotta had held on to her share and was well out of it, in Leamington, though there was something queer about taking a kitchen-maid as a companion. But if there was money again, surely they wouldn't grudge her a little whisky from time to time, to quieten the palpitations. Now there was this awful woman with the steel spectacles and rough hands, there wouldn't be much chance of the nice looking footman bringing a little drop up from the village. Not that she could have kept going like that, because there weren't any more silver trinkets on her dressing-table to give him. The best thing was to do as she was told, then they might allow her a toddy. But this was an awful business, having to get up at eight the next morning, so she'd better get some rest, before the hauling began again. Mind you, it was nice to be clean, in fresh sheets, though that bitch had tricked her with the medicine and torn her precious nightdress. It hadn't been in a cool clean bed, the first time with Sandy, though: a couple of minutes against a tree in the

Soldiers' Garden at Kamptree, hitching up her dress to the fiercest heat she had ever experienced, the whalebone corset left off, for once.

Mrs Livingstone was speechless when Maggie brought Mama's teeth into the kitchen, to scrub them at the sink. She sat with a fresh pot of tea, demanding a full account of what had happened upstairs, making louder exclamations of disgust at every revelation, the bit about the castor-oil leaving her with open mouth.

'That's the trouble with nannies,' she said when she had recovered. 'They get above themselves, though they're only servants, like you and me. They might be able to read a bit better, but books aren't everything, you know. And she's got a face on her just like Miss Carlotta. I don't know how the young Mistress could get fond of a creature like that, and why she should bring her here. Pushing around the poor old soul like that, after the life she had with the old laird, though you'll not get me speaking about *that*. That's not the way to get her off the bottle. No, girl, there's too many changes too quickly, and it won't work out, you mark my words. You're wasting your time scrubbing at these teeth. Leave them in baking soda till the morning.'

The trees turned to autumn, the leaves becoming brittle, scraping along the avenue, the slaters' hammers sounding sharper in the cold mornings. The drawing-room walls had been prepared, and now an artist from Edinburgh lay on his back on scaffolding, restoring the gilt on the scrolled cornices with a thin brush and palette while Morrison the architect watched anxiously below. In a week's time they would be moving up to the bedrooms, but there was a problem. The bill he had submitted to the Edinburgh lawyers to pay part of the roofers' and decorators' accounts hadn't been settled. They needed the money for wages, and wouldn't go on without it, so he had had to go to Invernevis, who promised to write immediately, to speed up the payment.

A week later Richardson sent the cheque with a covering

letter, ordering all work on the house to be suspended because the expenditure was already exceeding the estimate. Besides:

> Work has come to our attention which requires to be done on the estate which the trustees could not have anticipated when they agreed these improvements to the mansion house. At least the roof is watertight now, which was the original reason for the work.

Invernevis told the irate architect that the work was only being suspended, not abandoned, but did not know what he was going to tell Mary Rose. He decided to stall for time by sending Richardson an angry reply, protesting that he was being put in an impossible position with his wife and the tradesmen, who would not get work again at Branglin from Campbell.

Mary Rose was wakened at eight each morning by Farquhar the piper stamping in reveille round the mansion, stopping under her window, his brogues crunching gravel as he fingered: 'Hey Johnnie Cope, are ye wauking yet?' Before the pipes had expired she was tilting the cooling pitcher, feeling slightly sick but attributing it to the previous night's curds and whey, which she had taken so as not to offend the cook. She put on a white dress and stooped to tighten the laces of her canvas shoes.

In the front hall the two Skye terriers preceded her to the door, yelping and skidding in their desire for the bracing freedom of the morning. She took the tennis racquet and the ball from the hollowed-out tree and went down the front lawn. The net sagged in the middle, but that didn't matter. She bounced the ball on the taut strings while waiting for her partner.

Maggie's young brother Hector, hall-boy and apprentice piper, came sheepishly round the corner of the house. He sat with his back to the wishing stone, removing his boots and rolling up his trousers. He went to stand on the other side of the net, lobbing the ball over, and when she struck it, trying to catch it. Soon she was laughing at his antics as he lunged, arm outstretched, but missing, rolling. He laughed too, and the dogs joined in.

Invernevis stood in the bay window of his bedroom, watching them as he dressed. When she had started her early morning tennis he wasn't pleased with her for playing with a servant, but at least it was better than with Alexander's wife, who had refused her invitation. But as he linked a sleeve with gold, watching her head bobbing in the sun, then thrown back in laughter as the bare-footed boy rolled down the slope towards the summer house, he couldn't help smiling. How Laura would have loved playing with her. How like Laura she was, the same infectious enthusiasm. But Laura had been backward: if anything, Mary Rose was too progressive. It didn't do for a laird's lady to be too outgoing, too sporty. It was dangerous to try and break down class barriers in the Highlands. Hadn't her brother Jamie tried, with disastrous results, on his Sutherland estate, where the tenants fleeced him while he drank himself to death? Tennis wasn't a dignified game. Far better to take a dog-cart up to the village, to show herself to the tenants.

Still, he could forgive so much because of her beauty and grace. He saw the ball bouncing beyond the hall-boy's outstretched hand, and one of Mama's terriers chasing it, trapping it between his paws, lifting it in his jaws to shake it. Mary Rose had run down the lawn to retrieve the ball, and she was stooping, asking the dog to give it up when the landscape began to tilt.

When she was carried up to the house, and Doctor MacNiven summoned, he pronounced her three months' pregnant.

BOOK TWO

CHAPTER 6

Chain-smoking, Invernevis paced the front hall, hoping for a boy while Doctor MacNiven and Nanny Gunn as midwife were closeted upstairs with Mary Rose.

It was a silent evening in May. The hammers on the roof had ceased, Richardson having written to warn him that with a child due there would be bigger domestic bills, a new burden on the already stretched estate. Only half of the roof had been replaced, and there were no dormer windows to the servants' quarters. Redecoration had been confined to the drawing and dining rooms, with Laura's room made into a nursery. To Mrs Livingstone's relief the kitchen had not been reached.

Though it was not yet dusk the birds in the policies had stopped singing, as if in anticipation of the first birth in that gloomy house since that of Laura over twenty years before. It was the silence, and the remembrance that his sister's had been a difficult birth which had almost killed Mama, that was making Invernevis smoke as he paced, stopping regularly at the foot of the wide darkening staircase where the burnished pendulum of the grandfather clock swung in its narrow mahogany case. As he waited he kept glancing over his shoulder, looking up as if someone was kneeling on the landing, watching him through the bars.

It was too quiet, no sound of a child crying its way into the world, though she had been in labour since early afternoon, his gold hunter told him. He was turning once again at the drawing-room door when the scream rang out, and it was still sounding in his ears as he stumbled up the stairs, audibly cursing the impediment of the game leg, certain that there was something very far wrong. Memories of local women who had died in labour returned, magnified, with Doctor MacNiven criticised.

But when he tried the door on the landing it was locked. He used his fist and then his voice, stopping in pain and exhaustion, groaning, forehead pressed against the lintel. *Somebody* was dying or dead behind that door.

The lock shifted, the door inched open, and Nanny Gunn's furious face appeared.

'Don't make such a racket,' she hissed.

Invernevis was too distraught to check her insolence.

'What's wrong? What is it? I want to see my wife.'

'You'll see her soon enough. Now go back downstairs and behave like a man.'

It was too much for Invernevis. As the door was closing he put his shoulder against it and pushed, sending its keeper staggering and shouting.

Doctor MacNiven was standing at the bottom of the bed in his waistcoat and shirt sleeves, holding the brown wrinkled thing upside down by the ankles and slapping its buttocks. The way it swung reminded Invernevis of a skinned rabbit.

The only sound was the thud of the doctor's palm. Mary Rose lay with splayed legs in the bloody litter of birth in the big canopied bed, her face averted from the swinging child, a look, not of loathing, but of resignation, as Nanny Gunn hurried forward to pull up the bedclothes.

'Not breathing properly,' Doctor MacNiven said in answer to Invernevis's silent entreaty. He stopped swinging and pressed his ear against the child's breast.

'Just breathing and no more.'

It was then Invernevis saw that it was a girl.

Doctor MacNiven handed the baby to Nanny Gunn, took off his gold-rimmed spectacles and mopped his steep shining brow.

'I don't know if it's going to make it,' he said factually. 'I'm telling you this in case you want it baptized.'

Invernevis could only echo the word. Things were happening too quickly. Nanny Gunn was now closing the heavy brocade curtain round Mary Rose's bed, and Invernevis caught her wrist, a chill at his heart.

'Your wife's all right,' Doctor MacNiven assured him. 'It's the child. I doubt if it will live, and it's the custom to baptize.'

'What shall I do? Send for Father Macdonald?' Invernevis asked helplessly.

'There probably won't be time. It's all right, I've stood in for him before. We have an arrangement. I need some clean water.'

'I'll get some from the ewer in my bedroom,' Invernevis said, turning to the connecting door.

'It's all right,' the doctor called. 'There's some here. What I *really* need is a name.'

Invernevis realised that he and Mary Rose hadn't discussed names, never mind sex. He approached the bed, and, pulling back the brocade, spoke gently.

'What name shall we give it?'

But she clenched her fist to her mouth and turned away.

He didn't know what to do. Even if her turning away signified her contempt for Catholicism, there wasn't time to send out of the district for a Church of Scotland minister. The religion wasn't important: the child had to be baptized. But what *was* important was a name. Even though it would only live a matter of minutes, it had to be linked with life. Names went racing through his head. Laura. Damn Alexander for stealing that precious name. Constance: Mama's. Too much of a mouthful. No, it couldn't come from his side. Oh what in God's name was her mother called? With an L. On the tip of his tongue.

'Lucy!'

Doctor MacNiven held the naked child in the crook of his arm, turning it to the mother lying in the bed, her face still averted. Invernevis and Nanny Gunn were silent witnesses as he dipped his fingertips into the bowl of water, sprinkling the baby's skull and saying: 'I baptize thee Lucy, in the Name of the Father, and of the Son, and of the Holy Ghost. Amen.'

As he stood forcing himself to watch Invernevis remembered the night that Laura had died in the cold room along the passage, her hands stretched between himself and Alexander until she had turned away, like the white blur of a salmon into darkness. But this child could not be mourned so much because it had never lived. It was luckier than Laura; it did not have to face the rush of life on un-coordinated limbs. He made the sign of the cross and turned away.

But as the water hit the child's head it seemed to waken it from its long sleep in the womb. Dusky skinned, its small face wrinkled like a malicious old woman's, it began crying, softly at first, puny fists raised, then growing loud and harsh, as if angry at the new world of light and water. Doctor MacNiven hugged it, shouting: 'Maybe I've got a better touch than Father Macdonald!' and he began to waltz with it in his arms while Nanny Gunn's mouth swallowed its own satisfaction. He passed the child to the elderly spinster, then went to pick up the mother's limp wrist, scrutinising his watch.

'A few days' rest should see you all right, after the fright about the little girl. But she's fine now; just a bit scared of so many people waiting to meet her, that's all.'

But there was neither movement nor grateful acknowledgement of the doctor's humour from the bed. As Doctor MacNiven struggled into his swallow coat, Invernevis stood staring at the revived child in the captive arms of Nanny Gunn. He was grateful for the miracle, but couldn't conceal his disappointment, since a boy would have secured succession. It put him level with Alexander, but the farmer's fertile daughter was probably pregnant again, no doubt carrying a male this time. It was as if Laura's spirit had triumphed through spite, even though a daughter might be a rival to her memory.

Then a horrifying thought hit him. Was the dark skin caused by the curtains being closed against the twilight, or a legacy from the little Indian girls? That thought was succeeded by the realisation that the crying, kicking infant could be affected by the disease that his father had died from. Though its eyes seemed to be open, how could he be certain that it was seeing? And suppose it had inherited the mental deficiency of Laura, which in her case had not manifested itself till she was about four years old, when her inability to make sounds become words had made Carlotta suspicious? It was not the infirmity that frightened him; it was the waiting to see what developed.

He took Doctor MacNiven down to the library and gave him a large whisky.

'A healthy baby,' the doctor assured him, accepting glass and chair. 'But your good lady seems a bit depressed. Any problems?'

'None that I'm aware of. Unless she's worried about her brother. He's a bit improvident, I'm afraid.'

'That's probably it,' Doctor MacNiven said, nodding. He peered over rimless spectacles. 'Try and cheer her up, make her happy here. I see you've been having some work done on the house.'

'On the roof mostly, though one or two rooms were decorated. It's had to stop, though; money, you see,' he added, embarrassed. 'My father got through a great deal, and what he had left, Alexander got.' There was bitterness in his tone, but the doctor gave no encouragement.

'*Slainte* to the new arrival,' he said, tilting his glass. 'I'm glad I'm up at the big house for something happy, this time. Next time it'll be a boy,' Doctor MacNiven assured him. 'If you want to make certain get the tinkers on your side. They can heal and bring about things where I can't.'

Invernevis just had to ask about the possibility of the child inheriting his father's disease.

'Put that out of your mind once and for all,' the doctor urged. 'That died with your father. Look at it this way: the wee one upstairs is a new start for this house, a chance of happiness after so much sorrow. It should help your mother too. Well, I'd better be going. I've calls to make in the village, another baby due.' He set down the glass and picked up his bag. 'Don't move, I'll see myself out.' He stopped at the door. 'Do try and cheer your wife up. Make her get out of doors, into the sunshine, take good long walks.'

Left alone with the decanter, Invernevis wondered if there would be any more children, with Mary Rose showing an increasing distaste for that side of marriage. To insist on his conjugal rights would be to treat the opposite sex as his father had treated them. But if there wasn't to be a son from Mary Rose, Cousin Hubert would get the place, which made the struggle futile.

Brooding wasn't any good. Doctor MacNiven was right: Mary Rose would have to start getting out and about, and so would he. He would take up fishing in earnest. The fifty six pound brute his father had taken from the Oak Tree Pool, was out there, suspended in the deepening shadows of the hall. If he could better that, it would be a blow struck in retaliation for the humiliation of being bound hand and foot by trustees. But he would be forced to use his father's rods because getting sporting gear tailored to shoulder and elbow was now out of the question, with a child to provide for.

There was something else he was going to follow his father in, but not in competition. The old laird had been honorary Colonel of the rifle volunteer company which had met on Friday evenings in the school, not to slope arms, but to tilt stone jars. With the death of his father, and the enlistment of the majority of volunteers for South Africa, the company had been disbanded, but now Invernevis had had a letter from the Lord-Lieutenant of the County, urging him to revive the unit in case of future threats to the stability of the Empire, and offering in incentive the rank of honorary Major.

Invernevis was tempted, though his game leg would be a serious impediment, and though what he had seen the Boers do had disillusioned him about military honour. If he accepted command, it wasn't going to be as a figurehead, like his father. He would create a company he could be proud of, and which would make its contribution in the field if called upon to do so. The idea became more appealing as his ambitions multiplied, but there were several serious obstacles. In the first place, Mary Rose might not approve of his spending time with the company when there was a child and other responsibilities at the house. She might feel she was being deserted, as Mama had done, though with his father, there had been manoeuvres other than military. Secondly, the village had contributed generously, with poor returns, to the South African war, and parents, wives and sweethearts wouldn't welcome a new call to arms, even for peace-time purposes, in case the same thing happened again. The bones of Invernevis men baked in trenches hacked from ironstone on the arid *veld*, under Magersfontein Hill and in other more fertile places where the Highland Brigade had pushed. Those who came home were being lowered from the train on stretchers, lacking limbs or with bandaged eyes, to lie on crude beds in cramped crofts, still shaking with the shock of the Boer shell explosion.

Invernevis realised that to get new recruits for the rifle volunteer company, he would have to enlist the services of Father Macdonald. There was no alternative if he was to comply with the Lord-Lieutenant's wishes. Recruits wouldn't come forward to his call alone. He had proved that a couple of years before, at the tenants' Hogmanay dance, when Laura had whirled into darkness, and he had requested more men for South Africa. It wasn't only Carlotta that had stopped them coming up the avenue to enlist. But though it rankled for a time, he knew his father's charisma had come from emptying stone jars at quoits contests and seducing maids.

His meeting with Father Macdonald took place over lunch, with Mary Rose still upstairs, recovering strength after the difficult delivery. Without Carlotta to watch him, the priest accepted a liberal port.

'I quite see that the volunteer company has to be revived,'

Father Macdonald conceded, taking Home Farm cheese on a water biscuit. 'They must learn that in serving the Monarch they also serve God. I shall make the necessary announcements at Mass, and we can hold a meeting in the school. That's easily taken care of.'

A blast from the quarry across the water broke up the water biscuit.

'As a trustee, I was against them resuming, but the estate can't afford to lose the income.' He said this in a tone which suggested that he was holding Invernevis personally responsible for the quarry's continuation. 'Speaking of the quarry, I'm afraid that all the blasting over the years has made the chapel by the ferry very unstable. It needs rebuilding, in stone, on a more sheltered site.' He had a new biscuit and cheese now, and was watching his hands moving. 'Miss Carlotta agrees. She's written to suggest the site down there.' He pointed with his knife to the Summer House Pool. 'I'll be bringing it up at the trustees' meeting in Edinburgh next month.'

Invernevis was alarmed by this news. He knew that his aunt had always coveted the meadow across the Summer House Pool as a site for a chapel which she had proposed financing herself until she had abdicated in anger. His father had been dead against the plan, and so was the son, because it would spoil the view from the principal windows and because the enforced devotions of the villagers would prove embarrassing. But more than that, the meadow was a shrine to the memory of Laura because there he had lain with her while she threaded daisies on the day he had left for war. Though a chapel was a shrine, its erection there would defile that place of precious memory because Carlotta had carried Catholicism to cruel fanaticism. Her choice of that site was not only to bring the villagers in homage to the bank of a river they dared not cross, but also because it was there that the Irish harper Diarmid O'Caibre was sundered between two horses for cutting the throat of Angus, son of John, Earl of Ross and Lord of the

Isles, progenitor of the Invernevis dynasty, with a long knife. No doubt Carlotta thought that a chapel there would heighten the barbarity of the clan her sister had married into, of the brother-in-law who had mocked Carlotta's faith.

Father Macdonald's revelation put Invernevis into a quandary. If he protested outright the trustees would overrule him, because Carlotta would manipulate all three. He would have to find a more indirect approach. An idea was already forming.

'But that meadow goes with the Home Farm. MacPherson would never agree to give it up.'

'Then we'll dispossess him,' the priest said abruptly, washing down biscuit with wine.

'It's not that simple,' Invernevis cautioned. 'Don't forget that the farming and crofting laws have been changed in favour of the tenants. MacPherson's a powerful man in these parts, and could make it very difficult for you to carry out your parish work properly.' He put into his tone the implication that this should be the priest's first priority.

'No one can interfere in the work of a priest,' Father Macdonald said harshly.

'MacPherson doesn't have that sort of conscience. I'd look for another site.'

'We'll see,' the priest said, extricating himself from a quarrel with his host, but at the same time showing it was a matter for the trustees. 'Incidentally, your aunt tells me that Colonel Hooker is pestering her. She's thinking of moving from Leamington.'

'Surely to God not back to Invernevis,' he thought in panic. She would finish Mary Rose within a month.

But the priest was reading his face. 'She hasn't said what her plans are. But Hooker is a bit of a liability. He doesn't attend trustees' meetings, and yet he expects to be paid his expenses.'

At least that was one less, Invernevis thought thankfully.

'Elsie is proving a great comfort to your aunt,' the priest continued. 'She seems a very capable and *caring* young woman.'

Which was clearly another criticism of her nephew's neglect.

'Not only that. She's become a Catholic, and not just to please your aunt.' He was dabbing his mouth with the snowy napkin. 'Which brings us to the proper christening of your daughter. Have you fixed a date? It should be done as soon as possible. I'll do my best to get the chapel as presentable as possible.'

'I haven't even discussed it with my wife yet,' Invernevis said evasively. 'But I will, once she's stronger.'

'Can I suggest that Carlotta be added as a name?'

'I'll pass it on to my wife,' he muttered, angry at the effrontery. Well, that settled it; no brandy for the priest, and, if at all avoidable, no more lunches, though he was a trustee.

But when the priest's trap pulled away, Invernevis was left with several major problems which required consideration over a large brandy and cigar in the library. How was he going to stop the building of the chapel in the meadow? He could drop a hint to MacPherson, but they weren't on friendly terms, and Father Macdonald would know it had come from him. Or alert Alexander; but he was too busy propping up the counter in the Arms, and the warning wouldn't get through. No, Invernevis would have to confront the problem himself. If necessary he would go to law with the trustees over the siting of the new chapel. Say it would spoil the view from his public windows, interfere with his privacy, the arguments Carlotta had used in an attempt to stop Alexander being allowed to build on the bank of *Poll Dubh*. Invernevis's confidence increased as his cigar shortened, and the decanter tilted again. Richardson wouldn't want it to go to court, and Father Macdonald wouldn't want to fall out with the laird, because if anything happened to Carlotta, he couldn't expect patronage from the big house.

If anything, the problem of the christening was more serious than that of the chapel. There was no guarantee that Mary Rose would want the emergency baptism confirmed by a

Catholic ceremony. She could easily plead that she hadn't been in a position to object when the baptism had taken place in the bedroom. A private ceremony in the bedroom was very different from a full Mass in the chapel. He had better go up and get a decision.

Mary Rose was sitting in a floral dressing-gown in a high-backed chair at her bedroom window overlooking the river, head bent to embroidery, the sun turning her hair into a million gold needles. He carried a chair over to sit beside her, to stay her hand and ask her if she was feeling stronger.

'A little better, thank you. I must try and get down to the garden,' she said wistfully, staring out.

'I can get Ranald to send a basket up.'

'No, no. They mustn't be cut till they're almost past their best, otherwise you deprive the bees.'

'So that they can make more honey,' he said lightly. 'For Mama, I mean.'

'No, for their own sakes,' she said, turning large eyes on him. 'How is your mother?' she asked.

'Still in bed, but Mrs Livingstone's going to get her up in a day or two.'

'I'm afraid Nanny's been neglecting her, but she's had the baby to look after. I don't have the strength yet.'

'That's what I wanted to speak to you about.'

'Then Doctor MacNiven spoke to you,' she said, relieved.

But he was confused now.

'I can't feed her, because I don't have the milk or the energy, so he said he would get a wet-nurse from the village.'

This was something beyond his experience and authority.

'It has to be a girl who's just had a baby,' she explained. 'A big healthy girl. I think the doctor's got someone in mind - Sheena, Betsy's grand-daughter. Does that name mean anything to you?'

His face showed that it did. Mad Betsy, who was said to have the second-sight, and was reckoned by some people in the village to be a witch. Surely not her, he thought in panic.

The girl would transmit her grandmother's madness in her milk. Besides which, he understood that the obsolete honour of being wet-nurse went to the girl closest by relationship to the big house. He was trying to work out who that was when Mary Rose said, irritated:

'There isn't anyone else suitable, and I trust Doctor MacNiven.'

He could have told her that his father hadn't held the same opinion, and that he himself felt that the doctor had been lackadaisical over Laura, letting leeches suck the last of her strength. But he could see that his wife was set on the girl. He decided to have one last try.

'Isn't the Home Farm milk suitable, if you boil it up?'

'No, natural feeding's best. I had a wet-nurse myself. So did Jamie. Anyway, Nanny will make the arrangements with the girl.'

So she was behind it, as big a manipulator as Carlotta. Well, no doubt she'd dictate the christening also, so he'd better ask.

'We'll need at least one more name,' he said.

'I don't think that's necessary. A middle name's hardly ever used - except in my case. I'd have preferred just the one name. Two sounds pretentious, but that was mother.'

'And the christening?' he asked.

'You mean where is it to be held? I'd like something quiet, here at the house.'

Which was going to put him in very bad grace with Father Macdonald and the villagers. But how was he going to get round the problem without upsetting her?

'We'd better invite your mother and brother,' he said, trying another approach.

'No, I couldn't bear having them here - not yet. Mother fusses so much, and Jamie's just a heartbreak. I want to rest, and if there has to be another christening, I want a quiet one, at this house.' She saw his frown. 'I don't want a fuss.'

Seeing that he could not change her mind for the moment about the place of christening, he wandered along the passage to the nursery, to find Nanny Gunn presiding by the lace canopy, steel needles clashing, small severe spectacles slipping down her nose. It was hard for him to believe that that room with its new floral wallpaper and whitewashed ceiling had been occupied by his sister Laura. He tried to tickle the child under the chin, but only made it cry, and its keeper rose to signal his unwelcome presence.

He went down to the library, worried by the domination by women. Perhaps having the baby had taken too much out of Mary Rose. There were as many problems as in the days of Carlotta, he thought as he rang for the ghillie. He would go down to the river and have a few casts to relieve his frustration, though the good spell was keeping the water low.

They went down the lawn, past the summer house which he had had rebuilt in granite as a memorial to his dead sister because it had been her most secure hiding-place from Carlotta and her cruel school-room. He could not help thinking that things would have been very different if she had lived. For the sake of her happiness he might have been prepared to relinquish the estate to cousin Hubert. His relationship with Laura had had nothing to do with birth or religion.

He stayed on the house side of the stepping stones, casting the small colourful fly where water rippled. The stepping stones stretched to the daisy-crowded meadow where he had promised Laura to return from war to protect her. Too late. Always too late. His father should have abdicated when the heir came of age, instead of leaving him to kick his heels in a static regiment. When there had been the chance of action, he had been invalided out before he could prove himself. If he had resigned his commission before South Africa, Mama wouldn't have become a drunkard and Carlotta wouldn't have killed Laura. Other things could have been prevented. The fly was forgotten because he had seen Alexander and MacPherson entering the meadow across the river, Alexander with a scythe slung across his shoulder, its curved blade flaring in the sun. He was wearing an open waistcoat over his collarless striped flannel shirt, and his leggings were lashed. MacPherson pointed, and his son-in-law unshouldered the scythe, pulling a whetstone from his trouser pocket and snecking it along steel.

It was not the sound of stone on metal that made Invernevis shout across the river. The curved blade was now a semi-circle of fire round Alexander's boots, and his brother was crying out because the daisies which Laura had threaded into a chain that precious afternoon before South Africa and war were being decapitated by steel. It was the desecration of a shrine by a wayward brother and the brutal tenant of the Home Farm, hence Invernevis's tantrum transferred itself to the tip of the rod, the fly lodging in rock, being jerked so violently that the line parted.

MacPherson and his son-in-law did not acknowledge the laird's presence across the river. While the older man stood by, Alexander swung the glinting steel down towards the river, daisy heads scattering round his black boots, the crumpled visor of his cap shading his face. At that moment his brother separated from him by sluggish water hated him as much as he hated MacPherson. Better the meadow went for a chapel, albeit built with Carlotta's money, than have the Home Farm profane the most precious memory.

'I'm going back up to the house,' Invernevis said, thrusting the rod savagely at the ghillie.

CHAPTER 7

From the high window Maggie stared beyond the shadowed hole of the wishing stone to the tip of the Master's rod waving in violent motion as the shining steel of the scythe manifested itself as Master Alexander in the meadow across the river.

The kitchen-maid was standing in the bay window of the old Mistress's bedroom. It wasn't ignorance of manners that made her keep her back to the figure propped up in bed, but Mrs Livingstone's strict instructions. You didn't stare at old arthritic ladies with loose teeth while they were crumbling hot scones.

But Mama was talking and eating at the same time, scone muffling the same old stories that made Maggie's mind wander where her eyes went. The cook had sent her assistant up with her own hot scones because the old Mistress considered the girl to be a good baker as well as a good listener. You could explain that you were once young, with red hair that reached down to your waist but which had had to go in the furnace of India. You could tell her about Invernevis in the old days, and how what the tinkers had said about the old cook had come true when she refused them food. But there were some things you couldn't tell the good-looking but pale girl: how you had surprised Sandy on the back stairs with a maid just like Maggie, with his spurs digging into the bare board, and the hem of her black dress between her teeth. Nor could you tell her what had really killed your husband, or the hellish life Carlotta had given you, or the cross of Laura, the shame of Alexander.

But Maggie wasn't listening to the shock-impeded mouth

behind her. She was watching the rising rod, the black figure of Alexander, fire scything round his boots. She knew that more than the river divided the brothers, but couldn't understand the bad blood, considering that Master Alexander had done the right thing by Kate MacPherson. The Master himself was married now, also with a baby girl, which should have brought the brothers closer. Master Alexander was always taking his little girl on his shoulder up to the village, but the Master spent very little time with the child lying in Miss Laura's room. Maybe he couldn't get near it. The other maids said that Nanny Gunn was a right bitch who wouldn't even allow them to look round the door at the baby, and if you rattled her tray, one look was enough. Worse than Miss Carlotta, they were saying, which Maggie found hard to imagine.

They also gossiped about the new Mistress, who hadn't been downstairs since the baby was born.

'They don't sleep together,' Jessie the house-maid had confided, giggling.

Maggie was trying to work out what that meant as she watched the dipping rod. It gave her a queer thrill, like the night of the big heather fire, when she had sat on the gig beside the Master and he had pressed his thigh against hers. She knew it was wrong to entertain such thoughts, especially as the man was married, but the Master looked so sad the few times she saw him, usually pacing, absorbed in a cigarette. Of course he must have got a terrible fright, the way the baby had almost died without hardly having drawn a breath, as Mrs Livingstone had said. The fingers that had sifted flour with such skill had been static all that afternoon and evening, fankled in a rosary, the rambling tongue mixing prayer with reminiscences of Laura's birth, which had almost ended in death. 'It's a pity it didn't then, the poor wee mite.' The cook had quickly corrected her blasphemy by crossing herself.

The sun was sparkling on the crude fingers of the standing stones on the hill above the Home Farm, making Maggie close her eyes. It wasn't the Master she was thinking about, but what Master Alexander had done to Kate. He was stockier, much more untidy than the Master, but there was something attractive about him, like the brother, expert plougher, whom she had lost in South Africa, at that hill with the unpronounceable name. Master Alexander was quite like Frank, the footman whose advances she had so far resisted. Frank, like Master Alexander, had a fair moustache, only Frank's was thicker. The Master had a black moustache which he kept clipped. He had a nice smile, blue eyes. The sun had its hands on her neck, caressing. She preferred the Master. It was getting very hot in the bay window, as if her body was on fire, burning at the fork, so pleasurable, near to eruption, until:

'Now I want you to do something for me,' the old Mistress was saying.

Maggie opened her eyes, saw that the tip of the rod had gone, the Master coming laboriously up the lawn, scowling as he stopped to cup his hands round a flame. What had happened? A row with her father? Surely not, because he worshipped the laird, wouldn't hear a word said against son or father.

'I said: I want you to do something for me, girl,' the old Mistress repeated, irritated.

It was what Maggie feared she had said the first time. Surely she wasn't going to be bribed to fetch drink from the village, which would put her in an awful situation. If she agreed, the Master would be very angry and might dismiss her. If she refused, the old Mistress would take a spite to her, and maybe make trouble for her father. What made it worse was that she had been off the drink for weeks, because of Nanny Gunn's vigilance, and even Mrs Livingstone thought she might reform. Maggie knew that Roddy the coachman had been the prime suspect for bringing the stuff from the village, but she didn't want to get involved.

Mama had something else on her mind.

'I want you to go down to Ranald at the garden and ask him

for a bunch of flowers. A big bunch. He'll ask you what they're for, and you'll say for your mother's grave, which won't be telling a lie. Now what you'll do is to divide the bunch, put half on your mother's grave, and the other half on my husband's. It's at the chapel, down by the ferry, not the wooden place my sister put up, but the old stone one. You'll not be able to recognise it right away, because I don't think my son's put a stone up yet; but take your time and look around; you'll see where the ground's been disturbed. You can't miss it, because it was the last space in the chapel. There isn't any room for me, but I'm quite prepared to go into the enclosure, at the back.' And, eyes now alive with intrigue: 'This is a secret between you and me, girl, and if you do as I tell you I'll give you five shillings.' She said this as if it was an immense sum of money, and her confident eyes met Maggie's.

The kitchen-maid nodded, but she wasn't at all sure. She had heard Mrs Livingstone say that the Master hadn't got on with his father. She didn't want to displease the Master by doing something behind his back. But the old lady looked so pathetic, propped up with pillows, waiting.

Her good hand had already slid the black bead bag from under the pillow, and was fumbling with the catch, two gilt serpents intertwined. Coins clinked, were sorted on the quilt.

'Oh yes, you'll take it,' she said indignantly. 'This isn't part of your duties, and I always believe in paying for what I get.' She waved Maggie towards the two half crowns.

'Now you're off on Sunday afternoon, aren't you, so you'll do it then. And make sure that Ranald gives you *nice* flowers, ones that will last.' She sighed. 'If only I could get down myself. But the next time I leave this house, it will be in a box, for the chapel.' It was said almost thankfully. She began to sob, bringing bunched lace to her eyes.

Maggie did not know what to do or say, so she stood by the bed, twisting her hands and looking away. Something warned her that it was safer to lift the tray and go, leaving the old Mistress to her grief, in case Nanny Gunn came and accused her of upsetting the old lady. Instinct and not thought worked better in that house, Maggie had learned.

'Well, how is she today?' Mrs Livingstone wanted to know as her assistant put the tray on the big white table. The cook was sitting at the end near the stove, the habitual cracked brown teapot within reach, swollen feet in slippers.

'Fine,' Maggie said. 'Talking ten to the dozen.' She put her hand in her apron pocket, to keep the two half crowns quiet.

'She's certainly taken a liking to you,' Mrs Livingstone said in a tone that suggested pride. 'See and keep in with her; you'll not be the loser by it.' Tea gurgled, a scone was broken, a bit passed down to the Skye terrier under the table. 'Aye, she's the best of them, the old lady. You always knew where you were with her. Never had much of a chance with that awful sister of hers. I wonder how *she's* faring. And Elsie. I never took to her; too forward.'

It sounded like a warning to Maggie, but curiosity had got the better of her.

'What like was the old Master?'

'Your father could tell you better than me,' Mrs Livingstone said stiffly. 'He was left a hundred pounds by him.' It wasn't the money; it was the slight because the butler, over whom she claimed superiority, had also got it.

But Maggie dared not ask her father and well the cook knew it, so, having delivered her rebuke, she went on.

'A great big man with a bushy beard and eyes that seemed to go right through you. Seventeen stone he was, and the old girl had a hell of a life with him. But least said soonest mended.'

Maggie was in a panic at having undertaken the chapel commission, convinced now that it was some kind of trick. She would return the two coins weighing down her apron.

'Och, he wasn't all bad,' Mrs Livingstone said, seeing Maggie's frightened look and feeling that she was doing the dead injustice, though she hadn't been left anything after all the bowls of beef tea she'd sent up in his lingering illness. 'And the old girl stuck by him through thick and thin, you've got to grant her that. Things would have been better between them if it hadn't been for Miss Carlotta.' For Mrs Livingstone had decided that it was the spinster sister-in-law who had stopped her from getting anything in the will.

'Is it all right if I have Sunday afternoon off?' Maggie asked, seeing no hope of returning the bribe.

'Why ask when you're due it? I always manage the tea things myself,' the cook said, as if her competence was being challenged. Then, seeing how Maggie had coloured: 'I hope you're not going to meet that footman. I see he's starting to hang about the kitchen again, though he's no business here. I don't trust his kind, the kind that gets a girl into trouble, then is up and off.'

'I'm going to take some flowers up to the cemetery.'

'Well, that's a nice thought,' the cook murmured, pleased there was no secret. 'Aye, you're going to be as good as your mother,' she said, swallowing the last piece of scone. Then, in case the girl got above herself: 'They could be lighter, mind you.'

Maggie went in search of the gardener and found him in the servants' hall, drinking tea and chatting in Gaelic to Farquhar as the piper repaired the reed of a chanter, Maggie's young brother Hector standing behind his tutor's chair, watching intently.

'Now that's how you do it, son,' the piper said, producing a moaning sound on the reed before putting the two parts of the chanter together again. 'But you have to take care not to crack the reed.'

While her brother practised his fingering in a corner, Maggie put her request to Ranald.

'Aye, I'll come down on Sunday afternoon and cut you a nice bunch of flowers, lassie. It'll please your father to see you remembering your mother like that. A fine woman. Straight as that chanter.'

After lunch for servants as well as family on Sunday Maggie went down to the walled garden, pushing open the creaking iron gate to find Ranald already there, in his sabbath black, stooping, snipping.

'I'm going to give you the last of the daffodils,' he announced, laying the severed flowers in the shallow basket. 'And some others for colour. They won't last, but they'll make a show for a few days. Anyway, it's not the flowers; it's the thought that counts.' He arranged the heads, and when he was satisfied, bound them with green twine. 'I'm doing this because it can be quite windy up at the cemetery,' he explained. 'I'll speak to your father about getting a stone holder, because that would give flowers some protection. There you are, then.'

Cradling the big bunch of flowers, Maggie went down the windless avenue vocal with birds, the scent of her burden making her light-headed, but brought back to earth by the black button boots inherited from Laura stubbing on stone exposed by iron-shod wheels. She quickened her pace at the blind bend where rhododendron bushes offered blooms in appreciation, but only to clutch and scar with tendrils, blood-flecked trumpets leaking their funereal sweetness in that place of chill Maggie and her mother had never liked.

But now the avenue was straight and sunny, primroses crowding to the verge, grasshoppers making the sound of a whisk against china. She noticed what looked like initials carved into bark and stepped on to the grass to decipher the marks, but the wood the blade had exposed was almost the same green as the tree, and it needed her fingertips on tiptoe to make out the L & N within the crude shield. Somebody long before her birth, Maggie decided.

She passed between the crumbling white pillars and took the road right, pausing, after the uphill exertion on Wade's Bridge, to rest arms as well as legs by lowering the flowers gently on the stone and leaning over to see if she could identify a fin in the ripples, a skill her father had taught her while taking her up to the big house as a child. The Yellow Pool looked so cool that she would have loved to have gone down to wade, but it was out of the question on the sabbath, even with Miss Carlotta departed, and besides, her father would give her the weight of his hand for scaring the laird's fish. She stared down, but could see nothing where stone shadowed the water.

Retrieving the flowers, she proceeded along the dusty road above the river, turning her head to the white mansion under the mountain, wondering if the old Mistress was sitting in the bay window of her bedroom, watching to make sure that the girl was discharging the five shilling commission. Maybe the Master was at the drawing-room window, wondering where on earth she was going with so many flowers. It made her nervous, stopping to look round at the fork in the road before taking the stony track leading down to the chapel and ferry. The loch stretched still and grey as she went downhill, almost losing her balance on hard bare stone, the wooden chapel that Miss Carlotta had had built now coming into sight above the swaying flowers in her aching arms. The salt winds sniped through its splayed boards, now that its benefactress had abdicated, convinced that local souls were beyond salvation but still subsidising Father Macdonald in cigarettes and those little luxuries Rome would not allow.

Maggie was terrified that the priest would see her and report her to the Master, until she remembered that there was no afternoon Mass. The silence was uncanny, and there was something menacing about the horseshoe scar across the still water, where six days a week, using all the light that the mountain above would allow, two hundred Irish navvies blasted and sawed granite into paving slabs for Glasgow. Some were even supporting the wheels and feet of London, Frank the footman had told her, back at his old game of trying to persuade her to go to the capital with him. When they became butler and cook in a house where sovereigns were left under Spode plates, they could become man and wife. She was tired of telling him that she didn't want to leave Invernevis, not only because of her father and brother. Just look at that view, mountains upside down in the loch, and off the rotting jetty where the penny ferry plied for the quarry, a swan circling, coy necked, white as starched linen.

There had been a lot of talk in the servants' hall about the Master allowing the quarry to continue, after the fights there had been in the Arms involving Master Alexander. Frank said he had heard in the Arms that the Master was short of money because of the improvements to the big house his lady had demanded, but Mrs Livingstone had checked the footman in front of the other servants, once again warning him that talking about the gentry, or listening to them being talked about, wasn't done at the big house or in the village. And besides, the cook had said, looking significantly at the butler, the footman shouldn't be drinking, in the Arms or anywhere else.

'But you're always saying to try and learn from them out front,' Frank said. 'I haven't caught up with the old lady yet.'

Then Maggie's father, who had been sitting in the corner on the gashed leather sofa, listening as his pipe spurted, started up on the footman, calling him 'a puffed-up fool who doesn't know any better, coming from the city,' and warning him to apologise to Mrs Livingstone or he would take him up to the stables.

Frank had gone white, looking up and down the table, and, seeing no support, blurting out an apology before his chair scraped and the door slammed.

The growing friction between her father and the footman was worrying Maggie as she turned left, through the trees to the burial chapel. She kept telling her father that she wasn't interested in the footman, but that only made him more angry, repeating endlessly how much her mother had loved truth, and how she had promised her mother on her deathbed to stick to her ambition of succeeding Mrs Livingstone as cook.

'Mrs Livingstone's legs won't last much longer, and you've got as good a chance as any,' her father had predicted. 'So don't go spoiling things by getting mixed up with that fool of a footman. Oh, I've seen his kind before. They come from the city, thinking we haven't got any wits.'

Hugging the flowers tighter where trees shadowed the path, Maggie scrambled up the short sandy slope to the rectangle of ruined stone in which Invernevis lairds and their ladies had been laid since the first Macdonald settlement in the sweep of the river nearly four hundred years before. Winter gales gusting across the loch had bent the protective circle of trees and carried away the roof, loosening lime-bonded stone, leaving the crooked arches of the ivy-lashed windows against the sky. Generations of jackdaws had made their nests in the crumbling curved masonry, bringing back in their bills the glittering spoils they had snatched off desks and dressing-tables at the open windows of the big house, half a mile south through the trees. Sometimes strollers from the village found these trinkets round the chapel arches, taking them home to tell their children they were gifts from the fairies, the hallmarks supernatural hieroglyphics. Some had even turned up as tender in the Arms.

To Miss Carlotta, the stubborn ruin had represented the morally squalid, war-mongering Invernevis dynasty, her wooden chapel on the knoll one hundred yards west meant to oppose as well as highlight. She would have had the arches pulled down when the heir was away at war, had she not been too proud to approach the Home Farm for horses and chains. Her method of destroying the Macdonald shrine had been to have the laird buried in the enclosure behind, instead of in the chapel proper, which his heir dared do nothing about on his return from South Africa for fear of contamination through exhumation.

Maggie had reached the iron grille at the entrance, and she stood with forehead pressed to it, recovering her breath above the sweet flowers. The locked grille was intended to keep the unauthorised out, yet there was easy access through the empty arches of the windows. The family croft was only a few hundred yards away, on the slope above the iron furnace, and she had often played at the chapel as a child, with her elder brother Donald, though her father had warned them against entering the sanctuary, on pain of a beating with the leather belt that supported his plus-fours. But there had seemed to be no harm in leaning, puny fists round the rusty grille, staring down at tilted lichened stone, the inscriptions eaten away by salt-laden winds. The biggest stone was the one that had frightened her most, even with her brother for company, and now, years later, with Donald dust under Magersfontein Hill, it still made her skin creep. Hacked from granite quarried across the loch ages before explosives, the six foot stone represented the recumbent figure of the first of Invernevis, son of Angus, son of John Earl of Ross and Lord of the Isles, fighter at Flodden. The top of his massive two-handed sword rested between his deerskin-shod feet, pointing towards her, the closed visor of his helmet indicating a cruel mouth, the muscular arms jutting from the chain-mail shirt making it seem as if he was about to lever himself into life again and pursue her through the wood. Behind her back she could hear her brother's Gaelic shout: 'He's moving!' and then his boots sliding down sand as he ran, leaving her to her fate.

It almost made her drop the flowers, until she remembered her mission. But where was the old laird's grave among all those urns and stones, some stuck to the crumbling walls? The old Mistress had mentioned newly disturbed ground, but there was no evidence of a spade among the cluttered stones. It was getting chilly, with a breeze from the loch stirring the trees, shadows sweeping where the dead lay. Should she dump the flowers at the grille, run back to the big house, return the five shillings, telling that she couldn't find the grave? But the old lady would create such a scene, like she used to do when deprived of drink. Besides, she was committed to carrying some of the flowers further because she had told the gardener that they were for her mother's grave. Ranald would tell her father, which meant that he would expect to see them the next time he went up to the cemetery.

Her mother had hated lies, and yet Maggie had been put into the position of having to deceive somebody. It was hopeless, really. You thought when Miss Carlotta had gone and you had got into the kitchen in Elsie's place that things could only get better, but now the Master's mother was turning out as big a bother, going to get you into as much trouble as her sister. Well, she wasn't going to take money under false pretences, so she would return the two half crowns, but not directly. She would put the five shillings into the collecting plate at her next Mass. That way, the old Mistress would be none the wiser about the flowers not having reached her husband's grave, which wasn't really a great sin, because Maggie had tried. What you didn't know couldn't hurt you, Mrs Livingstone was always saying. As for the flowers, she would lug them up to the village cemetery, a labour of aching arms to please her father.

She was about to leave the flowers at her feet, against the grille, when she noticed the small stone of glittering granite standing at the tip of the first chieftain's sword, the inscription new:

LAURA JANE MACDONALD OF INVERNEVIS
1883-1901
R.I.P.

Memories rushed back; a golden head racing a big wheel down the avenue on the day her brother the laird had left for the South African war; a freckled face bobbing at the scullery window, then the thin arm held up, round which the slow-worm was wound; black button boots disorientated after one of Miss Carlotta's verbal and sometimes physical assaults. Her life had been short and miserable, and now her stone looked small and forlorn among the large weatherbeaten slabs in the weed-choked rectangle.

Maggie loosened the twine and began to pull out flowers, leaning through the iron bars and throwing them, one by one, towards Laura's grave. It required the same skill as getting the small white balls into the goldfish bowls when the shows came to the common grazing. Some fell short, on to other graves, strewing the first of Invernevis's effigy, a broken-stemmed daffodil over the tip of the massive sword, but sufficient hit the mark to give the girl's resting place some colour and cheer, where the arched stone of a window shadowed. It didn't matter now that Maggie hadn't found the old laird's grave; strewing Laura's was a remembrance for both, and she could tell the old lady that the commission had been carried out.

As she turned away, tearful for the best friend she had had at the big house, she saw a figure leaning against a tree at the bottom of the slope. Because of the elevation she could only see the legs. Her first instinct was that it was one of the Irish navvies who had missed the last ferry the previous evening, and who was marooned because there was no crossing on the sabbath. Images of violation, murder even, made a magic lantern of her mind as she cowered against the iron grille, hearing her own heart. If she ran round the back of the chapel, along the shore and up the iron furnace slope, she might escape, but her legs rooted her. Her whole body was going to liquid, but as she forced herself to look down at the immobile legs again she saw they could not be Irish because they were not clad in moleskins. In light grey cloth, in fact, in contravention of local sabbath custom. When she looked again, cautiously, trying not to breathe for fear of being discovered, though she knew she was being watched, the crossed ankles in the shining supple boots became Frank the footman's.

What made it worse was that she had looked back a good many times coming from the big house, to make sure nobody was following her. It was eerie, the way he was standing there, the upper half of his torso screened by foliage, smoke from a cigarette drifting. She felt like throwing a stone to chase him away, the way one did to a dubious dog, but that would only provoke him. Then how was she going to get past him to go home? She would ignore his presence, take another angle through the wood. His advances didn't worry her as much as his spying. What he had seen with the flowers he would carry back to the big house, to Mrs Livingstone and the Master, or else there would be a price to his silence. The sad thing was, she had quite liked him before he had begun to force his attentions on her.

She went carefully and quietly down the sandy slope, passing within several yards of him. She heard the twig snap behind, but didn't increase her pace. Not that she could afford to be seen walking back with him, and she certainly wasn't going to take any secret routes. He had been with too many of the maids for that.

He was talking before he caught up with her.

'Doing your good deed for the day?' he asked, and she couldn't detect if it was a sneer.

She knew that not answering wouldn't save her.

'Putting some flowers on Miss Laura's grave,' she said. 'There's no harm in that.'

'Yes, but who asked you to? The laird? Oh, I know how friendly you are.'

He seemed to have forgotten that the last time he had pursued that line, she had slapped him.

'And these other flowers? Are they for me?' he asked, indicating the diminished bunch in her arms.

'I'm taking them up to the village,' was all she would tell.

He found the unfinished answer provocative, and held her wrist.

'Why are you always so nasty to me?' he demanded, turning her to face him, pressing her against a tree.

'I'm not,' she protested. 'Look out: you're crushing the flowers.'

But he was pulling her closer to the blonde moustache, his other hand going round her waist. The daffodil stems were digging through her thin Sunday coat, at the midriff. She was split into two, her body wanting to surrender out of curiosity, but her mind warning that she would have to pay a price for satisfying her curiosity. She had had the feelings before, when looking at the Master's photograph as she lay on her bed in her locked room, but this was not the Master but a servant, his close-set eyes bright and his breathing quickening.

To save herself from falling, her button boot lashed out, finding his shin, and as his oath broke the silence of the wood, she dropped the bunch of flowers and ran. He came after her, twigs and grass making way for his fashionable boots.

'You little bitch! You're going to get it this time!'

She was running frantically but fruitlessly among the trees, shoulder striking wood, knocking the breath out, spinning her round, precious seconds lost till she regained balance, only to go the wrong way again. She daren't look back because of what her imagination was making of the pursuit, the memory of a pedlar who had hacked through whalebone, a tale told by her mother as she hunched over reddening peats. Her hearing seemed to have become more finely attuned, so that the sound of his chase was an increasing panting and snapping, like a runaway horse.

The wood surrounding the chapel was a circle, and she was searching for light through the wheeling foliage, finding breath for the last effort, lunging away from his fingertips, which came and went at her shoulder. There, through the trees, was the wooden chapel. If she could only reach it, barricade the door. He would not dare force entry there.

As she burst out into the blinding light, she almost fell under the wheels of Father Macdonald's trap.

He had come to prepare for evening Mass, but really to reassure himself about the safety of Miss Carlotta's chapel. On several occasions drunk Irishmen who had missed the last Saturday night crossing had broken into the chapel, drinking the Communion wine and devouring the wafers before snoring, stretched out on a pew. Father Macdonald had duly reported the outrage to his patroness, and she had replied, condemning her nephew the laird for allowing the quarry to continue and sending a money order for five pounds to make her chapel lock-fast from the Celtic savages. Murdo the blacksmith had fitted a big hasp and padlock, but the navvies had gone in through the window. Suddenly, as he was thinking what a good woman Miss Carlotta was, sending him a hundred hand-made cigarettes, this girl shot out of the woods and almost under the hooves. He didn't have time to rein; the horse shied, almost overturning the trap, sending his black hat spinning, a wheel temporarily in the sky until he was bumped to earth again.

His instantaneous suspicion was of a tinker girl in the wood with one of the Irishmen, but as the metal round the horse quietened and the dust settled, he recognised Duncan the ghillie's daughter, the girl who had been Miss Carlotta's *bête noire*. She picked herself up, with no broken bones apparently, but one bleeding knee. But why such haste? A navvy lurking in the wood? The priest looked around, but it was all silence, as it should be on the sabbath. He began to feel irritated. He could have been killed, or his horse lamed. The girl wasn't going to volunteer anything. She merely stood there, head bowed, crying.

'What on earth's the matter, girl? There could have been a dreadful accident.'

She was trying to sort out her thoughts, and the consequences of the near collision. The footman had melted into the wood. She wasn't going to mention him, because Father Macdonald wouldn't believe her, and there had been enough trouble already. But to say anything else would be a lie, and to a priest. Best to keep it vague.

'Something frightened me at the old chapel,' she sobbed.

'And what were you doing there?'

She hadn't taken into account this natural question, so had to answer quick.

'Just out for a walk, sir.' She realised too late that she should have said 'father'.

But the title and answer pleased him, as he sat above her, holding the reins. The Catholic church prohibited a belief in spectres, since all souls either went to heaven or hell, with no more earthly reference. But in the case of the old chapel on the knoll, the priest felt that Rome would have made an exception. As Miss Carlotta had said, it was a barbarous heritage, with its fighting and fornication, and the idea of the old laird's diseased ghost haunting the pagan rubble to scare local women was quite credible. So the girl, to whom Miss Carlotta had taken such a dislike, had to be treated gently, and could be taken back to the big house in his trap as a hostage to his idea that the burial chapel ought to be demolished, or at least shut in by a stout fence. At the same time, he might get afternoon tea.

'It is rather an eerie place,' he said gently. 'Now I'm going to take you home.'

It was what she hoped for, in case the footman was still lurking, so she accepted the hand he thrust down and climbed in.

In the accident of her assistant Mrs Livingstone found confirmation of the tinkers' story that the old chapel was haunted. She quizzed Maggie about what she had seen. The girl feigned shock, but said nothing about the footman.

'Well, I'd better take the tea tray through to the old lady today,' the cook said. 'Father Macdonald's with her, so I'll put out extra scones.'

While Maggie sat at the big table, sipping sweet tea as instructed by Mrs Livingstone, she came round to the subject of the old laird, and asked as casually as she could where he was buried in the chapel.

'He's not *in* it, but *behind* it,' the cook confided, inspecting a bubbling pot and prodding with a fork. 'That was Miss Carlotta's doing, when the young Master was away at the war.' And, letting the lid drop: 'The old lady would never need to get to know, or it would put her back on the bottle.' She eyed Maggie suspiciously. 'Why are you asking? Was it him you saw? I always said he would never rest peacefully, with what he had on his conscience.'

Maggie shook her head quickly, and, moving back to work,

mourned the futility of the afternoon. It would have been so easy to have put the flowers on the old laird's grave, because there were no iron bars there. The rest of the flowers, intended for her mother's grave, were lying trampled in the wood. She hoped there would be no questions about these.

CHAPTER 8

Following Father Macdonald's call for recruits for the rifle volunteer company, about sixty showed up at the school. Invernevis was surprised and delighted, for it was more than his father had managed to muster. The few who had survived the South African war without loss of limb or other impediment also climbed the brae to the school. They were now veterans and could expect promotion. Frank the footman had joined, swearing that he wanted to sample the military life, though Mrs Livingstone said that it was just to get extra time off and a uniform to attract the girls.

Invernevis himself was raised to the rank of Major, and though it was only honorary, would be addressed as such by the district from now on, though his father, with the more prestigious rank of Lieutenant-Colonel sweated for in India, had simply been 'the laird'.

Dressed in scarlet doublets with yellow facings, Cawdor Campbell kilts, red and black diced hose and blue Kilmarnock bonnets, the company paraded on the dusty playground of the school, shouldering Lee-Metford rifles as their commanding officer, also kilted but feeling slightly absurd with his game leg, watched from the shadow of granite. They bore no resemblance to the company of Princess Louise's he had led in South Africa, but there was promising material there, once they had got over the glamour of the new uniforms. One thing was certain: he wasn't going to repeat his father's excesses. There was no question of passing round a stone jar to slake their thirst at the end of drill, no awarding silver medals when bullets thudded into the bulls-eyes of the targets fixed along the top of the school's enclosing wall. Even if he could have afforded them, there wouldn't have been silver medals, because that was buying popularity. Most of them were expert shots anyway through poaching practice. As for whisky, Father Macdonald, spiritual mentor and trustee, would have objected to the circulation of liquor where there were firearms in the fists of the temperamental.

No, you couldn't buy respect; you earned it by making agonising new boots stamp and wheel, bringing sweat to foreheads, making sure they kept their equipment spick and span. When it was all over for another Friday, they went, kilts swinging, smoking and laughing down the brae, past the priest's shrubbery-screened house to the Arms. There other young men, too timid to volunteer in case there was a war somewhere else in the limitless Empire, slapped their backs and put up large whiskies for them, while old men who had been with the laird in India and had seen spitted white babies, winked at each other as they sipped the strictly rationed whisky, while erratic darts thudded into the board and dominoes clicked.

After the drills Invernevis drove himself home in the gig, usually to find that his wife had retired upstairs to read the latest novel that had come by post that morning. He had thought Carlotta's temperance tracts desperately dull reading, but some of the books Mary Rose got sent were risky, advocating ideas that had no place at Invernevis. When he had told her that he was reviving the rifle volunteer company and would therefore be late for dinner on Fridays she had shrugged and said: 'I thought that most men got tired of playing at soldiers.' He was shocked by her cynicism, and put it down to bitterness at what soldiering had done to his leg. But surely she understood that it stayed in the blood, even after forced retirement through wounds?

Having dined alone at sombre wood, he went up to the nursery to see his daughter, to find Nanny Gunn sitting by the canopied heirloom crib, steel needles going, the tight grey bun of her hair transfixed by more steel. She answered his queries about the child's health curtly, as if a man had no business in a nursery, and when he approached the crib, she rose, blocking his view, warning him that the child must get its regular sleep.

He went downstairs to the library, to brood over the brandy decanter. The domination by women was as bad, if not worse, than in the days of Carlotta. Mama, Mrs Livingstone, Nanny Gunn; they all tried to boss him, as if he was still a boy. Such thoughts made him reach for bigger brandies until the decanter was drained, and he could hardly see his own hand in the dusk. It was at times like these that Laura returned to haunt his loneliness, as if at any moment the library door would burst open and she would come skipping in with Mama's terriers. Their relationship hadn't depended in any way on the physical, except when he had taken her hand on avenue or river bank to reinforce what already held their hearts together. But however pure and uncomplicated their relationship, it was wronging the young woman upstairs to have such thoughts. He would have to try to make things better between them, but he didn't know how.

The situation was worsened by the announcement that King Edward was to inspect the massed volunteer forces of Scotland at a Royal Review in Edinburgh in September. All the volunteer battalions of Princess Louise's Argyll and Sutherland Highlanders were to be present, and since Invernevis's company was affiliated to the Fifth Battalion, its presence was essential. Even if his company had not been going, he would have put his name to the duty roster of the King's Bodyguard of the Royal Company of Archers, having taken his father's place but not being able to attend two years' previously on Edward's first visit to Edinburgh.

There were problems over the transportation of his rifle company. The war office grant was not going to be big enough to cover the expenses of volunteers from remote areas, and the Invernevis share fell short. Local money would have to be found. The men couldn't afford their own fares, and their commanding officer was financially embarrassed. An approach to the trustees wouldn't yield a contribution, because of what had been spent on improvements to the mansion house.

The only way was a sale of work to raise funds. Invernevis realised that the arrangements would have to be put in the hands of Father Macdonald. He didn't like being beholden to Carlotta's ally, but was forced to invite the priest to lunch to state his proposals. Mary Rose was present, and after some small-talk, Invernevis came to the point.

'An excellent idea,' the priest said, using his napkin on his lips. 'Next to God, their king is due their reverence; that was one of your aunt's sayings. And I think we've already found someone to open the sale of work,' he said, leaning forward to smile at Mary Rose.

'I'll consider it,' she said curtly.

Father Macdonald was perplexed. Here was a state of affairs he would have to report back to Miss Carlotta, who had always sent her old clothes up for charity sales in the village. It was vital that the laird's lady set an example to the parish, by organising and encouraging. There had been an excuse for old Mrs Macdonald, with her husband's lingering illness and her subsequent drinking problem, but here was a young, healthy woman. Though he had looked forward to an after-lunch brandy and cigar in the library, the priest saw by the silent faces flanking him that there was no alternative but to withdraw, making the excuse that he had to prepare for evening Mass.

Invernevis saw him out to his trap, and returned to Mary Rose.

'Well, the sale of work should keep the women baking and making jam for weeks,' he said lightly. 'I suppose we'll have to get Mrs Livingstone to make a contribution. What do you suggest? A large cake or a lot of small ones?'

'I don't think taking the men to Edinburgh is a very good idea,' she said. 'They'll only get drunk and show you up.'

He was shocked to hear her echo Carlotta's estimation of the village, but knew it wasn't the real reason for her disapproval. She didn't want him to go because she felt unable to cope with the house in his absence.

'It will look bad if we don't go, when all the other companies are going,' he argued gently. 'They'll say I'm too mean to take them. After all, my father paid out of his own pocket to take *his* company to the Wet Review of '81.' And there was something else, which he might as well get over. 'It's not only a matter of raising money to take them. They'll need to go into camp with the other companies to sharpen up their drill, because they'll be parading as a body. I'll have to go with them,' he added.

'That's a pity, because I was wanting to go away myself.'

He looked at her in surprise. 'To see your mother and Jamie?'

'No, not that far north. To Pitlochry, for the Highland Lawn Tennis Championship. If I'd felt fitter after the baby, I'd have entered for the Ladies' Singles Handicap.'

'But that kind of public thing's not for a lady like you,' he protested.

'Oh don't be so stuffy,' she scorned. 'Gentlemen shoot in public for prizes and do other silly things, so why shouldn't ladies? Titled women play tennis, you know. Anyway, I was only going as a spectator, to pick up some hints. But we can't both be away from here at the same time, so I suppose, as usual, the man gets his way. After all, preparing for war is *very* important.'

'But your brother was a soldier,' he reminded her.

'Yes, and look where it got him,' she said bitterly. 'The world doesn't have a great deal of use for one-armed alcoholics.'

'He was in here this afternoon,' Mrs Livingstone confided to Maggie that evening, after dinner. 'Asking me to do a big baking for a sale of work in the school to send the volunteers to the big show in Edinburgh in September, the one the king's coming to. Well, it's for a good cause; I don't mind if the village gets its hands on my baking. *Our* baking, because this is your big chance to show what you can do. Scones and wee cakes, mostly. No, I was just thinking as he was speaking: now why doesn't Maggie go to Edinburgh to see the show? Look at the time you've been here, and no holidays. It doesn't do to let them think that you don't want holidays. Your father wouldn't mind, I'm sure, and there wouldn't be any problem about a place to stay because I've got a friend who's a cook, and I'm sure she'd put you up for the night, if need be.'

The idea of going to Edinburgh both frightened and attracted Maggie, who had never been beyond Invernevis. It would be by train, which was something she'd always wanted to do, and the Master would be there. Perhaps they would travel in the same carriage. Of course it would take money, but she'd faithfully followed her mother's dictate about thrift, and had quite a few pounds up in her bedroom. She would like to take her young brother Hector with her, but that would be a big responsibility and her father wouldn't allow it.

'Now don't go telling anyone about this Edinburgh business,' Mrs Livingstone was warning, 'or the other girls will start wanting to go too, and you can't all go. Keep it dark till nearer the time, and I'll have a word with your father. But don't think you're going to stand about, dreaming about it till then. We'll need to be thinking about tomorrow's menus, because the young Mistress doesn't seem to bother nowadays. You could put the same thing in front of her day in, day out, and you wouldn't hear a word. I don't know what's got into her. Of course I've heard the tinkers say that some women go queer after having a baby. Aye, you can smile, but the tinkers have powers none of the rest of us have. I heard one of them putting a curse on Miss Carlotta because she wouldn't let him have a can of tea, and now she's away. No, I blame that bitch of a nanny, too snooty to take her meals in the servants' hall with the rest of us. Well, I'm going to speak to the Master about this business of trays having to be taken up to the nursery.' She snorted. 'You would think the fairies were going to snatch the baby. In fact, you would think it was *her* baby, not the young Mistress's.'

'Maybe she isn't well,' Maggie suggested, feeling sorry for the golden-headed lady she had hardly seen.

'Oh she's not well, that's for sure, but it isn't the kind of illness Doctor MacNiven can cure. It's inside her head, like it was with poor wee Miss Laura, only she was happy, running about and laughing, until Miss Carlotta got her. I don't need to tell you that what I'm saying to you doesn't go outside this kitchen. I'm only telling you these things because you've got a good chance of getting my post when I retire. What I'm saying is: there's more to it than filling their stomachs when you're cook in a house like this. You have to be a good listener, but hold your tongue, because their class don't like taking advice. That's the hardest thing to learn, slipping in a word where you feel it might help, but it takes a long time before you can trust yourself to do that. But enough talk now; away out to the larder and see what might do tomorrow's lunch, and *don't* come back with salmon. They've had it twice already this week, and though the Master loves it, you *can* sicken him.'

As spring moved into summer, there was frantic activity throughout the village to prepare stuff for the volunteers' sale of work. Children pulled the first fruits of the season from the tangled hedges, to boil in brass and solidify in glass. Eggs were cracked into bowls in the unstated but fierce competition to beat the big house by producing the lightest baking. Arthritic fingers fed wool to flickering wheels, and nimble needles trailed thick sweaters.

The men took no part in these preparations, though some of the older ones were carving stick handles out of rams' horns, and the less cynical would volunteer to look after stalls where rolled pennies could multiply and the hanged Home Farm goose be claimed simply by guessing its true weight, a penny a try.

Most of the young men were preparing to go into camp

under their Major and laird to learn the discipline of marching *en masse* under the critical eye of the monarch. They went by train early in July, the hour's journey taking them into the peaceful fertile countryside where the other companies of Princess Louise's Fifth Volunteer Battalion were mustering. They were roused from their bell tents by the reveille bugle as the sun was rising, to parade and have their weapons and persons inspected. Those who had been too late or timid to apply a curved blade steeped in cold water to their jowls were sent to remove the shadow, hunched squinting into a mirror hung from a tent rope and flared by the sun while those who had passed muster crowded round the field kitchen, eggs sizzling on blackened iron attracting early flies, a twig turning rashers of bacon, regulation issue cutlery scraping on tin.

They were marched up and down the meadow, trampling the daisies until hundreds of pairs of heels came together simultaneously and rifles were inclined at correct angles to the relentless sky. When the officers were satisfied with the troops' discipline sham battles were staged between a blue raiding force and a red defending force. There was much smoke and noise, with kilted men crawling through grass, setting it alight with illicit cigarettes as they waited for the attack. When it eventually came it was inept, and in a real war would have resulted in massacre. There were near tragedies. Rifles that should have contained blank cartridges were carelessly discharged, and bayonets almost blinded unwary volunteers. At the end of the day, dozens of blackened faces crowded round the casualty tent, but the majority were grinning, as if a great battle had been won.

There were sports to induce comradeship as well as test their stamina. Burly moustached men, agricultural labourers in civilian life, stripped to their kilts, their sporrans swivelled out of the way as they crouched and circled for catch-as-catch-can, heels hacking at sun-baked turf till glistening sinews yielded, to be pinned down among flowers by knees. They ran races started by an officer's revolver; they climbed shoulders in wavering pyramids; they did hops, skips and jumps to see who could get the furthest. The thick rope with an officer's blue silk handkerchief knotted in the middle went taut in the tug of war competition, the teams of six men each straining, slanted back, heels dug in, hemp in friction with flesh as the handkerchief inched towards them.

There were prizes, but Invernevis did not contribute, as his father had done. He sat in the sun outside the row of officers' tents, watching the sports with other commanding officers, burly landowners in tartan trews and riding boots who had been comrades of his father's and who had brought plentiful supplies of whisky, availing themselves of gunmetal hip-flasks as they smoked, laughing hoarsely when the buckles of the wrestler's kilt broke or the runner's foot snagged.

Invernevis felt no affinity with them, though they were of his own class. As he sat with the sun in his face, his game leg stretched out on turf, he was thinking back to the camp at the Orange River Station, before the Highland Brigade had pushed forward to the Modder, Magersfontein and massacre. That was soldiering, laughter in sunlight before the mocking guns, but this only horseplay, an insult to the dead in the South African dust. What on earth had his father extracted from these annual camps but drunken excesses, sometimes joining in the wrestling himself? Yet those he sat beside in sunlight sang his praises, hinting that the son couldn't be half the man.

The officers also participated in the sports, spurs and whips urging their mounts over the jumps in the gymkhana while the ranks cheered. One bearded burly landowner, very like Invernevis's father, applied too much toothed steel to his black charger. It went down with the splintering barrier and was found to have a broken leg. Having put his revolver to its skull in full view, the officer ordered the men to drag it away and bury it. Invernevis turned his face away from the eyes of the fallen horse. He had seen the same look in gun-dogs being whipped for trivial offences by his father. His loathing for the landowner who had crippled his own horse was increased by the fact that the man was a Campbell.

After sundown the officers and men sat round the camp fires, tin mugs of whisky circulating, tenors adopting grave stances, making the surrounding hills return, amplified, the mournful Gaelic. Fire within and without quickened the mood, calling for pipes and dancing demonstrations over crossed swords provided by officers. Invernevis sat beyond the flaring noisy circle, smoking a cigar. To make his men withdraw to their billets for the night would be to spoil their collective harmony, and have criticism carried home. If that was what being Highland meant, getting drunk and dancing over crossed steel to clapped encouragement, he didn't want to be a part of it. Lairdship was about distanced supervision, not participation. The world was certainly changing for the worse, but Edward, the enlightened king, had given his blessing to decadence as Prince of Wales.

He looked up at the stars and thought of Mary Rose sleeping in her canopied bed in the shadow of the mountain, with the river audible below. Maybe things would change when he went home. But then, his ancestors had known that you didn't wait for things to change; you manipulated men and time to suit your own ends, hence their suzerainty of these acres in the sweep of the river. Mary Rose wasn't an adversary; she was his wife, upon whom the continuation of the dynasty depended because he needed a male heir to defeat the spiteful terms of his father's will. Things would have to be different when he got back from Edinburgh. Maybe he could persuade Jamie to come to Invernevis for a holiday, and if the decanter was kept out of his reach, that was bound to please Mary Rose.

Thinking of Jamie as he sat at the camp fire, with sparks climbing to the stars in the perfume of burning pine, brought back an episode from South Africa that had haunted him. After crossing the Modder Princess Louise's men had torn off their stifling tunics and unbuckled their sweat-saturated kilts to go running naked through sunlight, ploughing and plunging into the element that had almost defeated them, scooping, shouting: 'Chateau Modder, full of body!' because of the dead Boers and horses drifting down. Jamie had stood beside Invernevis, shielding his eyes, his tongue moving in a parched manner over his moustached lip as he watched the white clefted bodies stooping, appendages at the dark triangulations swinging without shame. It was confirmation of Invernevis's growing suspicions of his friend's predilections, which he had tried to accept without judgement, though the thought of the physical side was distasteful. Now at the camp fire he could see justification for such a relationship. There might be emotional justification where men were disappointed with women. Call it companionship. He didn't have anyone to confide in, least of all Alexander who had made such a mess of his life with women, and there was no one else of his social status in the district. He certainly wasn't going to confide in Father Macdonald, because he could almost believe in him betraying the confidence of the confessional box to please Carlotta.

Next day the volunteer company entrained for Invernevis, where the preparations for the sale of work were almost complete. Trestle tables heaped with goods crowded the school's two classrooms, the partition wall folded back, women standing jealously on guard over their baking, as if reluctant to sell what they had taken so long to make. In the kitchen of the big house the blast from the oven brought beads of perspiration to Maggie's face as she stooped to replace trays of scones and cakes, dozens already cooling on the big white table where Mrs Livingstone stood with agonising ankles, warding off wasps with the back of her hand as she buttered her fourth sponge.

'Well, I hope they put a good price on them. There won't be better ones. Kate Black might like to think she can beat me, but I've a way of doing it no one else knows.'

'Is the young Mistress opening the sale?' Maggie asked,

going to the door for coolness, but meeting raging summer.

'I suppose so, but she hasn't been through today. Too busy at that damned organ.'

Through in the drawing-room Mary Rose sat in a shaft of sunlight, feet on the pedals, fingers on the stops, playing Saint-Saens's 'Preludes' which had come that morning. The gilded pipes above her golden head sent the bell-like music through the house, and as she pulled and pressed she hummed, swaying in time. It was like being back at the reins of the dog-cart on the sombre Sutherland avenue, ribboned straw on the back of her head, the horse's ears pricking to her 'home! home!' to new-risen scones and a newly arrived brother in soldier's uniform holding her in two arms. The music seemed to surge through her, making her brace her body against pushed pedals and pulled stops for the crescendo. If only her husband could do that for her.

In the library Invernevis sat at his desk, writing Mary Rose's speech for the opening of the sale of work the next day. When he heard the music she was making, the fingers of his free hand began to drum. It was certainly more cheerful than what Carlotta had produced. He felt tempted to go through and tell her so, but didn't want to interrupt her recital.

The cheerful music carried across the river, up to the Home Farm, where Alexander was hosing down the byre, watched by MacPherson, the gutters grumbling.

'It sounds as if they're having a party over at the big house!' MacPherson shouted, voice rebounding from dim bare stone. 'Maybe another youngster on the way, a boy this time, eh?'

But his son-in-law kept plying the hose, flushing the stalls, the hissing water failing to drown out the organ.

'They say his wife's got very advanced ideas,' MacPherson persisted. 'Playing tennis with the servants, votes for women, now this fancy modern music. What next? I hope she doesn't start mixing with the servants the way your father did.' His laugh echoed, the organ lost.

Alexander shrugged and began to hose the dung from his

own boots before going to shut the stand-pipe off. As he stepped out into the sunlight his father-in-law said:

'You're looking very pale. Is there anything the matter?'

'I was late home from the Arms last night.'

MacPherson slapped him heartily on the back, making him stagger. 'Aye, you're the best of them, Sandy. None of these fancy bloody new ideas for you.'

Instead of following him in for dinner, Alexander stood listening to the recital that the mountain behind the mansion was amplifying, the music sounding like huge bells swinging.

Next day Mary Rose appeared downstairs punctually after lunch for the sale of work opening. Her outfit was the one she had worn on her first visit to Invernevis, a satin dress, the colour of salmon flesh, with spangles at the high throat and more at the hugging cuffs. Angled on the golden head was a wide brimmed straw hat of delicate weaving, with the same satin bunched in a flower at the band. To match the dress, a furled parasol, its mother-of-pearl handle a swan's neck.

Invernevis was wearing the kilt and carrying a ram's horn stick which he used to lever himself up on to the gig. He kept close to Mary Rose, but the blind bend was negotiated without incident, and once across Wade's Bridge, the horses broke into a brisk trot, Mary Rose sitting serenely, gloved hands folded on the swan's neck of the parasol. Her husband fumbled in his sporran and produced a piece of paper which he passed to her.

'This is your speech.'

She looked at him in surprise, laying the parasol by her side to scan his difficult writing.

'I can do much better myself, thank you,' she said gaily, gloved fingers shredding the paper and tossing the confetti over her shoulder. The parasol was taken up again and she resumed her throne-like posture, but with a mischievous smile under the tilted brim of straw. It made him apprehensive about what was to come. Surely she wouldn't let him down in front of the locals. After all, his father had always written Mama's speeches.

At the school they took their places on the temporary platform beside Father Macdonald, who insisted on a prayer of gratitude from the locals jamming the classroom, some strategically standing by home baking or jumble. The massed skulls of the village, young and venerable, bowed to the harsh Gaelic, warning them that to forget homage to monarch and empire was a mortal sin.

'It is far better to spend your money here than in the Arms. The one will send your sons to national glory, the other to an early grave.'

After the priest had crossed himself it was the turn of the laird's lady. She rose in a rustle of satin, and without a paper in her gloves, began to speak fluently and distinctly.

'I do appreciate the honour being paid to me by Father Macdonald and the committee in being asked to open this sale of work, which is to raise money to send our volunteer company to the Royal Review in Edinburgh next month. Now I know that several in this audience served in South Africa and have wounds to prove it; and I also know that some of you lost sons and husbands in South Africa. Of course you are proud of your volunteer company, but would it not be better if we didn't have to raise funds for such a cause?' She ignored the startled faces, including her husband's. 'Wouldn't it be better if such things didn't exist, because armies and weapons mean war, and war is a wicked thing that feeds on life and limb.' Her eyes were on Invernevis's game leg; his were on the floor; Father Macdonald's face was thunderstruck.

'We boast that we beat the Boer, but at what cost? I see no victory, and indeed the papers are suggesting that the Boer will get his independence from us and be able to keep his gold and diamonds for his own good. Which is as it should be. Some of you will doubtless say: but this is only a woman speaking.' Her voice rose. 'But may I remind you how important women are in society? Without women men would – '

The moleskinned trousered Irishman standing below her

took the broken stemmed clay pipe from between his stained teeth and clenched it in his fist as he pounded the platform, shouting: 'Aye, you tell the buggers, ledy. Me wife at home's got ten chuldren and has the lookin' efter the lot of them, and if this quarry's goin' to close as they say it will, well what will she do —'

But Invernevis was rising to interrupt the drunken monologue, to declare the sale of work open on behalf of his wife. It took several seconds for the locals to lose their astounded looks before turning to the stalls. Soon they were shoving and reaching, and in some instances kicking, home knitting stretched as competitors tugged, cakes squashed, children crawling up to jump queues, coins in grubby fists. The noise was deafening, angry arguments in Gaelic about ownership, the trundle of the wheel of fortune, and MacPherson roaring, demanding that they come and guess the weight of the Home Farm goose. Elbows ruined two of Mrs Livingstone's sponges, but the other two fetched half a crown each, a record for home baking. They were bought by a village boy sent by Invernevis, with strict instructions to give the sponges to the two oldest widows in the village and sworn to secrecy so that news of the laird's charitable act would never get back to the big house.

The Irish navvy who had applauded the lady's speech and a crofter were disputing the ownership of a shirt, the local clutching at the striped flannel, claiming in a loud voice that he had paid threepence for it, the other swearing by all the saints that he had had his hand on it first. But the garment, which was being stretched by the sleeves between the two, suddenly tore with a snarling sound, and as he fell against the stall, a fragment of flannel in his fist, the crofter cursed the 'shower of Irish tinkers'.

Though the crofter shouted in his own Gaelic, the Irishman understood, and let the amputated sleeve fall to the floor as he turned to face him, stroking his grizzled chin thoughtfully, as if pondering the gravity of the insult, then lunging, his fist making contact with the crofter's chin.

The crofter sprawled against the jumble stall, the old clothes cushioning his fall, but the force overturning the trestle table, the signal for the other local men in the classroom to come belatedly to his assistance because another navvy had appeared at his compatriot's side. Fists and boots flailed as the two Irishmen fought off the impossibly matched assault, their backs to the stall where no one as yet had guessed the exact weight of the Home Farm goose, MacPherson red in the face as he shouted abuse at the Irishmen. The goose, bound at the claws, was swinging dangerously on its supporting pole, until it splintered, making the women scream more.

The two Irish navvies were soon overpowered and propelled outside by half a dozen locals apiece, but the damage had been done, the sale broken up in confusion before it had got under way, blood on the floorboards of the school, and some of the women hysterical, having to be slapped quiet by their men.

Up on the platform Invernevis put his head into his hands and groaned, knowing that he would have to subsidise the disaster if the volunteers were to get to Edinburgh. Worse: having shamed him and the cause by her speech, Mary Rose was now helpless with laughter, doubled over the swan's neck parasol as she watched the hall being cleared. Father Macdonald stood glaring at her, as if he wanted to say something. He had had a further demonstration of the dangers of letting the quarry continue, and no doubt would write that night to Carlotta, reporting the revolutionary young woman at the big house. And MacPherson, who was stooping to retrieve the goose because technically it had not been won, would not fail to spread the word that the laird had been present but had done nothing.

Invernevis had Mary Rose roughly by the arm and was turning her towards the door, but she stayed, touching Father Macdonald's sleeve for attention.

'Could you do the christening next Sunday?' she asked charmingly.

The priest was so taken aback that he could only watch her

with wide eyes, and she repeated the question. Invernevis was staggered because he had been given no warning. Did she mean at the house?

'I shall get the chapel thoroughly cleaned, with flowers,' the priest said, stern expression staying. 'There is no reason, is there, why the villagers should not witness the ceremony? After all, it is the first child from the big house for twenty years or so, and such things are of great significance to the ordinary people.' His tone presumed superiority. He would use the ceremony to strengthen the hand of the Lord in the village by working in references to the evils of drink and indolence, showing the risks the innocent children were exposed to.

'No reason why they should not be there,' she said.

'Shall we say twelve o'clock?' And seeing there was no opposition, gave her arm to her husband so that she could be taken home, her salmon-coloured hem trailing through the shambles of the sale of work.

As the gig jolted homewards, Invernevis was beyond anger, into the emptiness of self-pity. The summer countryside had lost its charms, the sun was now harsh. Oh yes, he had scorned the legend of the sundered Irish harper O'Caibre, but there *was* a family curse working. His father, Carlotta, Alexander, Laura, Mama, and now Mary Rose. He could do nothing about the disgrace that was spreading behind them in the form of gossip, but her proud profile rankled with him, and as soon as they were passing under the ivy into the front hall he began to give voice to his anger.

'You suddenly raise this matter with Father Macdonald without having first consulted me. Do you think that's quite proper? After all, these things need planning.'

'I thought it was a good opportunity to get it over with.'

'Over with?' he said, shocked, barring her way into the drawing-room. 'The christening of a child's a very important occasion, especially in a family like this, and this is our firstborn. Invitations should have been issued. Your mother and brother, for instance.'

'We've talked about this before. I don't want them here,' she said abruptly. 'You're making this thing much more important than it really is. After all, it's not a male heir.' He searched her face for sarcasm, but saw none as she continued: 'Your brother and his wife can come from your side of the family. Surely that will be sufficient.'

'He's not going to set foot inside this house,' he said, really angry now.

She turned to confront him, her hand on the cut glass door handle. 'But you've just said a christening's a most important occasion so it's only proper that your brother should be present. In fact, I insist, or there'll be no christening.'

'But the child was to have its name confirmed by a proper ceremony,' he almost shouted, wondering what he had married. 'You know very well what Father Macdonald and the locals will say if Alexander's there.'

'Why should we care what they say?' she asked indignantly. 'The christening *will* take place on Sunday, as I arranged, and your brother and his wife *will* receive an invitation.' Pushing into the drawing-room, she shut him out.

Invernevis was left standing in the hall, searching his pockets for a cigarette. He was hurt and angry, hearing in her imperatives Carlotta's harsh voice. Invite Alexander? *And* his wife. That was outrageous. It could only be to embarrass him in front of Father Macdonald, who was sure to transmit the insult to Carlotta, which would cause trouble with the trustees. No, she wasn't the woman he had married. He blamed that bitch Nanny Gunn for bringing all the troubles of Sutherland with her and upsetting Mary Rose.

Invernevis determined to get rid of the tyrant at the first opportunity.

CHAPTER 9

Without first checking with Invernevis, Mary Rose sent the coachman down with Alexander and his wife's invitation to the big house after the christening ceremony; and the same to Father Macdonald. Then she went through to see Mrs Livingstone, who broke the news to Maggie after she came down with the old lady's afternoon tea tray.

'Great God, she's wanting a christening cake for next Sunday,' the cook announced, forced from her feet by the request. She counted on her fingers. 'Five days.'

'Surely we can manage something by then,' Maggie said.

'You've a lot to learn, girl,' Mrs Livingstone said, shaking her head mournfully. 'It's not the making, but the maturing that's the art. Fruit cake's like whisky; it improves with age. Something in the fruit. You need to leave a wedding or christening cake for a good few weeks, the way I do with the Christmas puddings. I ask you: is this the way to run a house, coming at the last minute? And they tell me she made an awful mess of opening the sale of work. Now the laird will have to dig into his pocket to send the volunteers to Edinburgh, and he hasn't got it, because of what *she* spent on clothes on honeymoon and the expense of keeping that bitch of a nanny.' The cracked brown teapot gurgled. 'Anyway, girl, we'll just have to do our best, because she's determined to have the christening on Sunday. She says there'll be five for lunch, but she's not saying who. Roast as usual. It's the cake that's the worry. Well, girl, we'd better make a start,' she said resolutely, gripping the table edge to ease herself up. 'We'd better go and see what we've got in the way of fruit. It's too late to get any more from Glasgow.'

Invernevis was kept in ignorance of these preparations, and became convinced that his protests had led to the postponement of the ceremony until Mary Rose said at Saturday lunch:

'I've made all the arrangements myself for tomorrow - except the wine. I can't remember what one drinks with christening cake. Champagne? But first there'll have to be wine at lunch, with the roast beef. Red. Then instead of a sweet, we'll have the cake.'

'I didn't realise you were proceeding with it,' was all her husband could say.

'Oh yes, it's time the child was properly christened,' she said brusquely. 'There'll be five of us - Father Macdonald, your brother and his wife.'

Instead of waiting till the library, Invernevis lit his after-luncheon cigarette at the dining table, waving the match out before he said: 'But we've already discussed this business of Alexander coming up to this house. It's most embarrassing for me, and it'll only lead to trouble in front of the servants, especially when there's drink.'

'But he's your brother, the only close relative you've got left - except your mother,' Mary Rose said. 'You've never given me a satisfactory reason for not getting on with him. If it's his lifestyle that worries you, he seems to be quite happy, so you should be pleased for him. I do wish Jamie was as settled. Anyway, Alexander's accepted to come tomorrow with his wife, so it would be unforgivable of you not to give them a warm welcome. Besides, I want Alexander to be the godfather.'

'Godfather?' he echoed incredulously. 'But I thought it was more usual to have a godmother, and that would be Mama. I assume she's attending the christening.'

'She's not fit enough to come downstairs,' Mary Rose said calmly. 'Even if she could it wouldn't be safe, with drink about. As for her being godmother, she's that already, of Alexander's little girl.'

'But Mama hasn't had a drink for ages; not since we came home from honeymoon,' he protested.

'Yes, but you know what would happen if temptation was put in her way.' Then, seeing his scowl, she added quietly: 'I think you'll agree that I've had enough experience with Jamie.'

'But how is one going to explain to her that she can't come? She's going to feel not wanted. She hasn't got anyone else.'

'It isn't necessary to explain anything,' Mary Rose said firmly. 'I'll send up a piece of the christening cake.'

He was angry. His wife was treating his mother as his aunt had done, as if Mama was a child without a mind of her own. If Mama wasn't shown some trust, then she would deteriorate into a senile bedridden child.

'What does one drink with christening cake?' Mary Rose repeated.

'Oh, that's settled already by you inviting Alexander. It'll have to be whisky and plenty of it. And when he gets drunk, who's going to control his tongue? Certainly not Father Macdonald; he'll be taking everything in for transmission to my aunt.'

'It doesn't have to be whisky,' she said dismissively. 'Anyway, I must go and see how Mrs Livingstone's getting on with the cake.' As she swept out he knew he had lost a very important battle. She seemed to be cultivating Alexander's company in order to embarrass him. As he lit another cigarette in the library and had a supporting brandy he was beginning to regret his marriage. It had been too hasty, panic because of Laura's death, his fear of being left alone in that large house with a drunk mother. Having known Jamie since schooldays, he should have realised that the sister would be as impulsive and moody.

The cook was standing at the big table, applying icing with a knife to the brown circle of the basic fruit while Maggie stood watching.

'You mustn't put on too much at the one time,' Mrs

Livingstone cautioned. She dipped the tip of the knife into a bowl of water. 'Take your time and get it as smooth as possible.'

Mary Rose stood in the doorway, watching in admiration, so silent that neither the cook nor her assistant was aware of her presence till the knife skidded, scoring.

'You *have* done well,' Mary Rose said, coming forward.

'There wasn't enough time, Ma'm,' Mrs Livingstone said decisively, as if indemnifying herself against the cake between her hands being a failure. The top tier was still cooling on a wire rack further down the table. 'The fruit needs a long time to get firm, and I doubt if this icing will be properly dry by tomorrow.'

'Never mind, you've done marvellously well,' Mary Rose complimented her, sampling icing from the tip of her finger as she went out. 'Five for lunch, I think I said; Father Macdonald, my husband's brother and his wife.'

Mrs Livingstone had to sit and order her assistant to make a fresh pot of tea.

'My God, what a place this is becoming, creeping up and spying on you like that. We could have been speaking about anything. And this business of Master Alexander coming here after the christening. Asking him is bad enough, but his wife as well. I mean: Kate MacPherson's a nice enough girl, but what does she know about mixing with gentry? Oh yes, her father will claim that he and the late laird were great drinking friends, but the laird never made a close friend of anyone, unless it was a woman. No, it seems to me that the young Mistress is up to mischief here, making trouble between the two brothers, as if there wasn't enough already. I don't think *he* should have rushed into marriage.' She looked significantly at Maggie, then said peremptorily: 'Pour two cups and we'll get on with the icing.'

The next morning punctually at ten the best gig left Invernevis House, bearing the laird and his lady, and, in the back, Nanny Gunn and the baby. Mary Rose was sheeted from throat to ankle in white silk ornate with lace at cuff and neck, and carrying a parasol. Nanny Gunn was severe in black, grim mouth hidden by a veil as she clutched the child in its christening robe of fragile lace and Tay pearls. The gig rocked down the ruts, through the flickering shadows of the high leaves and out on to the public highway, Nanny Gunn clutching the child tighter as Wade's Bridge loomed, the springs moving with the motion of a boat in rough seas until the crest was behind. They turned the bend towards Alexander's house, the reins tightening in the coachman's fists. Alexander came out in a badly fitting black suit and high starched collar with stud showing, boots on his feet and a scuffed black hat in his ingrained fist. His wife followed, head bowed, pulling a shawl round her long rustic dress, Sunday shoes stumbling in the ruts of the driveway Alexander was supposed to have laid, instead of spending fine evenings in the Arms. Putting his hand under her buttocks, he heaved his wife up on to the back of the gig, and hoisted himself beside her. Nanny Gunn clasped the child as if it was about to be snatched by the rough new arrivals, her eyes horrified behind the thick lenses.

They ran above the river, Mary Rose turning to chat to the passengers, the road forking for village and ferry, the gig taking the latter and inferior one, stone now instead of dust under the iron-shod wheels, stragglers for the service and the merely inquisitive stepping up on to heather, the men removing their black hats and pressing them against their chests in attitudes of piety, the women waving as the big house gig lurched down, and when it was out of earshot, the revelation in shocked Gaelic that Alexander and the Home Farm girl were up there. It was said not because they had a spite against the girl, who was harmless, but because her father would be 'so bloody smug' at the fraternal reconciliation. By the next opening time it would be transmitted to the Arms that Alexander had gone back to his own side and was therefore not to be trusted with the secrets of the village.

The wooden chapel was coming into sight and beyond it the grey stagnation of the loch where the encasing mountains excluded the sun, the scar of the granite quarry growing weekly, its crushing machinery silent. Invernevis dared not look left, to that circle of trees shielding the family burial chapel on the eminence, suspended stone glimpsed between the tight trunks as the gig approached Father Macdonald, standing in reception outside Carlotta's recent wooden chapel, his ankle-length black vestments with the white surplice limp in the windless morning. The last time that Invernevis had come that way was to bury his sister Laura, with the priest standing in the same predatory garments in the same weather, sunlight on calm water where the shore sloped to the penny ferry for the quarry, the long boat moored, oars shipped, because a sabbath crossing constituted work.

More locals of both sexes in black and sober cotton stood at several respectful paces from Father Macdonald, Missals in their fists as the big house party braked, the first lady helped down, momentarily showing an ankle. Invernevis's game leg was revealing too much under tartan, Alexander's wife coming down without assistance, an undignified jump, then the precious cargo, the baby passed from Nanny Gunn's arms to its mother's until the bird-like spinster could be helped down and stand, brogues firm, on the raised beach. The child was restored to her care, to be carried, preceding its parents and godfather into the chapel.

Boards splayed by storm, the chapel was crowded with bare wooden chairs that Carlotta had imported from Glasgow to stop the spines of the collected sinners of the village from slumping. The Invernevis family pew was a long bench at the front, with a red cushion, rarely used because Carlotta had not liked having the rabble behind her as she communicated with God. Instead, Father Macdonald had gone regularly each Sunday morning to the big house to hold a private Mass for Carlotta in the drawing-room, and, when necessary, to hear her confession, a silk screen separating them.

Carlotta's major outlay in the chapel had been the altar of light oak, carved panels depicting the saints, not made on the estate though there were joiners capable. It had come, like the organ in the big house drawing-room, from the south, and now Father Macdonald was praying at the altar of his benefactress, palms raised to the grey window overlooking the loch, too high and grimy to be a distraction to the congregation. He stepped down, stood in front of the crowded big house pew, with Nanny Gunn at the end, the child docile on her bony knees. It was in English, the preferred language of his most important worshipper.

> 'Dearly beloved brethren, I certify that on second May, and in Invernevis House, this infant, being then in peril of life, was duly baptized with water, in the Name of the Father, and of the Son, and of the Holy Ghost. And, Almighty God having of His mercy preserved her life, she is brought hither, that the true confession of that faith wherein she was baptized may be made openly in the presence of this congregation; and that we may publicly testify her reception into the Church and congregation of the Lord.'

He was reading from the Gospel, and Invernevis was dreaming, remembering the occasions - Christmas and other holy days - when he had sat beside Laura in the drawing-room of the house, letting her fidget as her simple mind fled the ponderous language, with its threat of eternal damnation. He wished she was there with him instead of the other occupants of the pew. Mary Rose inspected her hands, her expression betraying no sign of her attitude to this new religion into which her daughter was being received. Alexander sat, or rather slumped, fiddling with the bottom button of his waistcoat, his hat between his boots until Kate nudged him, reminding him where he was.

The priest was asking about renouncing the devil, all his works, and all evil spirits; the world, all its glory and vanities; and all sinful desires of the flesh.

'... so that thou wilt not follow, nor be led by them?'

The child was gurgling, waving its fists under Nanny Gunn's stony face.

The priest was standing over Invernevis, frowning as he whispered: 'You must answer for the child. Say after me: I renounce and abhor them all. Say it loud and clear.'

Invernevis did as he was told, though he had forgotten what the response referred to.

> 'And dost thou believe in the Holy Ghost; the Holy Catholic Church; the communion of saints; the remission of sins; the resurrection of the body; and everlasting life in the world to come?'

The last phrase made him imagine Laura running, barefooted, head thrown back, laughing through blazing light.

'Answer: All this I steadfastly believe,' the priest hissed.

'All this I steadfastly believe,' though he had grown cynical because of the way Carlotta had imposed her Catholicism, with hand and tongue.

'Answer: I do submit myself, and will obey.'

'In testimony of these thy good resolutions, I call upon thee to worship and adore the living and true God.' He signalled with both hands for those on the big house pew to come forward, but there was confusion, with Invernevis looking at his wife, and Alexander looking in alarm at the priest.

'The child is to be brought forward, with its Sponsors,' the priest said impatiently. 'Who are the Sponsors?'

The question was not directed to Mary Rose, but she indicated Alexander and Kate. At a sign from the priest Alexander and Kate slipped down on to their knees. There was a glare from Nanny Gunn as the priest directed her to hand down the child to Kate.

They knelt, Home Farm manure between the tackets on Alexander's soles, Kate with the child's face at her shoulder, her palm supporting its back.

'Repeat after me,' the priest whispered, and together man and wife said:

> 'I worship and adore the Father, the Son, and the Holy Ghost, One living and true God, being of one substance, power, and majesty: to whom be praise and glory. Amen.'

Alexander's voice was hoarse and unnatural, his brother hearing in it an attempt at subjugation of the big house accent, and annoyance at being forced to submit to something he thought he had escaped by defecting to the Home Farm.

At the next response, it was only Kate who said, in a clear voice:

> 'As it was in the beginning, is now, and ever shall be, world without end. Amen.'

Father Macdonald then stooped to raise the child by the armpits and turn with it to the altar, cradling it, then laying his hand on the small skull and saying:

> 'We receive this child into the congregation of Christ's flock, and do bless her in the name of the Father, and of the Son, and of the Holy Ghost.' He made the sign of the cross. 'And be thou blessed and kept unto everlasting life.'

Then the Lord's Prayer, and a prayer of gratitude which Invernevis only received in snatches because he was so angry at Mary Rose for having made Alexander and his wife Sponsors of the child without the father's prior approval. Well, her cunning move to bring the brothers together was going to come to nothing, he would see to that, because he didn't want Alexander coming about the big house again.

'Amen,' the congregation said collectively, in a tone suggesting that no mental effort was involved.

But the service wasn't over, for Father Macdonald had some advice to give, and he gave it from the authority of the altar, standing between the silver candlesticks Carlotta had provided.

'You may think that being Sponsors is a mere formality, but it is not,' the priest cautioned, his eyes on Alexander and his wife. 'As Sponsors you have the responsibility of overseeing the future physical and spiritual welfare of this child. Or so it seems. No. The parents will look after its physical well-being, and the church the spiritual. Your task is to set an example for the child by righteous behaviour, by abstaining from these temptations that degrade the physical and spiritual. That means regular attendance at this house of worship as surety for your good conduct.'

All the time the priest was lecturing them, Alexander's face was getting darker and darker, and he would have risen and gone, had not Kate detained him by the sleeve, biting her lip as she watched the priest. As if seeing that he was in danger of taking his sermon too far, Father Macdonald suddenly stopped and, coming down from the altar, blessed Alexander and his wife by making the sign of the cross above their heads. Then, ordering the congregation to kneel, he raised both hands:

> 'The grace of our Lord Jesus Christ, the love of God, and the communion of the Holy Ghost, be with you all evermore.'

They said 'Amen' and resumed their seats until the big house party had left, as they had been taught. Nanny Gunn led the way with the child, hugging it as she hurried up the narrow aisle, covering its head to deny the locals a look. The laird and his lady came next, Invernevis nodding right and left where reverence was being shown; then Kate and Alexander, he shambling, with a silly grin, his hand straying to his trouser pocket till his wife pulled it away.

Out in sunlight again they boarded the gig, taking the same seats, but at a slower pace, so that Father Macdonald could catch up in his trap. No words were exchanged, and not only because the baby was now crying querulously. Invernevis was apprehensive about what the rest of the day would bring, and wished that his brother and wife would dismount at their house. But Mary Rose had made the arrangements, and the gig jolted over Wade's Bridge and up the avenue, the exhausted child settling to sleep in the thin retentive arms of

Nanny Gunn, its father watching the repeating shadow of the nearside horse succumbing under the wheel, wondering if the child behind him was going to have as unhappy a life as his sister.

They went into the drawing-room to await the arrival of Father Macdonald and luncheon. There was silence for some time, Alexander working with his fingers, Kate rummaging in a little string bag, suddenly producing a badly tied small parcel and placing it on the table between herself and Mary Rose, nodding to her hostess to take it.

Mary Rose exposed the small christening cup with the monogram LM, murmuring, as she passed it to her husband: 'You shouldn't have done this. It's beautiful, isn't it, Niall?'

He held the cold silver and nodded in assent. But the initials reminded him of another child whom Alexander had neglected. He saw the cup as an attempt to buy favour.

'The engraving might have been better, but by the time we ordered it from Glasgow —' Kate was saying, then reddening as she realised that she was using the lateness of the invitation as an excuse.

Mary Rose made it easier for her by asking: 'And how is your little girl?'

'She's fine,' Kate said, relaxing as they reached common ground. 'My mother's looking after her up at the Farm.' By simple extension, she asked Invernevis: 'How is your mother?' The tone was one of respect.

'She's quite well, thank you.' He couldn't bring himself to acknowledge her drinking problem to someone he didn't consider to be a member of his family.

But Alexander was not going to let the truth go. 'Still tasting, is she?' he asked, grinning, trying out one of the new phrases he had learned in the Arms.

'As a matter of fact she hasn't touched a drink for months,' his brother said stiffly, in a tone which demanded that the subject be dropped.

But Mary Rose was taking it up. 'No, she's been very good

lately. What I don't understand is: how it got such a grip in the first place.'

She was looking round for enlightenment. Invernevis on the sofa beside her was going rigid, trying to catch his brother's eye, daring him to discuss their father's illness and death. But Alexander was looking the other way, so Invernevis knew that he had to turn the conversation with the first thing that came into his head.

'Are you liking your new house?' he asked Kate.

'Oh yes,' she said, shaking her head eagerly, like the girl she was.

But it was a silly question, for it allowed Mary Rose to lament: 'Oh I *do* wish we had a place your size instead of this great draughty barracks. You probably know we had some work done, but nothing to alter the character of the place. That's what I don't like, the atmosphere, as if – how shall I put it without it sounding silly? – all the Invernevis dead are still walking.'

'It's just your imagination,' Invernevis said dismissively, an edge to his voice because he was determined that they weren't going to carry to the Home Farm and hence to the village evidence that the lady of the big house was unsettled, queer even.

'No, I agree with you,' Alexander told her, ignoring his brother. 'That's one of the reasons I left this place. Think of lying upstairs in a gloomy room, listening to *that*.' He pointed to the gilded pipes of Carlotta's organ flaring in the sun. 'Morning and night; she was never away from it. Something I've never told anyone.' He looked at Niall. 'My father once offered me five pounds to put the organ out of action for good, by pouring syrup into the pipes, but I didn't have the courage.'

Mary Rose laughed. 'You make your aunt sound like an ogre.'

'She was certainly that,' he agreed. 'But Niall must have told you all about her.'

'Niall's told me very little about your family,' she said, giving her husband a benign, reproachful look. And to Alexander, with a warm, almost intimate smile: 'You must come oftener and tell me more, when no one else is about. I'll play the organ for you.'

Invernevis turned, wondering if she was falling for Alexander's famous charm, of which he had never seen any evidence. But her long fingers were wrapped round her tall thin neck as she laughed away her invitation, Father Macdonald's wheels over gravel taking her out to welcome him, then leading him in by a black arm. Seeing Alexander and his wife, the priest frowned, but allowed himself to be led to a chair. When he was settled in the scuffed sagging linen, he put the tips of his fingers together and surveyed the company, as if it was a board game, with one of them to make the first move. The ornate clock on the mantelpiece filled the silence he had created.

'Luncheon won't be long,' Mary Rose said, smoothing her silk lap as she searched for a theme. 'Your chapel is certainly in a lovely situation, Father. I can just see the roof from my bedroom window.'

He considered her statement for several seconds, pouting his lips before replying. 'If you mean the outlook - no.'

She looked surprised, spreading her hands to signify that she was lost, and Invernevis frowned at what he saw as a violation of manners, embarrassing a woman.

'When Miss Carlotta first built the chapel, there was a lovely view across the loch, but the quarry has ruined it. That great ugly scar - no, a sore - on the mountainside, and the noise. I couldn't count the number of panes we've lost since blasting began. Worse: they miss the last ferry on Saturday night, burst the padlock and sleep on the chairs.' His voice dropped dramatically. 'They have even drunk the Communion wine and eaten the holy wafers. The building has been wrecked, and there is no point in rebuilding it, because the same things would happen again; Miss Carlotta agrees.'

As he said this he looked steadily at Invernevis, to show that his aunt, though in exile, was still a power in the land.

'Then what shall you do, build in the village?' Mary Rose asked with genuine concern.

Father Macdonald shook his head. 'It would be no better protected in the village than down by the ferry, I regret to say. The solution is to build a new chapel closer to this house, so that villagers and Irishmen alike will respect it. The site I have in mind is the meadow across the river. You can see it from that window,' he said, turning, but no one followed his finger.

Alexander stiffened visibly. 'Is this your idea?' he asked the priest, in a tone devoid of respect. He seemed to be looking accusingly at his brother.

'Your aunt's,' Father Macdonald said calmly, stressing the pronoun. 'It was in her mind long before she departed. She has since been in communication with the trustees, and has proposed that she will put up the money, provided that the site is granted in perpetuity to the church.'

Invernevis was alarmed, having thought that the proposal had lapsed. He was also angry at the priest's lack of discretion in bringing up such a subject at such a time.

Alexander was already speaking. 'It's a bad idea, using good agricultural ground, which is leased to my father-in-law. *He* won't give it up easily. And what do you think, seeing it's going to affect your view?' he asked, turning to his brother.

Invernevis felt himself go red. He was being put into an impossible position, and it was all Mary Rose's fault, for her stupidity in inviting them. Now Alexander had him at his mercy, as so often in the past with their father, and anything he said would be reported back to the Home Farm via Kate, who was sitting, white-faced, beside her spouse. Even more menacing, Father Macdonald would transmit his opinion to Carlotta. There was no possibility of withholding an answer, for they were all watching him, waiting.

'I don't think it's the most suitable site,' he began cautiously, feeling for ground, like walking the boggy bank of *Casan Dubh* in darkness, 'though I agree that rebuilding the present chapel wouldn't be the best solution. This is where Father Macdonald and I differ slightly. He pays us a compliment by assuming that a chapel under our walls, so to speak, would ensure good behaviour through respect, but I feel that a place nearer the village would be safer through your proximity, if not presence, Father. It would also be more convenient for you and for the congregation – having less distance to travel in bad weather, and especially in winter, when ice makes the road so treacherous.'

'Your congregation didn't show a great deal of respect at the sale of work, did they, Father?' Mary Rose said lightly, angering her husband further.

'That is true,' the priest said mournfully, 'but it was the Irishmen who started the trouble.' He sighed. 'They are becoming a very serious problem.'

'They're all right, if they aren't provoked,' Alexander put in.

The priest turned cynical eyes on him, and spoke slowly, for effect. 'I haven't spent much time in their company, apart from the night I had to go down to the Arms and prevent them from murdering the locals. You remember that night?' he asked casually, as if Alexander could forget being discovered unconsious through drink and an Irish fist, under a toppled table.

At that moment Symmers the butler beat the circle of wrinkled brass in the hall, a souvenir of Carlotta's Indian days, to announce luncheon, and the conversation stopped, Mary Rose leading the way through, arranging the seating. The meal was mostly chinking silver as guests gave their full attention to the succulent beef. The butler's unsteady hand replenished wine glasses as soon as the level dropped significantly, but Kate's was inverted, the symbol of her aversion to the liquid fire that was threatening to consume her marriage. She took water instead, excusing herself with a blush, saying that alcohol made her sleepy. Father Macdonald nodded sympathetically, fingers feeling for the crystal stem again, to wash down his red meat.

The speed of Alexander's consumption meant that another cork had to be drawn audibly behind the silk screen, where the butler tested it before allowing it to proceed to the table. Alexander's elbows were on the table, and there were stains on the mahogany round his plate, where he had lifted gravy with a spoon.

'Going back to what you were saying about the Irishmen; I don't think they're as bad as you make out.'

It took Father Macdonald several seconds to realise that he was being addressed. He lowered the wine glass slowly, watching Alexander over its rim.

'It is not *my* judgement, nor that of the trustees. Their behaviour condemns them. They are like animals when they have a drink in them.'

'That isn't a very Christian thing to say,' Alexander protested, the wine now sheening his forehead.

'Drink in excess is the enemy of Christianity and civilisation.'

Invernevis was grateful that the conversation was being deflected from himself, but alarmed at the turn it was taking through Alexander's truculence. The only reason he did not stop him was because he wanted to hear how the priest as trustee would reconcile the continuation of the quarry with the trouble it was causing. Was Invernevis going to be blamed, for taking the decision to renew the lease? If so, he would protest, though time and situation were inappropriate.

'What the hell are big words like Christianity and civilisation supposed to mean?' Alexander asked angrily. 'These men live and work in terrible conditions. Have you ever been across to see their living quarters? No, I thought not. Well I can tell you it's a race between themselves and the rats who gets the food first.'

'Please, Sandy, not now,' his wife implored him from across the table, but was ignored.

'Rats and rotten food. If physical conditions were improved, then you might see a spiritual change.'

'I think you exaggerate the condition of the camp,' the priest said, with a slight smile. 'Even if what you say is true, you must accept that there are some people who do not wish their physical conditions to be improved, because then they lose their excuse for not reforming. Your aunt used to say that about the natives of India. As you no doubt know, Ireland is a very primitive country.'

'Where *your* church has got a good grip,' Alexander said heatedly. 'As for anything my dear aunt said, I treat it with the contempt it deserves because she was nothing but a cruel bitch.'

Though he was secretly delighted at his brother's attack, Invernevis knew that he had to intervene, for the sake of the two wives.

'That's *enough*, Alexander.'

'Yes, quite enough,' Kate called across dark wood. 'Why have you always got to let me down in company?' And to her host: 'I'm very sorry about this. I knew we shouldn't have come.'

'Of course you should have,' Mary Rose said calmly, folding her napkin through the silver ring and swinging her legs out. 'Now let's cut the cake.' She cranked the bell by the fireplace. 'We'd better get the principal guest brought down,' she said with a smile.

She led them to the end of the room by the fireplace where a white-covered circular table supported the christening cake, its two tiers separated by silver pillars, the top tier with an icing plaque embedded, with LM and the date traced out in wavy symbols by Mrs Livingstone. Kate was lost for words at the cook's skills at such short notice, with Mary Rose saying how lucky they were to have her, though her legs were so bad. Meantime Invernevis, to avoid making conversation with his brother and the priest, was directing the butler to open one of the two bottles of champagne resting in a bucket beside the cake. The wire cage came away easily enough, but the butler's thumbs had difficulty coaxing the cork. As he was levering it out, it left the bottle suddenly, the metal crown striking the high, dim ceiling, which produced laughter all round. Invernevis had to take the frothing bottle and direct it to the nearest glass, to prevent the carpet getting most of the champagne.

Then Nanny Gunn came in with the child, evidently not pleased because when she was summoned the child had just settled to sleep after its first excursion. Mary Rose offered her a glass of champagne, but the elderly woman would not relinquish her charge. She warned the mother that the child was stirring in its swaddling cover, and would cry soon.

'I think we'd better cut the cake,' Mary Rose advised, calling them round it. She put the silver knife into her husband's hand and directed the blade to the bottom tier. Then she put her hand over his and applied pressure, the knife sinking into the icing, to a hearty cheer from Alexander, which was met by a scowl from Father Macdonald, peeved that he had not been asked to say a short prayer.

Nanny Gunn bore the child away, also carrying on a blue plate a small piece of cake, minus marzipan and icing, which she would consume in the privacy of her room. Portions of the cake were passed round, and the butler circulated with the tray of champagne glasses.

Mary Rose came up to remind Alexander that he was the godfather, and grinning, he called out: 'Here's health to the wee girl. May she have a long and happy life,' before downing the sparkling glass in one swallow, and taking another from the tray.

'Not so fast! I've another toast!'

As they turned, he lifted the new glass, slopping some over his boots. 'Here's to our aunt in Leamington Spa. I hope she gets what's coming to her.'

Everyone was watching Father Macdonald for his reaction, and it was not long in coming. He set his empty glass down beside the cake and turned towards the door.

'I can't stay here and listen to a good Christian lady being insulted.'

'Good Christian lady, my arse!' Alexander jeered.

The priest was making for the door, with Alexander standing rocking with drink and laughter by the cake. Invernevis knew that he was going to have to choose between priest and brother. He didn't need time to make a decision; there would be plenty of trouble with the trustees when Alexander's insults got to Carlotta.

'I think *you'd* better go,' he said evenly.

'Aye, I'll go. I should never have come.'

'No, no,' Mary Rose pleaded, crossing to detain him by the arm. 'It's only a misunderstanding.'

'If it's only a misunderstanding, it's lasted an awful long time,' Alexander said, eyeing his brother. 'We'll never get on.'

As he turned to go the toe of his boot snagged in the frayed carpet and he staggered, saving himself against the table bearing the christening cake. As Kate shrieked the cake swayed, then came to a rest at a precarious angle, the separating pillars embedded. The champagne glasses on the table hushed their chiming as Invernevis strode across to take his brother by the arm, propelling him across the room.

'Never darken my doorstep again.'

He went, shrugging, Kate following, looking back imploringly as the priest's iron-hooped wheels sprayed gravel outside.

'I'll walk with you down the avenue,' Mary Rose called, 'if you'd like to wait in the hall a moment.'

When they were alone, beside the tilted cake, Invernevis turned accusingly to his wife.

'I *told* you it was a bad idea.' He had never been so angry with her.

'It was all right, till you ordered him to go. You could have handled it better.'

'*Me?*' he echoed incredulously.

'Yes, you could have made a joke of his toast. Why must you always be so solemn, so serious?'

'Because I'm the laird,' he reminded her, 'and because Father Macdonald is not only a man of God; he's also a trustee, and they can make a lot of trouble for me if they choose.'

'There are some things more important than status,' Mary Rose said, salvaging fragments of icing from the cake. 'Brotherly love, for instance.'

'Brotherly love,' he snorted. 'He never showed me any. It's a long story, and I'm not going to distress you with it. I've made up my mind; he's never to come here again.'

'It's harsh for such a little thing. I hope you don't live to regret it. Anyway, I'm going to walk them down the avenue. I need some fresh air.'

She was gone before he could protest. He stood, drinking champagne without appreciation of its vintage. He did not bother to go to the library window to look up the avenue because he knew she would carry out her threat through spite. Everything she did seemed to be directed towards disgracing him. My God, what a mistake he had made in marrying her. Because of his social position and religion divorce was out of the question, so he would just have to endure, as his sister had done with Carlotta. It had killed her. He tilted the foil-encased neck again, but the bottle was empty. He was making for the library and brandy when the commotion broke out in the front hall. He heard Alexander's voice and what he took to be scuffling.

By the time he had got to the dining-room door the two terriers had joined in, lunging and snapping round Alexander's heels as he stood at the bottom of the stairs, with Mary Rose in his arms weighing him down.

'Don't just stand there!' Alexander panted. 'Come and give a hand. She fainted on the bend.'

But help was arriving from the servants' quarters with

Mrs Livingstone pushing through the baize door, followed by Maggie and the ghillie. As they carried her up the stairs, the golden head turned, imploring eyes fixed on Invernevis.

'For God's sake – never again – that black thing.'

BOOK THREE

CHAPTER 10

On 17th September, 1905 the Invernevis company of the Fifth Volunteer Battalion Princess Louise's Argyll and Sutherland Highlanders entrained for Edinburgh and the Royal Review.

It was a Sunday, but Father Macdonald had given special dispensation for travel because the railway companies could not be expected to cope with the civilian as well as military invasion of Edinburgh on the Monday morning.

The Invernevis contingent left in the late evening, hoisting aboard their kit as though they were seasoned soldiers preparing to leave for a war in some far-flung outpost of the Empire. The whole village was there to see them off, Farquhar the piper from the big house risking the wrath of his laird by playing the regimental tune 'The Campbells are Coming' as he strode the platform, pushing a path for his deafening drones. Wives and sweethearts pressed round the windows, standing on tiptoe to offer chocolate and tobacco for the journey. The veterans of South Africa and earlier wars under the old laird had hobbled down from the Arms, and stood in the shadow of the serrated roof, squirting bitter black juice at their boots.

Mary Rose had not come to see the Major off because of her fear of the blind bend, and he was conscious of critical mutterings in Gaelic among the crowd as he mustered his men. But Maggie was there, being seen off by her young brother Hector, her father having already taken leave of her in the servants' hall with the admonition to behave herself and not to give the time of day to any man, however respectable, who might approach her in the streets of Edinburgh.

'Watch that footman, lassie. If there's any funny business, go straight to the Major. Very likely he'd leave him in the city, where his kind belong. It's not only me you should keep in mind; it's your mother, God rest her soul.'

Mrs Livingstone also wanted a word with her before she left.

'Shut the door,' she ordered, before fumbling in her clothes and producing a sovereign, pressing it into Maggie's palm, though the girl protested that she had sufficient.

'Take it and get yourself a treat,' the cook urged. 'What chance have I got to spend money here, and who have I got to leave it to? No, a wee cottage will do when I retire, and I've got enough put by for my needs. Now about company for you,' she went on brusquely. 'I got a letter back from my friend, saying how pleased she'd be to look after you for the day. There it is, with the address. We'll expect you back late tomorrow, with the others. Now that footman,' a finger wagged. 'Just you watch he doesn't try anything, when he gets you away from here. I'm only saying what your mother would have said to you. Now off you go in case you miss the train.'

'I wish you could have come with me,' Maggie said, ruffling Hector's hair as she leaned out of the train window. 'But I'll bring you back something.'

The awkward boy in his first pair of long trousers shrugged, though she could see by his eyes how much he wanted to go. He was about to leave school, to be hall-boy full time, setting out the veined plates in the servants' hall and polishing the Major's shoes, but in free moments learning the art of piping from Farquhar, beginning with the basic chanter. Farquhar said the boy showed real promise and could be as good as the brother who had died playing under Magersfontein Hill. Instead of going into the army, Hector hoped to succeed Farquhar as the laird's piper, circling the house to waken him at eight sharp each morning.

Hugh the porter was unfurling the red flag, and Maggie kissed the top of her brother's head before withdrawing into the compartment she was sharing with the few local women who could afford to go and see their volunteer husbands and sons parade in Edinburgh.

The special train was pulling out, sent on its way by cheers and the pipes, Father Macdonald, who could not go because of evening Mass and the probability of Last Rites, giving his blessing with two fingers to clanking iron. Invernevis settled back in his first class compartment, his company travelling third, at concession fares. The last streaks of a spectacular sunset were fading behind the standing stones as the train took the curve above the river. He remembered taking that line in a violent thunderstorm on the night he had left for the Boer war, with the mansion under the mountain momentarily illuminated by lightning, as if a million lamps had been turned up simultaneously. Then his father was dying in sightless agony behind stagnant muslin, but Laura was still unharmed by Carlotta's blows, her body thrusting towards womanhood. Now the house was dull and sinister in the last of the light, Mary Rose no doubt having a nightmare about the blind bend in the big canopied bed while Nanny Gunn guarded the child.

At her third class window Maggie's excitement at her first trip from Invernevis was subdued by a glimpse of the family croft occupied by another family now. Her mother had been as sparing with words as with coins from the caddy on the mantelpiece above the black grate, and she would have regarded such a journey as an unjustifiable extravagance, even though the laird was also travelling. It made the girl feel guilty, because at the back of her mind she knew that she had taken up Mrs Livingstone's offer of time off, not because she wanted to see the capital of Scotland or the men of the village parading before their monarch, but because the Master would be there, and might have more time for her than he had at home. Her own eyes and ears, and Mrs Livingstone's monologues, had convinced her that the Master was not getting on with the new Mistress, and though she knew it was wicked to have such thoughts, she hoped that somehow the young

Mistress would go home to Sutherland, leaving the Master to be looked after by Mrs Livingstone and, when she retired, by Maggie herself. Miss Carlotta had ranted and raved, sometimes resorting to physical violence, but the young Mistress was making the house just as gloomy with her silences. But it was bad to have such thoughts, so she settled back as the train entered the dark pass.

An entire third class carriage had been reserved for the volunteers, and they crowded to the windows, pushing for last views of Invernevis as if some of them would not see it again. They were in high spirits and there was a good deal of horseplay, with Kilmarnock bonnets snatched and exchanged. Only Frank the footman did not participate, sitting cross-legged in a corner, smoking a cigarette, sporran swivelled to the side, an experienced traveller who knew the world beyond Invernevis and liked it better. The Major had strictly prohibited the consumption of alcohol, on pain of not being allowed to parade and ignominious dismissal from the company on return to Invernevis, but there seemed to be no harm in cards, with small coins exchanged.

Though good at games of chance, the footman refused a hand. He was scowling, because there was no access to the next carriage where Maggie was, and even if there had been, the Major would dismiss him from the big house as well as the volunteer company if he found him with the kitchen-maid. It wasn't only because of appearances, the footman suspected. He slid from the seat, edging past the card players kneeling round the drum, and pretending to admire the sunset availed himself of the contents of a gill of whisky from inside his doublet, one that the old Mistress had paid for with a silver trinket but which had never reached her. He hadn't been running errands for her recently, which was a pity, because it was the only way of getting a little extra at Invernevis and the wages were so poor.

As the night darkened outside the hurrying windows, cards were slapped down and coins bounced on the drumskin, the carriage polluted by pipe and cigarette. Someone asked the company piper for a tune but he refused, in case the Major in the first class compartment further up the train heard the din and thought there was drinking.

He was now nodding into sleep, again crossing the Great Karroo with his company in the closing months of the late century, the sliding doors of the box cars open, Gaelic mouths agape at the sight of horned and feathered animals that could not be accommodated in their colourful tongue. When his sister Laura had first fallen ill he had planned to take her to convalesce in South Africa as soon as the Boer was beaten, but death had defeated him. Now he was dreaming that they were travelling together across the desert, her fists pounding glass as she shrieked in delight at the sight of the springbok bounding, trying to outdistance the clattering intruder. Then she became the animal, racing alongside with anguished face as she had raced the big wheel of his gig down the avenue on the day he had left for the South African war.

Metal locking underneath awakened him, and there was a long wait at Callander while the carriages were coupled to the engine of another railway company. Tired after the excitement of the send-off, and knowing they had a strenuous day in front of them, the volunteers restored cards to sporrans and stretched out as best they could in the cramped compartments, kilts riding up their splayed legs as they snored. But the footman was still wide awake, rubbing the window with his sleeve to look out on the Perthshire hamlet, wondering if he shouldn't risk moving up the train to Maggie's compartment. He trampled his cigarette and stuck his head out of the window.

Railway lamps were hazed by the nocturnal mist as he opened the doors, avoiding the legs of a sleeping man. Grasping metal with both hands, he lowered himself backwards, foot feeling for the ground, making contact with the rail, the cold going up under his kilt. The sounds of shunting metal and the shouts of invisible railwaymen muffled his shoes on the cinders as he groped his way along the side of the train, levering himself up to look in windows. An empty compartment. He cursed, lowered himself and moved on to the next window. The women were all sleeping, askew in their seats, knees apart, mouths wide, clutching their bags to their breasts. Maggie was next to the window, sleeping, her fist under her cheek. Though it hurt his fingertips, the footman hung there, held by her beauty behind the steamed glass. It was a face devoid of scheming, of disturbed dreams, like the expression on the face of Miss Laura, the Major's sister, when Miss Carlotta had made the servants shuffle in respect past the coffin.

But when he heaved himself further up he could see the sagging indentation of her dress where the legs splayed, whiteness exposed above the rim of the stocking. He was loosening a hand to rap glass when a window slammed down along the train and a thrust-out head demanded: 'What's going on there?'

The fright made the footman let go, and before the cinders bit into his bare knees he recognised the Major's voice. He lifted himself up, and, turning his back, hitched up his kilt, shouted, trying to make his voice Highland:

'Just relieving myself, sir.'

'Well, hurry up and get back aboard in case this train moves,' the Major said gruffly, conceding nature's call.

The footman found the first door and climbed aboard, and though it wasn't his compartment, stepped over the splayed legs and squeezed into a corner. Damn the Major, just when he was about to make it. A few minutes with Maggie beside the track, in the mist, was all he'd wanted. Very likely the Major had had the same idea, only he'd take her into his first class compartment. Oh, it must have happened a good few times before, the way her eyes went when his name came up. It was always the same, he thought bitterly; *their* class had the first pick of everything. The side of beef went in hot but came through cold, picked clean to the bone, which had to go to *their* dogs. And to crown it all, his quarter bottle had broken when he dropped at the Major's call. It was a soggy mess inside his doublet, but at least there wasn't any blood. His cigarettes were squashed but still serviceable.

The train pulled into Morrison Street station, Edinburgh, in a fine mild dawn, one of several troop trains using that goods terminus, guided in by gas standards and oil lamps swinging in the fists of shouting linesmen, the volunteers leaning from the windows, cheering. The Major mustered his men, shepherding them across the railway line, shouldering their kit. He lined them up in the street for their march to their billet at South Bridge School. They tramped through cobbled streets where early spectators cheered their swinging kilts, and raucous voices of both sexes hawked Review programmes. At the grey school large kettles were laid on so that the soldiers could shave, stripped to the waist, sitting at desks, laughing, wielding cut-throat razors as they squinted into the shards of mirror propped in inkwells.

After a big breakfast of bacon and eggs some of the Invernevis contingent wandered out into the streets, crowding round picture-postcard booths, selecting views of the castle to send home, though they would be back before the cards. There was the difficulty of writing a suitable greeting. Though they knew how the words should sound in Gaelic, they weren't sure how to put them down. But, satisfied with their scribbled phonetics, they licked the king's profile and posted the cards. Then the Major came mustering them again, and they were formed up in the street and marched to the rendezvous in the East Meadows.

As soon as she stepped off the train, Maggie separated from the other Invernevis women, who were going to look at the shop windows before the Review began. She left the station, Invernevis volunteers calling after her to be sure and have a good day, and to look out for them. Footsteps were hurrying after her, and as she thought it was the footman, who had been leaning against a pillar, watching her leave the train, she increased her pace, her little case swinging, bumping against static soldiers. But when a voice called on her to stop she recognised the Master, and, face burning, waited without turning round. Was she going to get a warning about behaving herself? But he had her by the arm, had pressed a coin into her free hand with the cheerful admonition: 'Now *do* have a nice time,' and he was gone, before she could tell him that she had enough money.

She stood at the kerb, staring down at the sovereign in her palm, Mrs Livingstone's in the leather purse in the pocket of her dress. It was an awful lot of money, too much to spend on herself in the one day, more than two months' wages. She was not aware that a small cab had pulled up in front of her, a bowler-hatted driver leaning over smiling, long whip at the ready, the horse's front hooves idling, snorts visible in the chill morning.

'Where to, Miss?'

It put her into an agony of indecision, her face on fire. Apart from one or two lifts on the gig from Roddy the coachman (and even then only to the gate of the big house) she had never travelled by horse and vehicle before. The idea of paying to ride when she could walk, asking directions from policemen as Mrs Livingstone had instructed her, brought back her dead mother's constant injunctions about wasting money.

But the cabman was climbing down to open the door and help her up by the elbow, as though she was a lady of some importance. She got in because she was sure bystanders were watching her.

'Where to, Miss?' the cabbie called over his shoulder when he was restored to his seat, and waited while she fumbled in her pocket for the piece of paper Mrs Livingstone had given her.

She gave the number in the New Town and the whip flicked, the horse transcribing a circle, along Princes Street, though there was a far shorter way to her destination. The hood was down, mist dispersing with the dawn, promising sun. She couldn't take her eyes off the castle on the rock, its serrated stonework puncturing the mist, like an engraving in her fairy story book, the one her mother had picked up at a jumble sale. Statues stood among trees on her right, where the gardens sloped, and she gasped at the size of the figure seated on the roof of the columned building. Was it Queen Victoria, whom the old lady at Invernevis was always talking about? No, Maggie had seen the figure before, on a coin, sitting with wheel and trident.

A glittering display of shop windows unrolled on her left, sightseers from early trains pressing and pointing. Horses clattered by, blinkered, though the clock on the colossal North British Station Hotel had not yet reached seven.

Maggie began to relax against leather, to sense the excitement of a day in which she would actually see the new monarch in the flesh. The old lady had briefed her endlessly: to report back in the fullest detail about the king's dress, the extent of his beard, how much he resembled his 'dear mother'. But Mrs Livingstone had warned: 'Don't you go breaking your neck, just to have a look at the king. Just you have a good time.'

The cab turned left, running along a broad street flanked by high buildings, past a statue which looked like a king. Her neck against leather, Maggie was now imagining that she was a queen, waving to loyal subjects lining the pavements. But the wheels over cobbles jolted her back to the grey morning. The horse was now going round what seemed to be a square of curving houses, with a circular garden in the centre protected by railings.

'Here you are, Miss,' the cabbie called over his shoulder, bridling for the number she had given him.

The cobbles had made Maggie squeamish, and though the cabbie had the door open and was groping at her feet for the small case, she waited until the towering grey buildings with the huge columns had steadied. He was carrying the case up the steps, towards the circular fanlight when she called after him.

'It's the back door.'

He turned and came back down, smiling. 'There aren't any back doors in this part of Edinburgh,' he said, leading the way down a flight of steps to a door below ground-level flanked by barred windows.

'How much will that be?' Maggie asked anxiously, the Master's sovereign sweaty in her palm.

'Well now.' He pushed his bowler back and scratched his forehead, screwing up his face as if it was a difficult calculation. 'That's a run along Princes Street and down George Street. A mile at least, I would say.'

Maggie was beginning to fear that there wouldn't be much left out of the coin she was clutching, which she now wanted to keep as a souvenir.

But the cabbie had finished reeling off the route. 'I think we'll forget about the fare, seeing it's your first visit to Edinburgh, lassie. I can always add it to some of the fancy folk I'll be getting off the trains today. See and enjoy yourself, and give a *big* shout when you see the king.'

He was up the steps and on his seat before Maggie could protest. For the second time that morning she had been thwarted in her desire to refuse money, something that would have made her mother very angry. As she turned to the forbidding door with its brass knocker in the shape of a gargoyle, she heard the clip-clop of hooves going away above her, and wished that she hadn't come. It wasn't like the back door at Invernevis House, which was always open, with dogs as well as humans coming and going. Her hand was on the knocker, but she was wondering if she shouldn't climb the steps and go to the Review by herself. But Mrs Livingstone, who had made all the arrangements with her friend, would be furious. She waited, heart sounding. The door was opened by a maid who looked her up and down, her eyes staying on Maggie's black button boots, a legacy from Miss Laura.

'Well – what do *you* want?'

Maggie managed to blurt out: 'Mrs Chisholm.'

'The cook? What do you want with her? There's no jobs going here.'

The door was closing, but Maggie didn't care. Tears blinding her, she was stumbling up the steps. The maid was more horrible than Elsie, the kitchen-maid whom Miss Carlotta had taken with her baggage from Invernevis.

Then the Master's sovereign slipped from her fingers and bounced down the steps, ringing against the closed door before it came to rest. Maggie stood on the top step, the gold on grey stone below shimmering in her misted vision. She didn't want to go back down to that door. She didn't want the coin. She wished she hadn't come, and would get the first train back to Invernevis, telling Mrs Livingstone no lie when she told the cook that she'd gone to the address. But the coin had been given to her by the Master, and her mother had always said that it was wicked to waste money. If she left it, the horrible maid would pick it up the next time she answered the door.

She went down slowly, and was stooping when the door opened. She saw battered shoes, and swollen legs like Mrs Livingstone's, a bulging expanse of white, a round friendly face sweating from the stove.

'Come away in, girl,' she urged, lifting Maggie by the elbow, 'and pay no attention to that one who answered the door. She didn't know I was right behind her. Aye, she's a forward one, on her last warning, and after what's she just done to you, she's going today, Review or no Review. Now come away in and see if my breakfast's any better than Kate Livingstone's. How is she, the warrior? I haven't seen her for years, since we were in service together. A quick tongue, but a heart of gold.'

At that moment the massed guns of the castle sounded, and though Maggie was used to the blasting at the quarry across the water from Invernevis, she fell into Mrs Chisholm's sturdy arms.

'It's all right, dear,' the cook reassured her, laughing and patting her. 'It's only the king arriving at Waverley Station.'

CHAPTER 11

Thousands of people from all over the country were pouring into Edinburgh to see the king. The streets were jammed. Horse trams sprang the points, the passengers hedged in by advertising boards on the open top trying to climb down and complete their journey on foot, but being stopped by the press. Behind them, the horns of motor cars honked impatiently, the long-caped drivers at the tall wheels getting redder, the ladies behind sitting stiff-spined in their wide, flower-encrusted hats as inquisitive urchins poked sticks through the spokes.

The combined noise of men, machines and nervous animals was deafening as the solid mass choked Princes Street, pushing towards the splayed roads that would take them to Queen's Park, under Salisbury Crags, where the king was going to review his loyal volunteers. Since dawn people had been scaling the Crags to get the best vantage points, and some of their perches were precarious as they sat, waving. Arthur's Seat was already crowded as over 38000 officers and men began to march into Queen's Park, to their stances by the markers put down for each battalion.

As he marched his company through the Albert Gate to take its place in the ranks of Princess Louise's Argyll and Sutherland Highlanders, to the right of the Black Watch, Invernevis was remembering a different morning in a different land, when Princess Louise's had marched in a thunderstorm from the Modder, to get caught up with the Black Watch in the tenacious thorns under Magersfontein Hill, the Boer rifles blazing before they could get into battle order. This time, on

Queen's Park, under a dull grey sky, there was no hitch, no hidden enemy. He was proud of the appearance of his men, who had received a share of the cheering from the hill.

Then came the King's Bodyguard of the Royal Company of Archers, led by pipes playing 'Highland Laddie'. The Archers were in their dark green uniforms faced with crimson, eagle feathers slanting from their Scots bonnets. Their long bows were carried in their left hands, and at their sides, a quiver of arrows, a gold-hilted sword.

Though he was some distance away, among the massed volunteers, Invernevis recognised his brother-in-law Jamie Mackay by the missing arm, as he was turning to take his place as part of the Guard of Honour in front of the grandstand. Invernevis was worried. Jamie's exaggerated stride and the way he kept his spine parallel with his bow, walking like a clockwork toy, suggested that he had a good drink in him. Surely not so early, and in front of the king. Jamie would be forced to stand stock-still for several hours on guard, and his brother-in-law doubted that he had the stamina.

The distant, almost pathetic figure in front of the grandstand decked with Stewart tartan made Invernevis think of Mary Rose. He wondered if she was still in bed brooding about the blind bend, or bent over her embroidery in the big, lonely drawing-room. No, if Jamie was drinking, he couldn't be invited back to Invernevis, because that would only upset his sister.

At twelve minutes to eleven a gun informed the massed thousands that the king had left Holyrood Palace on horseback. Anxious eyes upturned were rewarded with a miracle as the royal salute sounded. For the first time that morning, the grey clouds rolled away, the sun thrusting through, gleaming like the burnished barrel of a cannon. It would stay like that for the Review.

Maggie and Mrs Chisholm heard the gun as they struggled among the crowds still trying to get into Queen's Park. The stout cook in the shapeless coat and battered hat, grey hair wisping, was panting from the climb from the New Town but determined to get a sight of the king, using her big body to push her way through the crowds, dragging Maggie after her by the wrist. The girl was confused and exhausted. Her boots seemed to be filled with fire, and elbows knocked the breath from her body. It had taken them over an hour to get from the New Town, and there had been no time or opportunity to stop and admire the sights of Edinburgh.

But Mrs Chisholm was making progress, and they were inside the park, struggling towards a slope, because, as the red-faced cook, chest heaving, shouted over her shoulder to her captive: 'There's no use in coming all this way just to look at the backs of people's necks!'

People glared, and some made threatening gestures, but Mrs Chisholm pushed upwards regardless, her stout shoes sliding, heavy body steadying.

'This will do,' she announced.

As Maggie reached her side, the bearded king, plumed and in Field-Marshal's uniform, and wearing the jewel and ribbon of the Order of the Thistle, rode into the Park, surrounded by a scarlet entourage. He was too far away from Maggie for his features to be visible, and a head in front kept bobbing, blotting out her view, though she was standing on tiptoe, but she saw sufficient to commit that minute forever to precious memory as the king swung in the shaft of sunlight towards the grandstand. All around her, below and above, the multitude was erupting, thousands swaying on sloping turf, those perched on the precarious rocks of Arthur's Seat waving small flags and surrendering their Sunday hats to the bright sky as the national anthem was struck up, cheers punctured by the guns completing the royal salute. It was a sight Maggie would never be able to find words for even in Gaelic, never mind reconstructing it in awkward English for the old lady back home. Beside her stood Mrs Chisholm, her lower lip trembling before the tears came. Maggie was puzzled as to why she should be crying for the king, until she saw it was sheer adoration.

Below, in the ranks of the volunteers, the same sentiments were affecting Invernevis. He had known pomp and circumstance in that city before, when, as a serving soldier in Princess Louise's, he had formed part of the escort when Czar Nicholas and the Czarina landed at Leith in '96, *en route* for Balmoral and Victoria. This was different, more rapturous, because it was their own monarch whose short reign had already swept away the constricting conventions of his seemingly immortal widowed mother; conventions, down to the perpetual widow's weeds, that Invernevis's own mother had aped, with her sister Carlotta enforcing the high morality. It did not seem to matter that the name of the bearded figure waiting for 38000 men to march by, had been linked with married women and uproarious dinners in London. He recalled to Invernevis his own father. The new laird felt a growing understanding, if not sympathy, for the problems his father had faced at Invernevis, in particular in being in a minority with women.

There was a line of Indian Mutiny veterans, some with medals pinned to their long coats, others so weak that they had to remain seated in the presence of their monarch. It occurred to Invernevis that some of them might have served with his father. Then the Archers' Guard of Honour, with Jamie stiff, only hand grasping the long bow. It seemed to Invernevis that his brother-in-law was swaying, or was it an effect produced by the now bright sun on gun barrels?

The king was at the saluting base, ready to survey the march past, and the crowd hushed in expectation. But before the bands could strike up and boots stride, a black and white collie dog appeared, loping up and down in front of the grandstand. The king was laughing, the crowd whistling, but the bewildered dog kept running up and down until an Archer ran forward, stooping, prodding it out of the way with his long bow, which produced laughter. The collie slunk into the crowd, but its antics had upset an officer's horse, and as it reared, he lost his feathered bonnet, which a boy darted forward to restore. He reminded Maggie of her brother Hector, and she laughed with Mrs Chisholm.

'He should get knighted for that,' the cook said.

All was now ready for the ranks of volunteers to move forward. Invernevis was anxious about his men keeping in step, though he had used up most of the short period of their training drilling them in moving as a co-ordinated body. Anxiety became horror when he saw Jamie sway and pitch forward under the grandstand.

The king's head turned; the crowd was hushed after the spontaneous gasp. For a moment Invernevis had the impulse to go to his brother-in-law, but he was too far away, and besides, to break rank would be a serious breach of discipline, and would only confuse the men ready to march behind him. But help was already at hand, for two Archers had gone forward to carry him behind the grandstand, out of the sight of the king and the tramping feet of thousands of men.

At last they were ready. A signal was given, military bands struck up, and the volunteers began to move towards the saluting base, company by company, battalion after battalion, a disciplined mass of guns, troops and horses. There were even cycle companies wobbling past under the monarch's steady stare.

There were hitches, of course. Men losing the rhythm of the march had to run past the king to catch up with their comrades, and bagpipes went off tune. Rifles slipped and men stumbled, but it was an impressive display from part-time soldiers.

It was now the turn of the Invernevis company to move forward, and from her vantage point on the hillside Maggie identified the Master by his game leg. A lump came into her throat as she watched the villagers marching behind him, Frank the footman with his small moustache, Kilmarnock bonnet angled on his fair head. Though the pace set by their Major's game leg was an awkward one, their diced shins swung in co-ordination behind him, rifles sloped on their shoulders, hands going up simultaneously, saluting the king as they passed. Only then did Maggie let her breath go and begin to clap furiously, Mrs Chisholm cocking an eyebrow and saying with benign suspicion: 'Oh, so *your* young man must be in that lot that's just gone past.'

The Invernevis men were clear of the king's critical eye, but the Major was still worried. Archers had fainted before, and some had even died from standing too long in the sun, but it wasn't that hot, and Jamie was still a young man. If it was drink, the Captain-General would hold an enquiry and have his name removed for good from the Duty Roster. The disgrace would get north, to his mother. It would affect Mary Rose.

But as they were leaving the parade ground, Jamie was driven out of Invernevis's mind by the way the crowds were pressing round them in the euphoria of the music and the marching. They were cheering, boys bobbing up to snatch at Kilmarnock bonnets, to touch the barrels of guns, and bright-eyed women fondled kilts and doublets. There weren't enough policemen to keep control, and as their officer Invernevis could only order his men to break rank and get clear of the field as quickly as possible before there was a serious accident. His game leg was succumbing to the strain, and he was beginning to get angry with the yelling faces all around.

On the other side of the park Maggie was also in trouble, clutching Mrs Chisholm's arm as the crowd swayed and shouted above them, stones bouncing down, dislodged by the boots of men and boys who had scrambled up cliffs to get better views, and now wanted to come down to follow the soldiers from the parade ground. A jagged stone struck Maggie's ankle, puncturing the leather boot to bruise and draw. She cried out with the pain, but had to keep stumbling downhill, for to stop was to be trampled and suffocated. She was terrified at what the day of jubilation had turned into, a human accordion emitting groans and breaths fouled by drink and tobacco. It was what she imagined being dragged down into the black depths of *Casan Dubh* below Invernevis House would be like, with Mrs Chisholm's arm the stout branch saving her. In the crowd behind, a hand was where it should not have been, though she kept striking it away repeatedly, crying at the assault.

It took them an hour to get clear of the park, and another half hour in the nearby kitchen of one of Mrs Chisholm's friends to recover their strength and composure over a pot of tea and hot scones. Maggie removed her boot, and bathed her ankle in warm water, Mrs Chisholm insisting on a liberal application of iodine.

'You could spit peas through these boots,' the cook said contemptuously. 'I'll need to write to Mrs Livingstone and tell her to get you more money.'

It would have taken too long for Maggie to explain that sentiment and not poverty made her keep wearing the boots.

'Aye, maybe you should stay in Edinburgh and get more money,' Mrs Chisholm said, half jocularly, for she had taken a liking to her temporary charge. 'Being stuck in the wilds isn't good for a young girl, and Mrs Livingstone tells me you're coming on as a cook.'

But Maggie had had enough of the city, and when Mrs Chisholm insisted that they go up to the castle to see the view, she would rather have stayed in the chair by the fire till it was time for the train. They climbed cobbles between tall tenements which, the breathless cook in the wobbling shoes explained, formed the old part of Edinburgh, still the haunt of thieves and loose women. There had been murders in the past, with the bodies sold to hospitals for research, but Mrs Chisholm couldn't remember the names of the two villains involved.

'It's not an area we would take help for the house from,' she confided to Maggie.

The view from the battlements beside the big cannon was

frightening in extent, with water glinting beyond the radiating streets. But it was Princes Street that fascinated Maggie. Like a river being fed by tributaries, people were pouring down the streets of the West End, to jam the principal thoroughfare as they crowded the windows of the big shops. It was a seething mass of tartan, feather hats, and the black sheen of horses, and in the crowded gardens below, a military band was playing, instruments dazzling in the sun.

Her fingers were in her coat pocket, in search of the sovereign the Master had given her, but when they failed to meet metal, they went deeper. It wasn't there. Frantically she turned out the other pocket, her face registering her panic.

'How much?' Mrs Chisholm asked wearily, hand on the barrel of the cannon.

'A sovereign; I had a sovereign.' She had lifted the hem of her coat and was feeling the lining.

'Pickpockets,' the cook said. 'Aye, it might be a beautiful city, but it's full of criminals. Drunkards, loose women, thieves. They're at it all the time, down there on Princes Street, begging and soliciting, bumping against folks and slipping their hands into their pockets. Today was a godsend for them, especially with all that pushing to get out of the park. Is that all the money you've got with you?'

'No, no, my purse is here, in my dress. But that sovereign —' She was still searching, unable to believe that anyone could do such a thing. You never locked the door of the big house, even with the tinkers about.

'Whoever it was is probably pouring it down his throat at this very minute. Well I hope it chokes him,' Mrs Chisholm said emphatically.

But Maggie wasn't listening. She was going to have kept the coin as a souvenir of her visit, to wrap it in cotton wool and take it out from time to time to remind her of how kind the Master was. Oh yes, she had another sovereign, the one Mrs Livingstone had given her, but it wasn't the same. She wished it was time for the train.

Down on Princes Street Invernevis had disbanded his company till train time, with strict instructions to do nothing that would disgrace them; but after the euphoria of having paraded so well, they were bound to have a drink or two. He couldn't stand guard over them because he had to find Jamie, to discover the cause, as well as the effect, of his collapse in front of the king. He was probably up in Archers' Hall, but it was worth trying the club. On his way Invernevis hesitated at large windows, surveying the season's fashions, wondering if he should buy a dress for Mary Rose. It would be embarrassing as well as exhausting to shoulder his way among milling women. Besides, he didn't know her size, had never bought a dress before, not even for Laura, whom Carlotta had clothed in drab cotton. No, it would please Mary Rose better if he made sure that her brother was all right.

He was thankful to climb away from the crowded street, into the spacious peace of the club, where he found Jamie sitting in a leather arm-chair, drinking in a circle of Archers, still in ceremonial uniform. One was wearing the gold tabard of a herald, his baton of authority on the table among the brandy balloons.

'Now don't say anything,' Jamie cautioned, holding up his only hand. 'In front of - what? - a hundred thousand people, as well as the king. I'm never going to live this down. And it *wasn't* drink. Everything suddenly went blank; that was all.'

Invernevis was irritated by Jamie's flippant dismissal of the incident. He obviously wasn't going to move from the company to speak to his brother-in-law in private. That was worse than bad manners, and Invernevis could see the defiant hostility in his eyes. This wasn't the man who had clutched his hand, crossing the Modder. Was it because Invernevis had deprived him of his sister's company, leaving him at the mercy of his formidable mother?

'Have you seen a doctor?' Invernevis asked anxiously.

'*This* is my doctor,' Jamie announced, holding up his

balloon to the laughter of his friends and swirling the amber contents.

'Why don't you come back with me for a few days?' Invernevis was embarrassed at having to issue the invitation in public.

'I'd love to, but I've got things to attend to here. Got to see the lawyers, to make sure I'm not bankrupt.' He laughed wearily. 'Then it's home to mother.'

Invernevis saw that there was no point in pursuing the matter. In fact, he had the feeling that Jamie could turn nasty at any moment. He had done as much as he could.

'And don't worry about Mary Rose seeing my name in the paper,' he called after his brother-in-law. 'The Captain-General knows the editor, so they won't even say an Archer collapsed.'

At the door he looked back at his best friend since boyhood, like a malicious sprite in his dark green uniform holding court in the exclusive sect, the face so gaunt and pale. He raised his hand in a weak salute, and went down into sunlight to search for the Invernevis contingent, but they were scattered the length and breadth of Princes Street, giving silver to blind hawkers in exchange for matches, eating pies, eyeing the long-skirted women in wide feathered hats in the gardens where a military band played.

Frank the footman sat alone on a bench under the Scott monument, swigging a gill of whisky, watching hems trailing by and thinking bitterly of Maggie. He had seen the Major slipping her the gold coin at the station, and to the footman it was final confirmation that there was something physical between them. The gentry had it every way, he thought, kicking the empty bottle under the bench. They paid you in pennies and thought they owned you body and soul, and as soon as they snapped their fingers you were supposed to come running, day and night. Oh, if he stayed in Edinburgh he could easily get another job, with far better prospects, but they were always making a fool of him in the servants' hall at Invernevis, calling him a 'city gent'. If he deserted without leave that would give them victory, particularly Maggie's father, whose spite had almost come to physical violence. He would go back on the train and endure their sneers because he wanted Maggie, not as a wife – he wasn't the marrying type – but in the way he had wanted, and got, most of the other maids. They had been easy because they were silly frustrated girls working long hours in a big gloomy house and wanting some excitement, however brief, to justify their miserable lives. Maggie was different. She hadn't only rejected him, once with her boot on his shin; she had been openly hostile in front of Mrs Livingstone. Oh, *he* knew what was going on between the kitchen-maid and the Major, and so did the cook, but she thought the sun rose and set on him. No, he was damned sure he wasn't going to be beaten by a pompous fool with a game leg.

At five o'clock the Invernevis party began to congregate at the station. The train, which was due to leave at five thirty, was waiting at the platform, doors wide, and Invernevis was anxiously counting heads, sighing with relief when they came on to the platform, licking ices but with no drink in them apparently. Maggie arrived with a stout woman, and Invernevis nodded and smiled.

Only one to come, the footman, suspected of being the carrier of Mama's drink from the village, but though Invernevis had accused him, he had denied it. Better he stayed in Edinburgh, but he was in the uniform of Princess Louise's, and might disgrace it. Invernevis would get rid of him as soon as a suitable opportunity occurred.

Two minutes before the train was due to pull out, the footman came sauntering on to the platform, Kilmarnock bonnet tilted over his eyes. From his gait Invernevis could see that he was drunk. There was no time to do anything but push him towards the train because a railwayman was going down, slamming doors.

'Get in there,' Invernevis said angrily. 'I'll deal with you when we get home.'

The footman struck his arm away, slurring: 'I'm going in to sit with Maggie.'

'Nothing of the sort. You're under military discipline, and you'll get in with the other men.'

'Bugger off. I know what you're after.'

Their heads were crowded at the windows, and Invernevis didn't know what to do. If he started to struggle with the drunk footman, would his game leg hold?

But the blacksmith's son, veteran of Magersfontein, with a sergeant's stripes on his sleeve, was coming off the train.

'Take him aboard,' the Major ordered, and the Sergeant took him by collar and trouser seat, hoisting as if it was a rag doll.

'Now give my love to Mrs Livingstone, and come back again,' Mrs Chisholm was saying, helping Maggie aboard.

But she wasn't listening. She was watching the footman being put on the train, wondering what else he had said that made the Master look so angry.

CHAPTER 12

Next morning at eleven o'clock the footman was standing in front of the desk in the library of Invernevis House, his Master in the swivel chair opposite. The footman was back in livery, and there was an ugly bruise on his left cheekbone where the sergeant of the volunteers had had to strike him into submission on the train the previous night.

He was shaking but not through fear as he stood there, feet together, arms by his side, shutting his eyes against the strong light streaming in through the long window, making silver and crystal flare on the cluttered desk. He winced as the threadbare shaft of the swivel chair squeaked. God, but what wouldn't he give for a cup of tea or something stronger. He had been summoned straight from bed by the breathless butler, who warned that it was 'his books, this time. Bloody fool, why do you touch drink if you can't hold it?' The eyes flooded by a ruined liver had looked pathetically at him.

The Master seemed to be testing the breaking-strain of an ivory paperknife in his fists as he went to and fro in his chair, casting about for a suitable introduction. He hadn't dared sleep on the train in case there had been further trouble from the footman, and he hadn't had a chance to speak to Mary Rose, who must be awake by now. His dislike at having to take drastic action was modified by his lingering anger and shame. The crowd at the Edinburgh station - and there might easily have been newspapermen among them - had seen the fracas, a drunk and disorderly soldier and servant hauled kicking on to a train. No doubt that would get back to the club, to produce comments about the Major's ability to command. It would certainly be circulating in the village by now, reaching the ears of Father Macdonald for transmission to Carlotta as further proof that her nephew was weak, his servants drunkards and brawlers. It would be brought to the big house with the mail or the milk, and Mary Rose would think that they had *all* been drunk. That certainly didn't help him in what he had to report about Jamie.

But he had to say something to the footman, and he began, keeping his eyes on pliant ivory, his voice low but distinct.

'I needn't spell out why I sent for you. Your conduct, both as a volunteer and as one of my servants, was disgraceful. I gave strict orders about drinking yet you disobeyed me, and you disobeyed me further when I ordered you on to the train. You are a disgrace to the uniform you were wearing, a disgrace to the uniform you're now wearing, because I expect my servants to behave beyond Invernevis as they would here.

'I could, of course, have you court-martialled and dismissed from the volunteers, but what would that solve? No, I have to take more drastic action and dismiss you from my service. It's a great pity, because if you had continued to give the service you were giving when you first came here, you would have succeeded Symmers as butler when he retires, which can't be long now, I imagine. I cannot allow you to stay because I can no longer trust you. You will be given a month's wages to get you away from here and into another job, but I cannot help by giving you references. It would be very wrong of me to foist you on another house. I want you to get your things together and be on the evening train out of here. I'll give you the money due to you before you go, but you mustn't take that uniform with you. It will be needed, if I decide to get another footman.'

He was thankful that he had finished, and he looked down at the curving ivory, waiting for the footman to dismiss himself. He didn't even want an apology. But the footman had no intention of retreating. The expression on his face hadn't changed while his master was speaking, because he knew he was going to be dismissed, but for reasons other than were being given.

'I only drank a gill, sir,' he began. 'It was the excitement that went for me. I don't like crowds.' Then, seeing that there was no response: 'It's not because I got drunk that you're sacking me. It's because of Maggie.'

Invernevis ignored the heat of the words, and the absence of sir.

'There's also that too,' he admitted, in a reasonable voice. 'It seemed to me that you were trying to molest her. Don't think I didn't know it was you getting out of the train at Callander on the way down. I understand that you've been pestering Maggie for quite a while, and I also understand that she doesn't want to have anything to do with you.'

'Is that what her father said?' the footman asked angrily.

'I've got eyes and ears,' Invernevis said, becoming irritated by his insolence. 'It's my duty to protect my servants, especially young women.'

The footman stepped forward, planted his palms on stained leather and leaned over.

'Protect?' he sneered. 'Oh yes, we know how you protect Maggie. That's why you're getting me out of the road, isn't it, so that you can have her all to yourself?'

Invernevis was rising, speechless.

'I've got eyes too, you know,' the footman said, staying where he was. 'I saw you slipping the coin to her when we arrived in Edinburgh. Now don't try and tell me it was back wages.'

'This is outrageous —' But he was sinking towards the swivel chair again, memory robbing him of explanation. It was repeating itself. At that very desk. Carlotta instead of the footman, his portrait instead of a sovereign, and Maggie the main character on both occasions. He hadn't been able to convince his aunt that the silver-framed portrait was a harmless present, in place of the one she had failed through spite to give to the servant girl. Why had he to justify himself to a footman? But the situation was too dangerous to leave to outraged silence. Think what damage would be done to an already difficult relationship if the footman's accusation was to reach Mary Rose's ears, not to mention Maggie's father. It wouldn't take long to get to the village, to Father Macdonald, to be transmitted to Carlotta as final proof of the immorality of Invernevis, man and mansion. What made it worse was that he could see that his spontaneous generosity had been dangerous for a man in his position, though it had only been a little extra for the girl for having been so patient with Mama.

Now that he was in the swivel chair again, he felt more confident, though the footman's puffed face was still hovering, smug because he thought that he had had the last word.

'Though it's none of your business, I did give the girl a coin,' Invernevis said harshly. 'It was some spending money, because she doesn't get much wages.' That sounded ambiguous, so he added: 'It was her first time away from home, after all. Now go and get out of that uniform. I want you out of this house by late afternoon – or else.'

'Oh no,' the footman said emphatically. 'I'm not so easy to get rid of. Just like that, a month's wages after six, seven years' services in this godforsaken place. First of all your poxed father, then your mother on the bottle, wanting trays carried up to that stinking room, and your twisted bitch of an aunt who was after young girls. Now you with Maggie. Oh you're a noble family, all right, and your brother putting a farmer's daughter in the family way and fighting with the Irishmen up in the Arms. What a story it would make for a newspaper! I'm sure I could sell it for a hundred quid. You don't think I've got the brain to put it down on paper because servants are supposed to be illiterate. If they start to read and write, they get above themselves and want better conditions. You're damned right I do. No, I don't want to stay in this hell-hole. I wouldn't be your butler if you offered me five hundred a year because I'm as good as you, any day. At least I don't have to *pay* for my women. But I'm not leaving here empty-handed, after all these years. I want a hundred pounds in cash, and first class references for a butler's post, otherwise I go straight up the stairs and tell your fancy lady all about you and Maggie. You gave me until this afternoon to get out of this house: I'm giving you five minutes to make up your mind, and I'll wait right here.'

As he finished speaking he went to the arm-chair by the fire, stooped, struck a match on iron, and settled back, smoking.

Invernevis's hands were trembling on the blotter. It was even worse than the incident over his photograph, for then it had been one of his own family threatening him. But a footman! He knew what his father would have done; taken the man up to the stables and put him against a wall. But violence wasn't the answer in this case. There had been enough of that in the station in Edinburgh. The footman was no fool. He was after money, and he wouldn't go till he got some. But giving in to him would be a weakness, the kind of weakness Carlotta had deplored. Besides, what was to stop him coming back again and again for more money?

'This is blackmail, you know,' Invernevis said to the man at his back. 'You can go to prison for blackmail.'

'I couldn't, because first of all you would have to tell the police about what I was blackmailing you over, and you couldn't bring yourself to do that because you know they would find it suspicious, you giving a kitchen-maid money. No, you won't go to the police because you're too worried about your social position. That's the price you have to pay for being a laird, because if it got to the village about Maggie —'

Invernevis had no answer because he knew the footman was right. His status as laird had taken enough knocks from his mother's and Alexander's behaviour. But he couldn't give the footman a hundred pounds, and not only because he didn't have that kind of money; to give it would be an admission of guilt. What was to be done? Have the footman taken to the station, and forced on the train? No, because he would just come back with a bigger demand. Persuade him to take his job back, promise him the butler's post as soon as Symmers retired or, more likely, dropped dead from drink? No, because that would be giving him the upper hand, to use in the future.

'Your time's almost up,' the footman announced harshly.
'Well, which?'

What happened next almost made Invernevis change his mind about supernatural forces operating in that house. Preceded by a cursory knock, Mrs Livingstone made a dramatic entrance, her apron bunched in her fist. Giving the footman a grim look, she went to the desk, and shed her cargo. The silver trinkets – coronation chairs and footstools – from Mama's dressing-table tinkled and were still on stained leather, in front of Invernevis, half out of his swivel chair in astonishment.

'Found in *his* bedroom,' the cook said triumphantly. And, glaring at him: 'To think that the poor jackdaws got the blame over the years.' Knowing that her duty was done, she went out, shaking her head at the deceit of some servants.

'So you're a thief as well,' Invernevis said, not bothering to conceal his delight at having trapped the footman. 'Well, this could be a matter for the constable.'

'Oh no you don't. You're not getting out of it that way,' the footman warned him. 'I didn't steal that stuff. I was given it for fetching drink from the village for your mother.'

'So we were right, you *were* the one,' Invernevis nodded. There was a double bonus in Mrs Livingstone's detection: Mama's source shut off, and the insolent footman dismissed. 'Anyway, as far as I'm concerned, you weren't given them; you stole them.' He picked up a miniature footstool, balanced it on his palm.

'It's a bloody lie.'

'One bloody lie for another,' Invernevis said blandly. 'It's a fair enough bargain. So I send for the constable to say that silver's been going missing, and though we've got the man, we've only recovered *some*. The constable will have heard by now how drunk and disorderly you were in Edinburgh, letting the village down, so he'll not feel too well disposed towards you. You'll be charged with theft, and if you say anything about Maggie and money, we can easily add another charge: defamation of character. You might get three years. Now what do you say to that?' He leaned back, handling ivory again, but this time letting it keep its shape.

'I'll tell the constable that I got that stuff for getting drink for your mother. He'll believe me. Everyone in the district knows she's a drunkard.'

Though the slight rankled, Invernevis kept calm. 'No, he won't believe you. He has too much respect for the big house, too much respect for my mother. He knows that she's a lady. No, he'll see you as a common thief, something that's very rare in these parts. Before your kind arrived here, we used to be able to leave our doors unlocked. Yes, even with the tinkers coming. So you'll be charged.'

The footman's fist was clenched, his face contorted.

'You bastard. Why do your class always think they should have the last word?'

'Because that's the way it is, until a better system is found. No, I wouldn't advise you to add assault to the list of charges. I'll tell you what, seeing I'm a generous man. Rather than turn you over to the law, I'm going to give you your train fare out of this place you hate so much.' He felt in his waistcoat, produced a sovereign and laid it on the desk. 'Before you take it, there's one last thing. You walk out of here, you go up to your room and pack without saying one word to anyone. Then you come down the front stairs.' He unthreaded the gold hunter from his waistcoat, laid it on the blotter beside the sovereign. 'You only gave me five minutes, but I'm going to be more generous. I'm going to give you ten. So off you go now. I'll be counting the seconds.'

The footman hesitated, then barged out, slamming the door, Invernevis following, swinging round in his chair.

'Thank God,' he said, his hand shaking towards the cigarette box. He leaned back, exhaling, smiling. My God, Mrs Livingstone wasn't slow. He felt elated. The bit about more silver being missing had been a lie, but one lie cancelled out another, so there was no sin. The footman would go, and he wouldn't hear from him again. The lie about Maggie and the money wouldn't reach Mary Rose. But he was going to have to tell her the truth about Jamie, and how he had offered to help.

Within ten minutes the footman was down. He was wearing the pearl-grey suit he had worn on the night Laura had danced her life away at the tenants' dance, but now it was loose and shabby.

'Did anyone see you?' Invernevis asked.

'No one saw me.' He held out his hand. 'Now give me the money. I wouldn't take it, only you're due it to me in back wages, and I want to get as far away as possible from this bloody place.'

Invernevis dropped the gold coin into his palm with the injunction: 'Now don't go into the pub and start shooting your mouth off before you get on the train.' He wagged a finger. 'Remember: my threat about the constable holds till your train is clear of Invernevis. And I don't want to see you back in these parts again.'

The footman's fingers closed round the sovereign. 'Don't worry, I don't want to see this bloody place again.' He paused at the door, his pronounced Adam's apple moving above the soiled white collar transfixed by a pin. 'You think you're so clever, the way you've got rid of me. Well I hope your family cause you plenty of trouble. You can take that as a curse if you like.'

And he was gone, picking up his strapped suitcase in the hall, crunching away over gravel. Invernevis sat on, wondering. The curse didn't bother him; his ancestors had endured plenty of curses, but there was more trouble upstairs, with Mary Rose. He would have to go and see her, tell her about Jamie. Perhaps that would snap her out of her lethargy. He was quite willing that Jamie should be invited to Invernevis, to straighten himself out, though he doubted if he would come, even at the summons of his sister.

He found his wife standing in the bay window of her sitting-room, sipping coffee as she stared down to the river, the morning mail on the silver tray, envelopes slit by ivory. He kissed her forehead, but her eyes stayed in the distance.

'Have you been feeling better?' he asked tenderly, his brief absence heightening her beauty. How perfect her profile was in the mellow morning, with the sky not yet dulled by autumn. The silk encasing her shoulders reflected the light.

'A little, thank you,' she said formally. Then: 'I saw the footman coming out with a suitcase and going towards the avenue. Where was he going? Somebody sick?'

'No, I dismissed him.' He had to tell her.

'But why?' she asked, wheeling round, astonished.

He didn't want to tell her about the incident at the station because it didn't make telling her about Jamie any easier. But he saw that she was determined to have a reply.

'He got drunk and disorderly after I'd warned him several times. I couldn't trust him here, any more.'

'I see,' she said, nodding, her silence implying that there was more to it.

'Anyway, we'll manage without him,' he said, and immediately saw that it was a dangerous remark, which he tried to correct by adding: 'I now know he was the one who was fetching drink for Mama.' He sat down opposite her. 'I saw Jamie in Edinburgh. He was in the Archers' bodyguard.'

'Don't tell me; he's disgraced himself.'

'But how do you know?' he asked in astonishment. 'It only happened yesterday, and it's not to be in the papers.'

'Oh, I can read your face. And this.' She picked up a letter from the salver. 'From Mother. Complaining about how heavily he's been drinking. She tried to stop him going to Edinburgh.'

But he didn't want to read the letter, and she dropped it.

'I'm afraid it was in front of the king,' he said gently.

'Don't tell me the sordid details. I can imagine.'

'I tried to bring him back here, but he wouldn't come.'

'I'm not surprised,' she said bitterly. 'He's sick to death of his own family.'

He knew what she meant, and he was hurt.

'Perhaps if *you* wrote to him —'

'I won't write. It's not like the old days.' She sighed, her eyes swivelling to the river again. 'We were so close, like one person, really.'

'Then maybe you want to go north for a spell? The child will be all right here.'

But she shook her head. 'No, it's almost all over now. There's only one thing that will stop Jamie.'

Her factual tone made him shiver, bringing back her reaction on the blind bend. He was getting so tired of gloom, had had it since childhood, with Carlotta.

'Why don't we go abroad this winter?' he asked suddenly, clasping her hand, remembering the bliss of the honeymoon. They could ride up the avenue a second time to a new beginning.

'We don't have the money,' she said coldly. 'Have you forgotten that we couldn't complete the repairs to this house?'

'I can raise the money,' he said, to save his pride.

'How? By borrowing? That will only put us deeper into debt, and there'll be nothing for the children.'

'Is it money that's making you so unhappy?' he asked in desperation.

She shook her head slowly, her eyes on the distance. 'What I want cannot be bought.'

'What is it that you want?' he pleaded.

But she put her hand to her forehead to show the headache, and he went, wishing that he had never raised the problem of Jamie. Damn Jamie! No doubt she was wishing that she was still single in Sutherland, so that she could save him. There was something unhealthy in their relationship, more so since women didn't attract Jamie.

In the kitchen Maggie was trundling the rolling pin while Mrs Livingstone was upstairs, doing something. Maggie had patiently answered all the questions about Mrs Chisholm, how she was looking, the kind of house she worked in.

'I hope you spent the sovereign I gave you.'

Maggie had nodded, the rumble of the rolling pin saving her from speech. She hadn't been able to bring herself to tell Mrs Livingstone that there had been another sovereign, from the Master, but that it had been stolen. Oh, it had been such a horrible trip, she was almost in tears. She would never leave Invernevis again, no matter what happened.

Her brother Hector was happy enough, sitting in the servants' hall playing with the lead soldiers she had managed to buy him in Princes Street, and for her father, a briar pipe with a metal cap because he liked smoking while fishing.

Then Mrs Livingstone had reappeared, red in the face, smoothing down her apron, to slump down at the end of the table, knocking wood with her knuckles as she said enigmatically, her eyes on her assistant: 'Well, that's the end of him. Thank God I had a look in his room while he was away. Aye, the poor old soul may have got back her stuff, but she can't get back her insides. Just a rag, as your father said, though I only wanted to keep the peace. Now girl, pour two cups and sit down and tell me what happened in Edinburgh with *him*.' And, as Maggie turned, startled, she waved a dismissive hand: 'No, girl, there's no use pretending; I've been too long on the go not to know when there's something wrong, and I knew the minute you came into the kitchen this morning. Don't try and hide these things from me, because I don't hide anything from you. Remember there's more than cooking to working together in a kitchen. Your mother knew that. Now sit down and tell me what happened.'

Leaving her tea to grow cold, Maggie told of how the footman had come on to the platform drunk, had been abusive to the Master, and had been lifted on to the train by the blacksmith's son. She didn't say anything about him shouting that he wanted to go in beside Maggie.

'Does that mean he's been sacked?' Maggie cried in alarm.

Mrs Livingstone watched her assistant for a long time before replying.

'There's many, men as well as women, been sent down that avenue since I first came here, and most of them went because they had something to hide. He wouldn't have been any good for you, lassie. Just you be thankful that he hasn't left you with anything, or that you're not going down the avenue with a big belly.'

Later that morning Invernevis came through when Mrs Livingstone was alone.

'I'm deeply grateful to you for what you did about my mother's silver.'

'It was nothing, Sir,' the cook said, keeping her back to him, but not through bad manners. 'I knew there was something wrong.'

'But how could you possibly know?' he asked astonished.

'He was a clever one, but brains aren't everything, Sir. Just you ask the tinkers, Sir. I had one here last night, when you were in Edinburgh.'

But though he pressed her to elaborate, she would say no more.

CHAPTER 13

Lugging his bulging suitcase, the footman went down the avenue, pointed toe stubbing stone. The beauty of the landscape was outside his consciousness because he was still smarting over the speed and method of his send-off. What a dirty bloody trick, the cook turning him in. Of course he should have gone straight up to the young Mistress's room, but what was the point in making her even more unhappy, married to that swine? And it would only have dragged in Maggie, though the little bitch deserved it, taking money from such a man. No, he was far better out of that house, though he hadn't got much in his pocket, a sovereign after all these years of fetching and carrying for them, covering up for the drunken butler, enduring the ignorant gossip of the servants' hall. Even if he had come away with good references, he wouldn't go into service again, not even to a butler's post in London. He would get another job, where you didn't have to serve such people, and then, when he had made money, he would come back to Invernevis and expose that swine for what he was. And they were the ones who thought they had breeding. The old lady wetted the mattress and expected you to dry it out, and all you got in exchange were a few pieces of silver.

No, he wouldn't be writing to Maggie; there were plenty of other women who didn't give themselves to their masters for a sovereign. She would come to a sticky end, that one, though she thought she was so damned cunning, putting on the innocent act. Of course that bitch of a cook encouraged her.

He crossed Wade's Bridge and took the road above the river, stopping to rest his case on the compacted dust, glancing at the mansion under the mountain and spitting. It wasn't the dead you had to be wary of in that eerie place. They appeared at your back like ghosts, always watching you, as if they weren't getting their money's worth, making sure you always had something to do while they lounged about the drawing-room and library, waiting at the big mahogany table for you to serve them, as if it was an honour, and if you used the wrong serving spoons they frowned, as if you weren't worth wasting words on, but frowning to let you know that they were watching, watching. What privacy did you have? That bitch Carlotta used to raid your room, turning back the mattress, looking for God knows what.

He was hurrying now, anxious in his anger to put as much distance between himself and the big house across the river as possible. The suitcase bumped against his leg as he passed the track forking down to the burial chapel and the shore of the loch, the calm broken by the oars of a dinghy trawling for mackerel. Across at the quarry metal was snarling through stone, dust drifting, but he didn't pause to watch. All his energies were concentrated on getting up into the village.

He was running above the disused iron furnace, the stitch in his side slowing him, but gritting his teeth, determined to keep going. Suddenly the absurdity of it made him fall towards the wayside grass, to stretch, panting. If they saw him running, they would think that he had been driven from the big house for a crime that would be assault at least by nightfall. Besides, there wasn't a train till the early evening, and the daily coach south had been withdrawn because it couldn't compete with clanking iron.

He lay there, recovering his breath, looking up at the sky, with its fluffy clouds. It was so peaceful, to be out of service and free, to have possibilities to look forward to. It didn't matter what he did, so long as he wasn't inside, in a servile capacity. He would rather work out of doors, with his hands, however dirty the work. The idea appealed more and more. No uniform to keep clean and pressed, and when the day's labour was done a good drink without fear of censure. He would have time which he could call his own, and as he approached thirty he was beginning to realise how precious time was. You needed to get a woman before your hair began to thin; a woman you could depend on, who would keep the house and have your children. He was tired of flirting. He wanted something stable, serious. The big house maids were only sport. They weren't the type he wanted to settle down with. He would find a dependable woman in the south because he didn't like the Invernevis women. Too queer, with their Gaelic and the little Celtic silverwork crosses between their breasts, but when you came up behind them and raised your hands, they offered no resistance, leaning back against you, breathing heavily. Some of them you had had to have on the landing because they were sharing rooms. Like animals they were, biting and clawing, but not in defence. And when you were exhausted they were still waiting, like bottomless pails. That kind of lust was almost obscene, because if a man's pleasure was finite, a woman's should also be. They reduced you to sagging nothingness, the bitches, lying on the landing with white aprons hoisted, the coarse blackness on white under the skylight. That was why the old laird had died blind, broken. He could tame his dogs but not his maids, and the frightening thing was, to look at them you would think butter wouldn't melt in their mouths, big dark innocent eyes for the world.

He found himself laughing at the sky at the thought of the splayed knees in prayer on the flagstones in the servants' hall in Miss Carlotta's time, knees he had been between the previous night, but the white faces were lowered so peacefully to the touching fingertips. My God, that was women all over. He laughed and laughed. And to think that Maggie, the best looking one, had got away.

The gig braked beside him and MacPherson from the Home Farm was looking down on him, bowler pushed back, bushy eyebrows raised quizzically in the red, ill-natured face.

'Are you drunk?'

The footman scrambled to his feet and retrieved his case from the long grass.

'No, just resting.'

'Did you miss the train back from Edinburgh?'

The footman was momentarily confused. 'No, I'm going the other way, back down south.'

'Got your books, eh?'

'No, I walked out,' he stammered, going red.

MacPherson wagged the whip. 'Look, son, you can fool most of the people round here, but not me. I heard all about what happened in Edinburgh. Anyway, throw your case on the back and climb up here beside me so that I can hear *your* version of the story. As I heard it this morning, you hit the laird.'

'A damned lie!' He slid the case on.

'A pity,' MacPherson said, eyes gleaming maliciously. When the footman was aboard he flicked the whip over the long black backs, made the two horses turn again towards the village.

'I had a drink in me,' the footman admitted, watching his driver's face uneasily.

'It's no crime, not something you would send a man away for. There's plenty of drink been taken at the big house, and plenty of trouble with it.'

The footman could see that he was expected to fill the silence as the gig lurched along, briars sounding against the big wheels.

'He took a spite to me.'

'Well you're not the first and you won't be the last,' the grim profile replied. 'He did the same to his own brother. Ach, I've no time for that man.' He spat back over the big wheel. 'But why should he take a spite to you?' he asked, mock anxiety in his tone.

Because he felt he had found a sympathetic ear, the footman blurted out the story of Maggie and the sovereign in the

Edinburgh station. Immediately he said it, he felt frightened, though he would soon be away from Invernevis. He added hastily: 'Of course, there might have been nothing to it —'

A hand was clapped on his knee. 'Listen, son, you needn't be frightened that I'll go talking, giving the girl a red face in the village. Her father's a decent sort, and so was the mother. No, it's that bugger who's to blame. He's got to do it that sneaky way, away from home, because he hasn't got it in him. That's why his wife's nearly off her head. Oh, I've seen it in cows, when the bull's been kept away a long time. It's only nature. Well, his brother Sandy's different. He might have put my girl in the family way, but at least he was a man and owned up to his responsibilities. With the other one, it's all groping because he can't do it. A minnow's got more jump in it.'

They were going up the long steep brae into the village, the wheels quieter, MacPherson's voice more savage as he bunched the reins in his mottled fist.

'Aye, he thinks he can treat people like dirt, but he forgets that it's us who keep him in his place. Not much longer, though. They'll pass new laws to give us protection from the likes of him and his damned trustees. They'll not even pay for the mending of a gate. And here you are, thrown out, with not a penny, no doubt, and no references. Well, they say MacPherson is this and that. I'm not a fool, and I've got ears. I don't give a tinker's curse what they say. They'll whip off their caps and bow their heads to their boots while *he's* passing, but as soon as his back's gone by, they start tearing him to pieces. I'm not like that. I keep clear of the people in the village and I speak my mind to a person's face. I told him the night of the big heather fire to close down the quarry before murder was done, but nobody backed me. Now the bloody Irishmen are like rats, overrunning the village at the weekend, desperate for a woman and not caring how they go about getting one. I'm not going to stand aside and see a decent man trampled by the likes of him.' He reined the horses abruptly on the crest of the hill, the railway bridge, and pointed along the rails south with his whip.

'You take the train out this evening and he's got the better of you, and when you've gone they'll be saying all sorts of things about you, how you tried to rape the laird's wife, but he let you go out of the goodness of his heart rather than sending for the constable. Or you can stay and defend your good name. You might only be a footman, but your name's better than his, any day, and his father would never turn a man out. If you want to stay I'll give you a job up at the farm. It won't be waiting on tables; it'll be working outside in the fields, as long as there's light, in all weathers. The wage won't be big, but you'll have a room and good food. And you'll have self-respect, which he in his fancy big house across the river never had. I took his brother in when he was hounded out of his own home by his bitch of an aunt, and I'll do the same for any man. The choice is yours. Refuse it and I won't be offended.'

The gig sat on the bridge while the footman considered over a cigarette, staring down the shining rails. They led south, to freedom, to a trustworthy wife, bright lights and no grating Gaelic. He would get all these things if he went, but as MacPherson warned, he would leave behind a grotesquely distorted character. On the other hand it would be hard work at the Home Farm, heavy outside work he wasn't used to, in old clothes, getting soaked and no perks. But at least he would have his self-respect, the comforting knowledge that he was staying to defend his character. With MacPherson to back him, the brute across the river wouldn't dare make anything of the silver trinkets. And maybe something would come of it with Maggie, since he would no longer be working beside her.

'I'll take it.'

'Good man. I knew you had it in you.'

They shook hands on the railway bridge before MacPherson flicked the reins.

'We'll go to the Arms for a dram,' he announced, eyes gleaming with intrigue. 'We'll show them he doesn't have the power he thinks he has.'

CHAPTER 14

After her second horrifying experience on the blind bend Mary Rose would not venture outside, far less down the avenue. She lay late in the big canopied bed, the connecting door with her husband's bedroom locked from her side. When she eventually descended to the drawing-room it was to ask for a fire in summer. After the sticks had caught the house-maid withdrew, leaving Mary Rose in a big shapeless arm-chair.

She didn't play the organ, though more music had arrived. The needle between her weak fingers only picked at the sampler, making silly mistakes, slipping to draw blood. Sobbing, she sucked her finger. How she hated Invernevis, as if the malicious spirits of the past were conspiring to drive her out.

She was beginning to wonder if her husband's dead sister hadn't something to do with the manifestation at the blind bend. The girl seemed to have exercised a profound influence over all at Invernevis and was now working from the other side, to drive out the usurper. Or was it some power for evil left behind by the perverted aunt? Whoever was manipulating the black substance at the bend intended her harm. Her nerves were in shreds, and she could not close her eyes without being reassured that there was enough oil in the lamp till morning.

Even the drawing-room was eerie in the sunlight, with the shadow of the organ pipes a giant hand on the scuffed floral linen of the sofa. She shifted seats, but the thought of the hand behind her made her move again.

The needle pricked, leaving its silver wake in linen, but the design was still shapeless. Below the doleful movement of the

French clock, fire shifted fitfully. She couldn't stand it any longer and threw down the taut drum of the sampler to go and stand in the bay window, shielding her eyes from the sky as she stared down at Alexander's house. If only she'd married a man like that, without pretensions, not tied to tradition and unmanageable mortar. God knows how it would have ended if he hadn't been at the blind bend that day of the christening, to catch her in his strong arms.

Not seeing the young Mistress in the drawing-room, Maggie had crept in and was going through the pile of magazines on the sofa table when Mary Rose turned in the bay window.

'What are you doing, girl?'

Maggie was so startled she dropped the magazine. Mary Rose came forward and picked it up.

'The *Scottish Field*,' she read. 'What are you wanting with this?'

The kitchen-maid's face was crimson, and she had difficulty finding words. 'It's the one for July, Ma'm,' she stammered. 'We're allowed to take the old magazines away. The Master said so after Miss Carlotta left.'

'But what do *you* want it for?' Mary Rose asked impatiently. The way the girl was standing, with that innocent look irritated her. She hadn't forgotten the stuck-together photograph of her husband she had seen in the girl's bedroom, the first secret of that house which she had encountered on her return from honeymoon. A great deal had happened since then, for which she had received no satisfactory explanation. It was time to get some answers, and this girl looked as if she would have them.

'Why do you want this magazine?' Mary Rose repeated.

'I like to look at the pictures, and there's good reading in it,' Maggie answered, seeing there was no escape. 'You learn things.'

'But what kind of things?' Mary Rose persisted. She opened and read. '"A High-Class Journal devoted to Manly Sport and Out-Door Life". Now how can that possibly interest you?

The Master gets this magazine because there's so much sport in it.'

'It's not all sports, Ma'm,' Maggie said quietly. 'There's a bit about ladies' fashions.'

Mary Rose, who had not looked at the magazine before, fanned through until she came to a sketch of a woman standing by a river in a big hat and white cloth frock with draped bodice. 'By Mr Ernest', the caption said.

Maggie tried to correct the impression that she was only interested in clothes. Not that she had the money or opportunity at Invernevis.

'There's good reading, Ma'm,' she said earnestly. 'Articles on history, about the famous families and big houses of Scotland.' She got more intense. 'The magazine only started coming out a couple of years ago, but I've got all the old ones in my room.'

Mary Rose was sceptical. She thoroughly approved of servants, females especially, improving themselves; but with society magazines? What good would articles about big houses do the girl? There must be more to it than that. There wasn't a photograph of her husband in the magazine? But that was impossible.

She was in danger of making a fool of herself.

'Take the magazine for your collection,' she said abruptly, thrusting it at Maggie. Then, as casually as she could: 'How long have you been working here?'

Maggie had to calculate. 'About six years, Ma'm.'

'Around about the time the Master went off to the South African war?'

Maggie nodded, trying to work out what was coming next. She was beginning to fear that the footman had been saying things because he'd been sacked.

'And are you happy here?'

'Yes, *very*.'

The emphasis the girl put on the word made Mary Rose even more suspicious, but she knew that she had to proceed with the greatest care. It would be disloyal to her husband if it transpired that there had been nothing between himself and the maid. A cautious gentle approach was best, but she wasn't any good at that kind of game; witness the mess she had made of being an intermediary between Jamie and her mother.

'Do you have a young man?'

Maggie coloured and shook her head. She was convinced now that the interrogation had something to do with the footman. Perhaps someone had seen her with him at the chapel on that Sunday when the old Mistress had sent her with the flowers.

'No young man?' Mary Rose's tone registered her disappointment, but not for the girl's sake. It suggested that there was sufficient to interest her at the big house.

'Wouldn't you like to be walking out with somebody?'

Maggie bit her lip and nodded. The tears she was desperately trying to hold back weren't only caused by the pointed questions, but also because her father claimed the right to regulate her social life, as in the case of the footman.

'All right, go back to your work,' Mary Rose said abruptly, tired of the cross-examination.

The magazine which had started it all lay on the sofa. Mary Rose hurled it across the room, in the direction of the glass cases housing the heirlooms. She put her face into her hands and let her pent-up emotions go. God, she was sick of Invernevis, house and husband, because she was surrounded by secrecy and duplicity. The girl wasn't as innocent as she wanted to appear. It was like the blind bend; she would never get the true story, not even from her own husband. She had tried to make a success of her marriage; it wasn't her fault that she had failed. She would go home to Sutherland the next morning, taking the child with her. At least she knew all the ghastly secrets of her family, and could try to save Jamie from destroying himself.

'What on earth's the matter, Miss Mary?' Nanny Gunn asked, making one of her rare appearances downstairs. 'Who's been upsetting you?' She hurried to the sofa to sit down and put a consoling arm round the woman she had practically reared. But she only succeeded in making Mary Rose's anguish worse.

Invernevis heard the wailing from the library and hurried through to investigate. When he saw Nanny Gunn beside his distraught wife he stopped in the doorway. That bitch had obviously upset her. Right: this was the chance he had been waiting for. As a military man he believed that attack was better than defence, and as the thick lenses swung towards him he was ready.

'What have you been saying to upset her?' Nanny Gunn asked sharply.

'How dare you speak to me like that.' He gave his words force without having to shout. 'I was about to ask you the same question, but I'm not going to discuss my wife with the likes of you.' He stood aside and pointed. 'Now get upstairs immediately.'

She hesitated, looking to Mary Rose for support, but her mistress was too distraught to hear what was being said. Then she swept past Invernevis, warning: 'You'll regret this.'

He stood watching to make sure that she went upstairs before he pushed through to the kitchen, his plan already formulated. Mrs Livingstone was at the table with Maggie, instructing her assistant on the finer points of keeping salmon mousse light.

'A word with you,' he said to the cook. Maggie heard the signal in his tone and went through to the scullery, closing the door behind her.

'That Gunn woman's gone too far this time,' Invernevis began. 'She's upset my wife terribly. I want her away from here on tonight's train. You were a great help to me in getting rid of the footman, and I'm going to ask for your help again. I don't want her going back down to my wife, looking for support, because she'll never go. You go up and make sure she packs, then stay outside her door to make sure she doesn't come down again till I get the gig arranged. Will you do that for me?'

'Of course, Sir,' Mrs Livingstone said, the light of satisfaction in her eye at the thought of being asked to help to drive out the biggest bitch she had ever come across. 'I'll go up this minute. But what about the poor Mistress?'

'I'm going to send for Doctor MacNiven to give her something to calm her. Duncan can take a horse; it's quicker than the gig.'

Mrs Livingstone's face clouded. 'I'm afraid he's down at the river, Sir. I don't know which pool. And Roddy's got the gig up at the blacksmith's.'

'Then who else can go?' He had to get back through to his wife.

Mrs Livingstone thought for several seconds. 'Maggie's quick on her feet.'

'All right; send her,' he said, turning to go back through.

Maggie ran as fast as the button boots inherited from Miss Laura would allow, but the avenue was treacherous with ruts, and several times she almost went over an ankle, rhododendron branches cruel little whips. She was sure that she was being blamed for upsetting the young Mistress, and was being sent for the doctor as a form of punishment. But it wasn't her fault. All she had wanted was the magazine. It was the young Mistress who had done all the talking, with a queer look on her face, neither a smile nor a frown. The maids had said in the servants' hall that the business of the blind bend was all in her mind, and they giggled until Mrs Livingstone told them to stop. Maggie wasn't so sure now that they weren't right.

Her thought processes became distorted by the stitch in her side as she clattered over Wade's Bridge, taking the road above the river. Her boots ploughed the dust as they began to drag. Gasping, she leaned against the dry stone dyke, feeling the contents of her stomach coming up. It was no use; she couldn't go any further. The Master would be furious, after his kindness to her, but she couldn't help it; there was no more breath left in her body.

Then the shadow of a gig's spokes stopped on the dust behind her, and Master Alexander jumped down, asking what the trouble was. She managed to blurt out about the young Mistress being taken poorly, and how she was on her way for Doctor MacNiven.

Alexander's two hands held her at the waist and hoisted her up on to the gig. Then the whip was plucked from the socket, and though it only touched the two horses lightly, they began to gallop, heads down, hauling the rocking gig through the quiet countryside, big wheels showering the thorn hedges with dust.

On the seat beside Alexander Maggie clasped his bare arm and closed her eyes, not only because of the force of the breeze lifting her long hair. It was exhilarating as well as frightening, the wheel beside her blurred, her hands clasping his hard muscle. When she opened her eyes momentarily she saw the traces of a smile as well as determination below the fair moustache.

She almost wished the journey would go on, but the gig was braking outside the doctor's, Master Alexander hurrying in to tell him he was wanted at the big house. The doctor came out, clapping on his black hat and carrying his bag. It was arranged that Maggie would go back on his gig.

Meantime Mrs Livingstone was standing with folded arms outside the bedroom door while Nanny Gunn packed her trunk. There had been a good deal of argument and insult, with the Sutherland woman insisting that her job called for far more skills than a cook, because a nanny had to deal with the living product. Besides, she was far better educated.

'Brains aren't everything,' Mrs Livingstone said indignantly. 'You've also got to have something here.' She put her palm over her big bosom, at the heart. 'You try to make yourself out to be so superior, the way you speak to people, but I've never heard the gentry speak to people like that, not in all the years I've been feeding them. They've got breeding, you see. Anyway, you've said all you're going to say in this house.

If you don't go, you'll starve, because I'm not sending up another bite.'

Conceding defeat, Nanny Gunn began to pack her trunk. Downstairs Invernevis tried to get the cause of her upset out of Mary Rose, but she was incoherent. Doctor MacNiven arrived sooner than Invernevis had expected, and, having spoken gently with her alone for five minutes, prescribed a week in bed.

'Nervous exhaustion,' he told Invernevis in the library, after she had been helped up to bed.

'Yes, but what caused it? Did she say anything?' her husband asked impatiently.

'She's in too bad a state to make sense. It's often the way,' the doctor said calmly. He was watching Invernevis.

'I blame that damned Nanny she brought from Sutherland,' Invernevis said angrily. 'Well, she's going.'

'It could be that, or just general strain,' the doctor shrugged. 'Nervous trouble can build up over a period of time, then come to a head.' He looked at Invernevis over his spectacles, eyes watering after decades of diagnosing by poor lamps. 'Is there a personal problem I should know about?'

'No, nothing,' Invernevis said coldly. He knew what the doctor was getting at. Well, if his father had sat discussing his sexual life with Doctor MacNiven *he* certainly wasn't going to. It was too private, and besides, it had nothing to do with nervous trouble.

The doctor's gig trundled off to the village, to be replaced an hour later by the oldest big house gig, with the coachman nodding to sleep as he waited on the high seat, his hat tilted over his eyes. As the day dulled towards evening Nanny Gunn's trunk was taken down by the ghillie and the gardener, and slid on the gig, jolting Roddy awake.

Then the woman herself descended, prim and erect, like a queen going into exile, the mouth a firm line below the steel spectacles as she refused an offer of a hand up on to the gig.

The whip flicked and, sitting sideways on the back, she was

dragged away to the late train, Invernevis watching her slate-grey hat bobbing away from his bedroom window. Carlotta had gone the same way. Then he hurried along to the nursery to play with his daughter.

Mama was sitting there, holding an unintelligible dialogue with the baby on her knee. Her skirt hadn't been put on straight, and the cuffs of her blouse were unbuttoned because of her weak hand, but she was sober and smiling, telling her astonished son:

'Mrs Livingstone let me know that awful woman was going and asked me if I would go and look after Lucy. Well, as I told her, I looked after three of my own, so I've had plenty of practice. And don't go bringing any other nannies here while I'm still living,' she warned with a mischievous smile, turning to her charge again and tickling her under the chin. The son saw that the chuckling child was the image of its new custodian. Smiling, he closed the door quietly.

Through in the kitchen Maggie was too frightened to tell Mrs Livingstone that Master Alexander had taken her up to the village, despite the bad blood between the two brothers. But the cook was still elated by the eviction, raising the thank-you sherry Invernevis had sent through and saying: 'Here's to a happier house, now that that bitch has gone.'

Later that evening Mary Rose asked why Nanny Gunn hadn't been along to see her.

'Because she's gone home.'

'But why?' she asked, sitting up in bed. She clutched his sleeve. 'Is Jamie ill?'

'No, no, nothing like that,' he assured her. 'It was personal.'

There was silence. Then she asked: 'Is the baby all right?'

'Yes, fine.' But he did not give the identity of the new nanny.

Too tired to enquire further, she sank back, into expanding blackness.

CHAPTER 15

At about nine o'clock on the last evening of October a series of lights bobbed over Wade's Bridge, then took the turning to the left, up the avenue to Invernevis House. Brightening as the trees closed in and travelling about four feet above the ground, they rounded the blind bend.

Maggie had gone into the scullery to rinse a plate in the absence of Morag the scullery-maid, who had climbed to bed complaining of a splitting headache, the trying start of womanhood. Maggie had lingered in the freezing stone cell, her hand staying on the big brass tap, struck into immobility by memories of the innumerable pots she had scoured in that deep chipped sink under the cruel supervision of Miss Carlotta until Mrs Livingstone had liberated her for the kitchen and more creative work.

It was pitch black beyond the pane, but the door into the kitchen was lighted behind her back, Mrs Livingstone sitting taking tea within hailing distance. It was from that window that Maggie had watched the Master go off to war with her brother Donald, only one returning; and into that same black frame Miss Laura's ringleted head had bobbed, her wrist shackled by the slow-worm.

Then Maggie saw the lights coming down the avenue, emerging from the rhododendrons. Yellow slits, like the eyes of animals. Sheep that had trampled a Home Farm dyke? But the eyes would only show if there was a moon. As she watched them approaching she was remembering the light she had seen going away up the avenue on the night Miss Laura had died; tales her mother had told in drawn-out Gaelic over dying peats of lights moving between the sick and the cemetery. But if they were coming up to the big house, who was it going to be? The old lady? She was well, no longer drinking, taking her duties as nanny very seriously. The young Mistress was all right, though lying down as usual. Surely not her father.

The irrational idea took hold that she should run through to the servants' hall, where he was dressing salmon flies, to warn him, but her legs were rooted to stone. Both hands on the big cold taps, she stood swaying, screaming, bringing Mrs Livingstone shuffling through with a poker, thinking it was another rat.

'Guisers, girl,' she said contemptuously, having peered out. 'Now for God's sake stop that yelling before you bring the Master through. We'd better go and see if we can get a laugh from the guisers.'

The scooped-out turnips with wavering candles behind the slit eyes and curved mouths stopped at the back door, Mrs Livingstone opening it, standing aside with the remark: 'You get later every year. You should be in bed.'

But her censure turned to a gasp when she saw it was two adults, and the way they were dressed. The taller one was wearing a long black silk dress tight at throat and cuff, a dark wig, and, to complete the likeness to Miss Carlotta, bunches of rusty keys dangling from a leather belt at the waist. But it was the grotesque feral mask that made Mrs Livingstone lean against the open door, covering her eyes.

'The Lord's sake, it's the work of the devil.'

But the smaller figure, coming into the light, was also cause for astonishment, for it was obvious by the outfit – apron over black gaberdine – that Elsie the departed kitchen-maid and Miss Carlotta's ally was being aped. The mask was equally repulsive. Though the source of the lights was manifestly human, Maggie was still weak at the knees because of what they brought back, even worse than the dead. For a second, as the taller one stepped inside, and before she had seen the mask, Maggie had felt sure that it was Miss Carlotta, come off the late train.

From the backs of the guisers' heads and their build it was obvious that they were men, but there was no clue as to their identities. The taller one set his turnip lantern down on the big white table while Mrs Livingstone told her assistant to stop standing with mouth open and to get some nuts and apples from the cupboard, where they had been laid in in expectation of guisers.

As Maggie stretched to the cupboard, the taller one began whistling and, clutching at his companion's arm, pointed at the kitchen-maid's legs. Red in the face, she let the bag of nuts drop. It burst and they rolled under the table, the two guisers now down on their knees, helping to retrieve them, a rough *papier-mâché* mask pushing against Maggie's face, a hand clutching at her knee. Jerking away, she banged her head on the table, saw stars.

Mrs Livingstone was standing by, helpless with laughter, hoisting her apron to take the tears away.

'Well, girl, Miss Carlotta didn't show you that much love when she was here!'

Maggie couldn't see any humour in the lunging grotesque mask, the keys at the waist jangling. She was more frightened by the identity of the person behind the mask than by the mask itself. It was obviously someone from the village, someone who didn't like her, the way he kept lunging, gripping her wrist, his dirty nails diggin in. The other one was more subdued, and gave Miss Carlotta's double a shake when he became too rough.

'We'll see how good you really are,' the cook was saying. She had filled a basin with water and floated some apples. She lowered the basin to the floor, beside a chair, winking at Maggie as she handed each guiser a fork.

'To do this you'll have to take off your masks,' she told them, well pleased with her cunning.

The taller one shook his head. Widening the mouth of the mask with the blunt end of the fork, he clasped the metal between his bright teeth and knelt on the chair, balancing his chin on the back, head held over the basin. The fork quivered between his teeth as he aimed, letting go, the prongs bruising the red skin of an apple before tilting, then ringing against tin.

'No use,' Mrs Livingstone announced. 'It's got to stick in the apple. Let's have the next one.'

The smaller man dressed as the defected kitchen-maid also widened the mouthpiece of his mask and knelt on the chair, the fork poised, then falling, embedding in an apple, rolling over and over, but the prongs holding.

'Now you're going to have to remove your mask to eat it,' Mrs Livingstone said triumphantly, plunging her arm in and retrieving apple and fork. He took the apple, but only to hand it to Maggie, and because they were all watching she was forced to bite into it, her face the colour of the skin, the sweet sliver almost choking her. But her ordeal wasn't over, for the taller one caught her by the waist and lifted her on to the chair, forcing her to kneel, Mrs Livingstone entering into the spirit and handing her the fork.

The pronged metal was swinging wildly in Maggie's mouth over the bobbing apples when the door swung open, butted by the head of one of Mama's Skye terriers, waddling through from the library fire for water. When the dog saw what it took to be the long black dress of its old enemy it went beserk, lunging across the room, teeth showing as it rushed barking round the silk hem. The other dog heard the commotion and came trotting through as reinforcement, age forgotten in its desire to settle the score against one who had hounded it throughout the house, pushing it outside, with a pointed shoe, whatever the weather.

The kitchen was in bedlam, with Mrs Livingstone trying to control the dogs, the taller guiser kicking out, the other kneeling on the chair, doubled up with laughter apparently. Maggie was cowering in a corner, biting her fist, not knowing whether to laugh or cry. Red in the face with exasperation through shouting at the dogs, Mrs Livingstone was running the tap.

'This will cool you down!' she shouted, turning and throwing a jug of water.

The two dogs stopped tearing the silk hem with their teeth, and stood there, stunned by the assault. Then, as the cold water seeped through their coats, they set up a pathetic chorus of yelps, scrabbling at the door to get back to the library fire.

But Invernevis's brogues were blocking the way, the rising noise having made him lay down the fishing book.

'What in God's name's going on?' he asked, seeing the pool of water, his eyes travelling up the tight black silk dress. Like Maggie he thought it was his aunt come back, until he saw the mask.

'Two guisers from the village, Sir,' Mrs Livingstone said weakly, now ashamed at the mess of her kitchen.

'I can see that. But what's the meaning of this - outrageous get-up?' Though he had never liked his aunt, the family name had to be upheld against the ridicule of the village because once that kind of thing started, it would spread back.

The two guisers stood in the pool of water, their masks turned on him.

'I demand to know who you are!' Invernevis shouted, shaking with anger now. 'I don't mind a bit of harmless fun, but this - Mrs Livingstone, lock the back door and put the key in your apron pocket. They're not leaving here till they identify themselves and apologise.'

The cook looked at him dubiously but shuffled forward to do his bidding, the lock protesting through disuse. The guisers looked at each other, then shrugged and put their fingers under their masks, levering them up and on to the tops of their heads.

The taller one was Frank the footman, the other Alexander.

Mrs Livingstone looked as if she had already guessed,

but Invernevis was speechless, unable to believe that either would have the temerity to return. From the silly smiles it was obvious that they were both drunk. He was having to think quickly. If there was any more noise, Mary Rose would come down. Then it might all come out about Maggie and the sovereign he'd given her in Edinburgh. No doubt that swine MacPherson was behind the visit; had probably supplied the drink to give them the courage in the first place. If he ordered them to clear out, that would only make matters worse. Besides, he didn't want to air family feuds in front of servants, though Mrs Livingstone and her assistant were both trustworthy. As usual Alexander looked stupid with drink and would no doubt go, but the footman was a different matter. Best to leave the problem with Mrs Livingstone, now she knew how angry he was with the noise and the insolence of the costumes. He pulled the door to behind him. If these two were getting together to drink, there would be plenty of trouble in the district, just as bad as the quarry. It would almost be worth-while to give the footman fifty guineas to get out.

In the kitchen the laird's arrival had deflated the high spirits of the Hallowe'en party. As soon as he had left Mrs Livingstone looked censoriously from Alexander to Frank, shaking her head in silent sorrow at their foolishness in daring to come, especially dressed like that. Any visitor, tradesman or tinker, was entitled to a cup of tea, but in this case to linger was to provoke the laird. She pressed Alexander's arm as she showed them to the door, and when they had gone into the frosty night, ordered Maggie to make a cup of tea before clearing up the mess.

'They shouldn't have come, though it was a harmless thing to do,' the cook said with a sigh. 'I blame that Frank. He's going to be a bad influence on poor Master Alexander. They say Frank's worked his way in with MacPherson. Of course there's another daughter desperate for a man.'

But Maggie wasn't listening. The Master had surprised

her, kneeling on the chair with the fork between her teeth. He would think she was involved in the capers of the two guisers, that she wasn't a serious person. Worse, he would feel she had betrayed him by fooling with the dismissed footman. She had seen the way the footman had looked at her when he took off his mask, the same narrowing of the eyes, the movement of the tip of his tongue along his lips he had used a hundred times, sitting opposite her at meals in the servants' hall. She couldn't shake off the feeling that he had come, not to entertain, but for revenge at what had happened in Edinburgh. She was disappointed that Master Alexander was with him; she had thought the Master's brother above that sort of thing. Miss Carlotta and Elsie might have made her life a misery, but that was all in the past and it wasn't fair to mock the absent.

'I don't know what this place is coming to,' Mrs Livingstone said, tilting the brown pot and stirring in an extra spoon for her nerves. 'We used to get guisers from the village, young ones that would give you a song and dance for a handful of nuts and an apple. All good clean fun, and I always managed to keep them quiet in case Miss Carlotta came through. But it's nothing but trouble now. I don't blame Master Alexander. This is his home, when all said and done. It's that footman, leading him astray. He's after *you*, of course!' she said accusingly to her assistant, 'and fine the Master will know it.' Holding up an admonitory hand: 'I know girl, but you know what I mean. Your mother would have wanted me to speak plainly to you, God rest her soul. It's you he wants. His pride's hurt, you see.'

Up in the nursery, Laura's old bedroom, Sheena, Mad Betsy's grand-daughter, was feeding the big house baby. The girl's stained blouse was open to the waist, her breasts exposed, swollen with the milk for her most recent child, this time to a woodcutter, who, like all the others, had denied paternity. The baby was absorbed into the overcrowded croft by Betsy, sympathetic because she had been the mother of half a dozen children herself, some outside wedlock; and the paternity of Sheena's own mother (now dead) had never been established. The girl was illiterate, had to be watched because at the lightest touch she would open her legs to anyone.

She sat in the severe wooden chair, her head lolling to the side, eyes glazed, mouth open with a look of infinite cerebral distance as the baby sucked, dribbling, making gurgling sounds of delight. Mama sat opposite, watching, remembering that she had fed three herself.

When the baby became restless, arm rejecting the sweetness, Mama demanded that it be restored to her lap, good hand tapping its back to expel surplus wind.

'That will do now. You can go, girl.'

Sheena buttoned up her blouse but out of alignment, and there was flesh showing as she arose, the tweed skirt detailing her attractions. She wobbled in uncertain shoes, grinning, as Mama handed her half a crown.

The girl went out into the passage lit by a weak oil-lamp stationed on a table, beside an Indian vase. She wasn't afraid. She had walked from the village in the darkness to give the big house child its evening feed, having fed her own. Darkness she found companionable: most of her happy moments with men, Irish as well as locals, had occurred in darkness, in the lean-to of the croft among the scolding hens or against the wall behind the Arms, where she sometimes did cleaning, Carmichael wanting to prove to the village his humanitarian principles. Also, folks couldn't stare, or mock her in darkness, tapping their temples and saying hurtful things in Gaelic.

She should have gone down the back stairs, through the kitchen and out into the night, to return the next dawn, but instead she lingered, looking at the oil paintings lining the passage, stabbing a finger against the full-length chieftain and laughing. The almond-eyed women with their creamy complexions and slender necks made her pensive. Why couldn't she look like that, instead of her mouth being all wrong, as the mirror showed? No, she didn't want to go home through the village because it was Hallowe'en and they would call after her that she didn't need to bother dressing up.

She left a gilt frame rocking behind her as she climbed bare boards, past bruised plaster. It was darker at the top of the house, with only stars sprinkling the grimy skylight. She opened a door, saw the candle burning down, Morag the scullery-maid curled in sleep under the rough blanket. Though she had been warned by her grandmother against handling fire, she lifted the candle on the saucer, going to the next room, again of basic furniture, black iron and dark wood, but this time with a dresser and a photograph standing in a frame. She set the saucer down, but couldn't make out the figure in the photograph, the way it had been stuck together, the tear across the face out of alignment, like the way she sometimes saw the world. The photograph didn't interest her, but the silver frame flared and shone in the candlelight as she handled it. She had never owned anything beautiful. For what they did to her the Irish and the locals sometimes gave her sixpences, but she gave these to her grandmother, not telling a lie by saying that she had earned them at the Arms.

Seeing no way of converting the photograph into money, she laid it down, picked up the candle and went into the next room. It was better furnished, but the rug under her shoes almost sent her sprawling, candle wax blistering the back of her hand.

She pulled at the top drawer of the dresser, and it yielded, squeaking, the reek of moth-balls released. She relied on her hands, rummaging through the linen, mostly starched, then making metal move at the bottom. She lifted out the small embroidered sack, tipping the contents on to her palm close to the candle, gasping at the way they shone. She couldn't count, but her hand wouldn't hold them all. One fell, to bounce against her shoe and roll into darkness, but she let it go.

Only once had she seen such a coin. It had been given her by a drunk Irishman after a session against the wall of the Arms during which she had had to do things she had never done before, but her grandmother had confiscated the coin, saying they could all live off it for a couple of weeks.

Stuffing the sovereigns into the pockets of her cardigan, she left the candle burning above the open drawer and made for the stairs. She had sufficient instinct to know that to carry on down the back stairs would mean getting caught by Mrs Livingstone or Maggie, so she used the landing with the lamp to make for the front door. The wide staircase yawned, but she couldn't resist stopping on the landing where the stained glass window of the Invernevis chieftain was dominant. Gasping at the multicoloured display lit by the lamp in the hall below, she stood on tiptoe, trying to peer through a blue fragment into the blackness beyond.

At that moment Invernevis was coming back through from the kitchen after his confrontation with the two guisers. Seeing the figure against the stained glass, he stopped suddenly. Laura was always doing that. It wasn't possible; it was a trick of his imagination, or light playing tricks. You *wanted* to see something, and so you saw. It was the same with sounds. His father had always scorned the legend of the sundered Irish harper O'Caibre screaming at the death of the Invernevis chieftain. Mama had dabbled in table-turning, pressing palms on the dining-room mahogany until Aunt Carlotta had discovered, taking her from the work of the devil. Because, as his aunt had argued, those without sin went to heaven and had no need to come back down; and those in hell (like his father) were too cindered to climb. But Laura had believed, and was always claiming encounters with the green lady on the front stairs or saying that she had come to her room to lay on a cold hand. Suppose Aunt Carlotta had been wrong: suppose disturbed spirits did come back to haunt the site of their unhappiness? If Laura was back to haunt her aunt, she was too late. Was she going to be condemned to wander that gloomy house forever in her lilac dress, the habitual one of summer, the one she had been wearing that day at the Yellow Pool when she wrestled with the salmon?

No, if it was her, it didn't frighten him. But he liked to think of himself as being a realist bred out of soldiering. When you pulled the trigger, you certainly didn't stop to consider that the man in your sights might come back to haunt you. All those Highlanders under Magersfontein Hill: unless ghosts could cross water, the only place they would haunt was the arid *veld*. A realist, yes, directing men to kill without letting conscience halt the action, but strange things happened, even among soldiers. On the day before Magersfontein, he had had to speak sharply to a man in his company who claimed to have seen blood on the forehead of Major-General Wauchope, killed in the dawn while leading with his claymore.

If it was his sister come back, he wanted to see her again, now that time could not touch her and there was no Carlotta to disturb her. Using both hands on the banister, he swung up, his heart sounding his growing apprehension as the silhouette against the stained glass loomed larger. Perhaps it was wrong to confront the dead when they had no tongue to tell, but she had never been able to answer back in life, when flesh was for striking.

'Laura.'

As his fingertips touched her, Sheena turned, screaming, and, knocking him aside with a powerful arm, ran downstairs, to wrestle with the handle of the engraved glass door and disappear into the night.

It had been so sudden and unexpected that he had not been able to identify the voice, but it was a woman's scream, and would have alerted the house. A thief? But why a woman, and how was he ever going to find out what was missing? The best thing he could do was to get back down to the library before Mary Rose came out.

The scream was not heard in the kitchen because of metal scraping on stone as Maggie mopped up the water from the bath of bobbing apples, Mrs Livingstone sitting with her tea, resting her ankles and lamenting the unexpected arrival of the Master.

'Well, this is one night I wish the Master had got tight earlier and fallen asleep in the chair,' she announced.

The two turnip lanterns were sitting on the big table, the eyes dark sockets now, and Maggie asked the cook if they were to go into the bin.

'No girl, just you leave them there. I'm going to give them to the milk cart in the morning. They can go back up to the Home Farm, where they came from, and I hope his sheep choke on them.'

When she eventually reached her room under the frosted slates, Maggie found her photograph of the Master face-down on the dresser. She sat down on her bed to puzzle it out, and reached the conclusion that it had been a rat. She would tell the gardener in the morning, and he would take up one of his wire cages, the kind the creature couldn't get out of again. That was one of the things you had to learn to live with in that house.

She was hoisting her sour black dress above her head when she heard the commotion next door, and then Mrs Livingstone came in, groping her way to the bed and sitting for a long time before speaking, not conscious that she was only in a corset, with pendulous breasts. She spoke in a dazed way, appearing to address the wall.

'All gone. I went to the drawer for my nightdress, and it was open. Not one left, and there were at least twenty. Two years' savings. Oh yes, I know they should have been put in the bank, but when do I ever get the chance to get away from here? I blame myself; I should have asked Hector to take them.'

Maggie went through to see for herself, but was no wiser.

'Sovereigns they were,' the cook elaborated. 'He always pays me in sovereigns, like his father before him.'

'But who?' Maggie cried, uneasily aware that her room was next door. It partly explained the toppled photograph, but she couldn't tell Mrs Livingstone about *that*.

The idea of it having been her assistant or any of the maids had never crossed the cook's mind. 'No, I know who it was, and he worked it very clever. It was that footman. That's why he brought Master Alexander up here. The guising was only an excuse. He would tell Master Alexander to wait till he fetched something he had left behind, then he would come up the front stairs. It isn't the first thing he's stolen from here.'

'You'll have to go down and tell the Master,' Maggie urged. 'He'll send for the constable.'

Mrs Livingstone shook her head. 'No, he's got enough worry as it is, poor soul, and it'll only make more trouble between himself and Master Alexander. I'm disappointed in Master Alexander, keeping such company. I always gave him the benefit of the doubt, but I'm glad now that he won't get back here.' She turned suddenly with the rebuke: 'It's a great pity that trash of a footman ever took such a fancy to you, girl. Well, let this be a lesson,' she said, rising to return to her own room, but not saying whose lesson it was.

Up in the village Sheena, Mad Betsy's grand-daughter had successfully negotiated Main Street without anyone jeering. When she saw the glow of turnip lanterns and heard laughter she kept to the shadows, clutching the pockets of her cardigan. Just wait till her grandmother saw what she had got. But how was she going to explain them? Safest to say that she had got them from the Arms. But that was an awful lot just for cleaning. No, she would keep them, hiding them in the byre until she decided.

In the library of Invernevis House the laird fell asleep in the arm-chair by the spent log, leaving an empty decanter and the mystery of the figure on the landing unsolved and not to be spoken of to anyone. In sleep she became Laura.

BOOK FOUR

CHAPTER 16

Autumn deteriorated into winter, with the dead leaves airborne on the avenue, and spray whipped up on the loch. The maids bruised their shins and knocked the breath from their black-clad bodies, lugging big-lipped scuttles to the gluttonous grates of Invernevis House, its dismal panes demanding early lamps. Now that the river was sacrosanct through spawning, Duncan the ghillie helped to carry the big baskets of logs through to the principal fireplaces.

Most days Mary Rose kept to her sitting-room, at the fire instead of in the bay window, but still sewing, the embroidery design taking definite shape, Egyptians in soiled loincloths bearing the body of a god across a blue river to a pyre kindled in scarlet thread on the opposite bank. Her needle picked, a sigh rising when it went in wrong, coal shifting by her shoes. Sometimes she nodded off, the needle trailing the blue thread poised in mid-air, until the maid knocking with the afternoon tea brought her back to ashes. She ought to go down the passage to see little Lucy, but she didn't have the strength. Besides, Mama had taken the child over, as if she was the mother. It was ironic, really. When she had come back from honeymoon Mama had been the hopeless one.

Invernevis kept to the library, reading estate papers in a pool of artificial light at his desk, and when these had been returned to Edinburgh, settling in the wing arm-chair by a flaring log, a fishing book on his lap, and by his right fist, a decanter of brandy. He was still dreaming about breaking his father's record, hauling a still larger fish from the spring flood, but his mind drifted from the glittering illustration on his lap into the dark reaches of speculation. He and Mary Rose were living as strangers. Most days she did not come down, and when he went upstairs, fired by brandy, it was to find the connecting door locked. It wasn't the pleasure, he told himself; it was the necessity for a male heir, even more urgent now that his break with Alexander was permanent. Some nights, when the decanter level had dropped significantly, he meditated over cigarettes about his father's conduct, outrageous but in some ways understandable. On how many nights, when the house was silent except for the buffeting wind and whatever sounds came from the past, had the big, bearded, burly man lifted the lamp by its fluted stem, bearing it up the betraying back staircase, to lay his long shadow over a startled maid's bed? Not one word would have passed between them, and not only for fear of waking the servant in the adjacent cell under the slates. They could have had nothing in common, except perhaps a heat in their bodies in that cold house. Though the son could not condone, he could at least understand the desire for physical satisfaction. He thought of Maggie, the only servant to have caught his attention. She had caused him a good deal of trouble, first with the photograph and then with the sovereign, but both had been resolved. She was kind to his mother and her father had been ghillie since his boyhood. These were sufficient reasons for dismissing such degrading thoughts, but he had gone to women late, and was conscious of the forties looming and the impediment of the game leg.

Perhaps it wasn't lack of interest in him that kept Mary Rose confined upstairs, but worries over Jamie. He hadn't been in touch since the Edinburgh disgrace, but Lady Mackay had written to complain about his increasing addiction. Apparently he was at it night and day, just like Mama had been when he was away in South Africa. After Christmas, when the weather eased, Invernevis would have to go north to see him, try to find out what was causing his instability.

If Mary Rose had worries about her brother, so had he about his. It wasn't that he feared an attempt by Alexander to return to the house of his birth because he knew that Mary Rose was well disposed towards him. On the contrary, he was confident that his brother would stay on his side of the river. It was the combination of Alexander, his father-in-law and the footman that worried him. The Hallowe'en visit had been the last straw. It was almost a repetition of Alexander's story, with MacPherson manipulating matters so as to get what he wanted out of the big house. Through Alexander he had got a wedding, but in the case of the footman the tenant of the Home Farm had motives which Invernevis couldn't quite work out. If it wasn't pure spite, what could MacPherson be after by giving the footman shelter? No doubt the footman would have told his twisted story about the sovereign and Maggie in Edinburgh, but how could that help MacPherson, unless he hoped to use it as a lever to get his rent reduced? That was a matter for the trustees, not the laird.

MacPherson's motives were worrying enough, but what would happen if Alexander and the footman teamed up and went up to the Arms together? Confidential stuff about life in the big house would spill out over drink, to become subject for derision or exaggeration. In that at least Carlotta had been correct: the villagers had too long and unruly tongues. Of course Father Macdonald would come to hear what the footman told, and would transmit to Leamington Spa, thus giving his patroness even greater moral superiority over the family she had deserted. It was a mess, but it had been a mess since he went to South Africa and war, the year the century turned. He could blame his lairdship, but it went beyond that, far back in time to the day when the Irish harper had been roped between two horses in the meadow across the river, the horses slapped north and south, his screamed curse becoming the blight of the Invernevis dynasty. All he could do was to sit drinking and brooding till the decanter was empty, and the log had crumbled. Then the cold climb with the unsteady lamp to his solitary uninviting bed, the momentary pause on the landing to wonder if he should climb higher for consolation.

Up at the Home Farm Frank, the ex-footman, had taken over many of the tasks formerly done by Alexander, who was spending more of his time at the Arms, going up at lunchtime now and adjourning to a crony's croft with a half bottle of whisky till opening time at five. Frank's uniform with the green piping down the leg had been replaced by corduroys lashed with leggings, blunted tacketed boots where there had been elegant pointed patent leather. Instead of rising at six to polish the silver because of the butler's incapacity through alcoholic tremor, he was down at five in the freezing dairy, collecting the enamel pail and going out into the bitter black dawn to cross frost-corrugated mud and dung to the byre, where the cows waited impatiently to be rid of their sagging cargoes. He pushed the three-legged stool under the first one and sat fumbling with the teats, much tugging and tweaking only producing a thin sporadic squirt because he had not yet learned the subtle art of manipulation, the warm stream often splashing his boots, the cow showing its contempt for the clumsy novice hands by arching its tail and making the dung explode in the streaming gutter. The smell of animal and excrement sickened him, and the byre was eerie beyond the weak lantern he had hooked above the stall, but he was determined to master the skill, to establish himself at the Home Farm, so he carried stool and pail from stall to stall.

Though MacPherson had fired his hatred of the man who had dismissed him so ignominiously, there was another reason for his tenacity. Annie, MacPherson's dark haired and voluptuous second daughter, assisted her mother in house and dairy. The first time the footman had come up behind her between the big basins of skimmed milk on scrubbed stone, putting his palms under her pronounced bust, there had been no resistance, only the momentary pause of the churn, the slurping sound of solidifying milk. He had already climbed with her to the warm stimulating hay of the barn and had been allowed to lift the hem and splay her legs, but full settlement of his desires wouldn't follow till she saw evidence that it wasn't mere lust, which she could meet anywhere in the district. It was an attitude he had not come across among the maids at the big house, and it irked his masculine pride as well as intriguing him. He was going to stay to claim her, and not only the nubile body. Her father seemed to have money, and would no doubt endow her generously when the right man came along, because he hadn't had to give much of a dowry with Alexander. There wouldn't be any necessity to move to a place of their own because of the spaciousness of the farmhouse. It was a matter of waiting and, meantime, mastering everything he was asked to do, so that MacPherson would continue to employ him.

It wasn't only his sweat he gave the red-faced farmer. After supper they sat on either side of the big black grate in the stone-flagged kitchen, MacPherson using a collie as a footstool and cradling a cold briar as he quizzed his new man about life in his previous employment. The footman knew he was being sounded out, but was willing to give, telling about the young Mistress's queer behaviour, the number of trays carried up to the grim custodian Nanny Gunn, the library decanter that had to be replenished every second day. When he saw disappointment in the face opposite, he embellished. Several times he had seen the laird going up the back stairs late at night, carrying only a candle, and it wasn't the game leg that had made him unsteady. If Maggie wouldn't entertain him, there were others, lusty islanders, under the cold slates.

Stem between discoloured teeth, MacPherson nodded sagely, his mental dossier against the laird growing.

'Of course he's not a real man, not like his father.' Spittle hissed on iron. 'Many a night he sat where you're sitting now, having a good dram and a chat. This was the only house he would come to, because he felt free, and he knew that nothing he would say would pass beyond these four walls. He was like Sandy, my son-in-law. He didn't fit in at the big house. He couldn't be bothered with all that fancy talk from the women, and the idea that they were above everybody. Used to say they weren't real women. That's not the way he put it, for he had a straight way of speaking. Liked to mix with his tenants, he did, and in more ways than one.' He winked. 'They used to say that for every maid that came, two went away.' He helped the joke by making an arc with his hands. 'But this one; he's hardly seen from one year's end to the other. I've heard the wags up in the village asking: "Is there still a laird in the big house?" And another saying: "Oh no, Miss Carlotta's gone." By God he did the dirty on you. I'm glad I was able to give you a corner, though I can't pay any more of a wage because of the rent the trustees are taking off me.'

Frank sat still. To make a sign, even the slightest movement of his head, would signify that he was happy with his lot, whereas he was only being paid a pittance. True, it was more than he'd been getting at the big house, for when MacPherson asked him his annual wage, he'd added several sovereigns.

'I can't match that,' MacPherson had said mournfully, deducting a couple of sovereigns, but it still came out more, and the Home Farm food was more plentiful if not better than Mrs Livingstone's. And his bedroom, though still coomed, was bigger and brighter, with a window overlooking the river, instead of a skylight filled with mountain slope. But the work was harder, the hours longer at the Home

Farm, and he was only going to tolerate these conditions until something came of it with Annie.

She was sitting at the scarred circular mahogany table, darning the heel of one of her father's socks in the circle of the lamp, her mother having climbed upstairs early, the pain at her side worse tonight. As her fingers worked the daughter listened to the conversation of the two men at the fireside, but she didn't contribute until the only sound was the sigh of a collie, and the lid of the kettle between them lifting, then settling as the peat underneath dulled.

'I hear something's going to happen about the quarry,' she announced.

'Where did you hear that?' her father asked sharply, twisting in his chair.

'I heard it in the village store this morning, when I was up for the messages,' she said simply, the needle still moving. 'Somebody said they had overheard Father Macdonald say it.'

'Damn it woman, make yourself plain!' her father shouted in exasperation. 'I've had to live with this for years,' he complained to the footman. Then to her again: 'Said *what?*'

'Said that the Irishmen weren't to be allowed over on this side any more,' Annie said, taking no notice of his tantrum. 'It's because of the fighting that's been going on in the Arms, and the things the Irishmen have been shouting at local women.'

'Why the hell didn't you tell us this sooner?' was her father's savage reaction. He turned again to Frank, closing one eye conspiratorially: 'So they've taken my advice at last. About bloody time too. It'll stop murder being done. But they should shut down the quarry.'

Annie hadn't finished her tale. 'The person who told me said they heard Father Macdonald saying that he blamed Alexander for the trouble in the Arms because of the money he was spending, getting the locals drunk, making them fight with the Irishmen.' She tried to keep her irritation at Alexander out of her voice, for she resented the way he had claimed her sister by first making her pregnant. It seemed to her typical of the treachery of the big house.

'Well, I hope you didn't stand with your mouth shut while that was being said,' her father warned. 'These buggers up in the village have nothing better to do with their time. Oh, I've known for years they've been jealous of me, just because I make a good job farming this place, when it's all hillside and stone. If they would get off their arses in the Arms and put the plough instead of pints into their fists, their crofts would be the better of it. Oh aye, they'll pour Sandy's money down their throats and tell him what a great man he is, but as soon as his back's turned —' He spat again. 'He's too good for them, that's what he is, too kind and trusting, like I used to be on the milk round, until the money stopped coming in. They would give you every excuse under the sun and swear you would get it the very next week, but you never saw it. The widows were the worst, with their poor mouths, whining that they lived on tea and couldn't take it without milk, and all the time you knew there was money under the mattress.

'As for the priest, I've not a great deal of time for religion because you're close to life on a farm, and some of the things you see, like the way the lambs are wiped out in the spring, makes you wonder if there's anything in it.' He acknowledged his daughter's sharp intake of breath by adding: 'Aye, religion's mostly women's stuff, but they don't always get to keep their babies. That priest: I've never trusted him from the first time I set eyes on him, and it must be forty years since he came to the village, as a skinny boy. He didn't bring the kind of comfort the women were wanting when their man was gone, and though he spoke out against drink, there was enough of it done behind the blinds of his house. Oh aye, he's fatter and better off now, because he had that bitch Carlotta behind him, and he's a big man in the district because he's a trustee. I never understood that, because the old laird couldn't stand the mention of his name. Called him the hoodie crow.

'The priest and this new fellow across the river are just like that.' MacPherson held up two crossed fingers. 'His trap's never away from the place. He carries up all the gossip from the village, you see, and likes nothing better than to sit at the big house table, because that's the only class of people he cares about. They've ganged up against Sandy because they're both so jealous of him. He gets on so well with everyone, you see, because there's no side to him. He should have been the laird instead of his brother. Oh aye, I know *that* one's the eldest, but Sandy was the old laird's favourite. He sat in that very chair and said so. Always took Sandy shooting with him and left the other one at home because he was too soft to climb the mountain. Sandy's *far* better liked than the priest, which makes him mad, so the laird and him put their heads together and try and do Sandy down, saying he's only a drunkard who spends all his time and money at the Arms. Even if he does like a dram, what bloody business is it of theirs? Now they'll be blaming Sandy for the Irishmen having to be banned from this side of the loch. But will they close down the quarry? Oh no, because that's bringing in a big rent, and he needs the money to keep his big house and his lazy wife going.'

He paused to apply fire to his black briar, cheeks sucking above the flame as he watched the footman closely. Annie stopped the diatribe by audibly gathering up her sewing, warning that she was making for bed.

'I'll take a run up to the village in the morning and see what I can hear,' her father said, pushing shut the grate door with his boot. He slapped the footman's knee. 'Well, son, you'd better go up because you can't lie in in the morning like that bugger across the river. But honest toil's better than living off the sweat of others,' he said, wrapping his huge rough hand round the stem of the lamp and lifting it to survey the kitchen as the footman's shadow rose and Annie's shoes sounded above.

Across the river at the big house Maggie was also preparing to climb the stairs after the day's labours in the kitchen, Mrs Livingstone having long since struggled up to give her swollen ankles relief. Maggie sat at the big scrubbed table by the benevolent lamp, cradling her last cup of tea, the glowing bars of the stove making her mind drift with the steam. She was so tired that she could hardly rise, but it was satisfying, having worked such a full day, with Mrs Livingstone delegating more and more duties, making more and more references to retirement. She had thrown herself into the work since coming back from Edinburgh, mainly to obliterate the embarrassing memory of the footman's departure. Though she knew it was drink to blame, she couldn't help feeling guilty. Perhaps she had been too cold towards him, though he had been forward. His staying on in the district instead of going south to a butler's post frightened her. She would have understood it if he had gone for a post up at Branglin, with Colonel Campbell, but the Home Farm, as a labourer? He hadn't the hands for such heavy work. His fingers were long and fine, not like her own, horned by immersion in water. He had been handsome in his own way, with that little blonde moustache, not unlike Master Alexander. But here she was, almost falling asleep beside the lamp, her elbows on the table she'd just scrubbed, thinking of him as if he was dead, yet he was only across the river. That was what worried her. Now that he was free of the strict rules of conduct of the big house, he would be even more forward with her when next they met. It made her frightened to take a walk on Sunday afternoon, especially after what had happened when she had taken the flowers down to the chapel for the old lady. On top of all that, she hadn't discovered why the young Mistress had quizzed her about having a boy friend. Maggie was sure that the footman had said something to her, and that she was waiting for the chance to use it.

As the days shortened, Mary Rose sat sewing and reading in her room, picking at the food under the silver cover when the tray came up. It wasn't only the friendless cold of downstairs that confined her, but depression about Jamie. She had an overpowering feeling that something terrible was going to happen to him. It had originated in a dream of a horizontal body, blonde moustached and booted, the torso in shadow. Night after night the hazy corpse had drifted through her dream, on a dark barge, accompanied by ominous music she had heard on honeymoon but the composer of which she could not identify, except she knew he was modern, controversial. She sat up, screaming her brother's name as the barge nosed forward, but her husband could not come through because of the connecting door being locked, and the canopied bed absorbing the sound.

It was that same feeling of impending doom she had twice experienced on the blind bend. Her dream of death seemed to be made more probable by the latest letters from her mother, each one more alarming about Jamie's drinking, more bitter in condemnation, words like 'degradation' and 'aberration' being used. Some malicious person had made sure the mother knew about the incident in front of the king in Edinburgh.

But not a line from Jamie, though she had written several times, inviting him to Invernevis to see if they could conquer his addiction together. They had been so close in childhood, spending the summer days together on the bleak moors of Sutherland, straying far from the family mansion despite strict maternal instructions. The punishment, bread and jam for supper, was worth it. He had waded through the deep heather with her, holding her hand and stooping to help her pick the wild flowers to press between the pages of a book. He had carried her on his back through the bog, parting the reeds to show her the blotched, olive-green eggs while the wedge-shaped bird circled and cried above.

She heard that high-pitched cry again as she sat in the deepening gloom of her Invernevis sitting-room, a woman and a mother now, and Jamie maimed, inside and out, unable to carry the burden of life. Having bred, the curlew had now forsaken the moor above the standing stones, and was back at the estuary of the river, stabbing the wet sand with its ibis-like beak, and when the boat ferrying the Irish navvies bumped the shingle, rising to wheel and cry. It was a wild sound, like a curse, and Mary Rose knew the Highland superstition of the curlew crying in darkness. Harbinger of death, belonging to the dark side of the moon which was now rising, waning in the perfection of fullness.

The maid came up with the lamp, to draw the curtains and hump the tin bath to the hearth, before lugging up the big black kettles. Even in the fragrant steam, with her back being circled by gentle bristles, Mary Rose could not relax, for the canopied bed loomed, with its dream of the drifting corpse.

Three days after Father Macdonald had circulated the story of the restriction of the Irishmen to the other side of the loch, confirmation reached Invernevis's desk in a letter from the Edinburgh lawyers, intimating that the trustees had taken into consideration the worsening tensions of the Arms and the damage done to the chapel. There had been a meeting with the quarry management, and it had been agreed that the navvies would be confined to their own side.

Invernevis was relieved by this solution, but angered by a letter on the same subject in the same post. It was a page torn from a notebook, scrawled in pencil, the writing large and childish, with spelling errors.

> I blame you for this business of the Irish boys getting kept on the

other side of the loch because you don't give anyone a chance. You listen to all the gossip that bloody priest carries down to you, instead of coming up to the village to see for yourself, the way our old man used to do. They're not savages, but decent men doing an honest week's work, and they need some kind of relaxation. *You* don't go without your drink, I hear. Even if I wasn't banned from your big fancy house, I wouldn't want to set foot in it again, or meet you.

Invernevis crumpled the note in his fist and tossed it into the wicker basket.

CHAPTER 17

On their last evening on the Invernevis side, the Irish navvies crowded the Arms, moleskins jingling with sovereigns. They insisted on putting up drink after drink for the locals, and there was little argument. Carmichael kept tossing gold coins into his drawer while strict turns were taken with raucous renderings of songs in the two types of Gaelic. Some of the Irishmen even supplied hymns, and even Carmichael was affected by the misty eye, the sign of the cross at the husky 'Amen'.

Alexander deserted his crofting cronies in the corner for a stance at the counter, his glass recharged with best Irish as soon as it was empty, a sovereign spinning in careless payment on the hollowed counter, Carmichael slapping it quiet, withdrawing it from circulation; Alexander even attempted a duet, his arm round an Irish neck as they rendered 'The Rose of Tralee', which drew appreciative cheers from both nationalities.

At closing time Carmichael had no trouble getting them to leave, for the navvies bought two bottles of the Power's apiece, thrusting them into the pockets of their moleskins. The locals went down the brae with them to the ferry, to see them off, and *en route* there were many halts to open bottles or flies.

The Irishmen gave the ferryman sovereigns to make an extra crossing that night, so that the locals could continue the *ceilidh* on the opposite shore, but the locals said no, for they had to be up at first light, to attend to their crofts. However, they wouldn't say no to a last drink, and as the bottles were passed round on the cold shore they wished the Irishmen well.

The locals then made to withdraw, but Alexander, who was hanging between two massive Irishmen, his boots clear of the shingle, insisted on accompanying them across. His crofting cronies tried to persuade him otherwise, warning him that Kate would be anxious, but the Irish mood was turning menacing in the darkness, so they went home.

Alexander slumped in the stern while the Irishmen gave the ferryman relief on the oars, singing as they pulled, and still pulling as their compatriots held bottles to their mouths. The boat was rocking through a swell and through the movements of the passengers. Alexander felt sick. He closed his eyes and voided the contents of his stomach over the side when the looming scar of the granite quarry began to contract and expand like a flexing fist in the fleeting moon.

When the keel ground shingle and he was helped out, he felt better. He felt better still when he was given more whisky as they made their precarious way up blasted stone to the huddle of ramshackle huts that had been an Irish colony for seven long years.

'Sure and be Christ, yer wan of the nicest fellas ever I met,' an Irishman said, clasping Alexander, and not even the whisky could anaesthetise the stench of moleskins. 'And I bet yer as strong as a horse too,' the Irishman added, feeling Alexander's bicep.

'He's a modest boy and doesn't answer,' another said.

'Aye, but the silent are always the strongest!' one leading the way shouted. 'And he's got what you haven't got: he's got brains. His brother is the owner of the place, and it was his brother decided to keep us to this side because he said we was animals.'

'Well he's not like his brother, is he? He's one of us.'

'We'll have to see about that,' the man in front said.

'And how do you propose to do that, Mick?'

'Well, we'll have to see him wrestling, won't we, just to make sure he's one of us. And to be fair, we'll put the boy against the smallest of us. You can't be fairer than that, can you, Danny?'

They led him past the camp, into the amphitheatre of the quarry floored with jagged aggregate, where a fistful of faggots made a brazier spurt. While a bottle of whisky was held to Alexander's mouth, fingers were groping his waistcoat pockets because this was to be a betting contest, with gold coins clattering on to the kitty of a shovel, held by the man in the battered stove hat who operated the crown & anchor board.

'Even money sez Michael will win, five to wan for Sendy!' As the coins kept coming, he chalked the names of the punters on a granite slab held up by an assistant.

'A sovereign on the laird's brother!' the man who had emptied Alexander's waistcoat shouted, tossing the coins with the others.

Stripped to the waist, his opponent now came into the glare of the brazier, the same height but thicker set, muscles rippling under the silk sheen of his skin as he flexed them, hitching up his moleskins by the studded belt, fingers combing through his beard, showing his rotten stumps as he studied Alexander.

'A count of ten wins!' the bookmaker shouted, and a hammer striking a shovel began the contest.

His opponent came forward, crouched, circling him in ritualistic simian suspicion, making to lunge, then drawing back as Alexander shifted ground.

'Stay by the brazier, so that we can see there's no fouls!' the bookmaker shouted.

The recent Irish whisky as well as the aggregate underfoot was making Alexander unsteady. The brazier was blinding, the frieze of bearded Irish faces distorting into gargoyles with yelling mouths, the collective smell of human uncleanliness overpowering, but it was vital to concentrate, to keep steady, to win. He had had wrestling matches with his father in the front hall, much to Carlotta's annoyance, when the big man in the riding boots had allowed him to get a grip and then, when he felt he had the ascendancy, throwing him hard on his back to show him that nobody was to be trusted.

But this was different. He was a man now but he was drunk, and his opponent was crunching towards him, knitting his fingers, then suddenly throwing the halter of his hands over his neck.

Alexander did the same. They stayed locked like that, boots searching for a stance on granite fragmented by dynamite, then spewed from the jaws of the crusher. The matted Irish beard was suffocating him, the hands round his neck tightening, making bone click. He tightened his own grip and heard the irritated rattle in the Irish throat, saw the protruding outraged eyes in the brazier light, the eyes of an animal, the smell of an animal, an animal that had to be stopped before it strangled him. Memory flashed an image of his father, in riding boots and breeches, stripped to the waist, what looked like burnt heather on his barrel chest, cigar clamped in the corner of his mouth as he trailed the whip stretched from a bull's penis while the gun-dog which had bitten a servant crouched trembling in the corner of the iron stockade at the stables. Then suddenly the dog had seen its opportunity, leaping to fasten its teeth in the arm now hoisting the whip, dragging down its tormentor. On one knee, his father had wrapped both hands around the dog's neck and throttled it till the tongue came out blue and stiff.

He made a great effort to throw as his father had shown him, crooking his knee. His tacketed boot gave and he was going down, swinging up the sheer grey walls of granite into darkness.

'One!' The shovel rang.

The Irishman was kneeling on his chest, pressing his shoulders down into the agonising stone, and though he squirmed, it was no use.

'Two!'

He opened his eyes, saw the leering bearded faces above, in the brazier's light, with the moon sliding behind the left shoulder of his oppressor. He felt neither anger nor fear now, only an immense weariness. Even if he could have found the word, he wouldn't have surrendered. 'Only fools and cowards surrender,' his father had told him, as he lay on the rug in front of the library fire, one cautious finger pushing the toothed spur on the riding boot as his father sat in darkness, drinking.

'Three!'

When they tore open his shirt and couldn't find the heart they got frightened and wandered away into the darkness, leaving the glittering gold on the shovel by the brazier. But they couldn't leave him lying out there, so they carried him into one of the shacks. They couldn't leave him lying on the floor because the rats would be attracted by the blood on his shoulders, where the aggregate had bit, so they lifted him on to the stained planks that served as a table, with a block of granite under his head, and a candle stuck on the white skin of his chest, so that they could see the face. They sat round him, swigging bottles, reminiscing about the good times in the Arms, the night the priest had found him under the table, and how he had opened one eye and wouldn't kiss the cross. Getting drunker and drunker, and deceived by the slight smile at the corners of his mouth, they addressed the ghostly white face in candlelight, calling him 'Sendy', making crude jokes, sometimes slapping him on a knee as they roared with laughter, and because their uproarious bodies were rocking the table, it seemed that he was laughing too. As the night advanced and the bottles emptied, they swiped away bold rats that had leapt up beside him, and as the light of a new day began to filter through the cracked filthy panes, two wavering fingers of the last man still conscious closed his eyelids.

In the grey light of morning the ferry took his body to the other side, Irishmen going with it as bearers. He was stretched out on one of the palettes that had been used to ship granite blocks for his new house. His hands were folded, and his boots pointed towards Invernevis, the solidified wax of the spent candle on his chest.

When he hadn't come home, Kate had assumed that he had been carried immobile with drink to one of the crofts, though that had never happened before. Though she was very worried, she couldn't go up to the Home Farm for her father, because carrying the little girl from her bed would give her a chill. MacPherson had come down at seven as usual, with the first of the milk. He whipped his gig up to the village, and when he heard about his son-in-law going across with the Irishmen, he went to meet the ferry, his gig parked by Miss Carlotta's chapel as he watched it nudging shingle, and seeing the stretched-out body, thought he was drunk. It was transferred to the gig and taken up to the Home Farm. Then MacPherson went down to tell his daughter she was a widow.

Invernevis heard the news an hour later from Archie, MacPherson's eldest son, when he came with the milk cart. Without going up to waken Mary Rose he immediately set out walking for his brother's house, so stunned that he forgot to take his Inverness cape against the autumn chill, and a cromach to counterbalance his game leg. As he rounded the blind bend, dew from a withered rhododendron bloom wetted his sleeve, a petal clinging. The avenue on which he had once known such happiness with Laura was now dismal, the birds silent, and a stubborn mist among the trees. He still hoped that it was a ghastly mistake, that Alexander was living, but in his heart he knew different. He would not look at the wound he had made on the tree when he had etched his own and Laura's initials with his *sgian dubh* the day he had left for war. Laura had pleaded with him not to go, and Mary Rose had pleaded with him not to break with his brother.

Crossing Wade's Bridge, he saw Doctor MacNiven coming out of Alexander's house.

'Is it true?'

'I'm afraid so; a sad business,' the doctor said, shaking hands.

'I wouldn't go in. She wants to be alone. Doesn't even want to see her own father. Apparently there's been a bit of a row. MacPherson wants the funeral to be from the Home Farm, but she's insisting that the remains are brought down here right away. Says she wants to wash him herself.'

'But how did it happen?' Invernevis asked, flinching from the details of death. 'Archie said it was murder.'

'That's what MacPherson's saying, but I don't think so. I questioned them, with the constable. They were just fooling about at wrestling, with drink in them. You know what the Irishmen are like.'

Invernevis couldn't determine if it was a rebuke, but Doctor MacNiven had turned away to swing his bag up on to his gig.

'But what killed him, if it wasn't murder?'

'His weak heart, of course.'

'Weak heart?' He was looking around for something to lean on. 'No one told me,' Invernevis moaned.

'It was *his* business,' Doctor MacNiven said, with a hint of a rebuke. 'I wouldn't go in there. Best go and break the news to your mother before it gets to her another way.'

But Invernevis detained him by gripping the spokes of the big back wheel.

'I never understood him.'

'Oh I understood what he was after, all right, but it

was impossible,' the doctor said factually. 'Anyway, I have to go. Sick people are waiting for me up in the village.'

Then Invernevis had to walk back up the avenue to rouse the two women. The tragedy had already been carried upstairs with the morning tea, and a white-faced Mary Rose met him in the hall, gripping his sleeve for confirmation, and when he nodded, putting her hands to her face. He put his arm round her shaking shoulders and steered her to the library fire where a new log sparked. Taking the opposite chair, he repeated the sparse details of the death.

'I never knew he had a weak heart,' Invernevis kept repeating, shaking his head incredulously.

'And these awful dreams I've been having: I thought it was going to be Jamie,' she moaned, still covering her face with her hands.

Her husband didn't ask for clarification. He was at the brandy decanter, preparing to go up to Mama. He swallowed the acrid stuff, grimaced and set his shoulders straight. 'Death is necessary to nature, so don't cry over it. At least, *real* men don't,' his father had warned him, and to prove the point, had taken Alexander and Niall up the back stairs to see the body of their old nanny who had passed away of a stroke in her sleep. Sheeted in white, she was stretched on the bare springs of the iron bed under the low skylight, waiting for cheap planks from the estate sawmill to encase her and convey her to the village cemetery because it was too expensive to ship her home to her beloved Barra. Because he was so small and because of the poor light, Niall hadn't been able to see her face, but the splayed feet were inches from his face. In proof of manhood, and to show that death was final, their father had made them touch the feet.

Alexander had gone forward first, and had touched without emotion. But Niall recoiled because of the horned translucent corns he had seen her attacking with an open razor. He had to be pushed forward, his hand held against the sole by his father. He had cried hysterically at the cold yellow skin, and Alexander had danced round the bed, yelling: 'Coward! Coward!' while their father stood smiling, hand on the lintel, leaning to strike a match on iron for his cigarette.

Mama was sitting up in the bedside chair in her dressing gown, Mrs Livingstone keeping her company.

'It *had* to happen,' she said as her remaining son stooped to kiss her cold wrinkled forehead. 'He was your father's son and that was that. But he was a beautiful child, wasn't he, Mrs Livingstone? Well I hope Carlotta's satisfied,' she said, crying again.

'You'd better bring her some brandy,' her son ordered the cook.

Mama held Mrs Livingstone's arm. 'No. It never did me much good when your father died, and it won't help now. I tried to pull myself together after Laura, and I'm going to keep on trying because with only one left you can't tempt fate. And the baby's depending on me. But my God, what a lovely little boy he was,' she moaned, her shoulders sagging under so many sorrows.

Invernevis left his mother with Mrs Livingstone and went back down to the library, to sit over more brandy. How disgusting, MacPherson and his daughter fighting over Alexander's body, using it to the last as a pawn, as if they hadn't done enough damage already. If only he had known about the weak heart. He had forced a doomed man to disinherit himself, had fought a man who had refused to defend himself. It was the final perverted legacy of his father's, far worse than the rest because it was guaranteed to cause a futile and fatal division between brothers.

With a pick bursting the surface of the cemetery, Invernevis sat drinking in the library, hearing the Jubilee clock dolefully dismiss the hours. Mary Rose and the rest of the house left him to his grief, appreciating that drink was the only anaesthetic. A coffin came off the late train, to be taken, swaddled in sacking, on the Home Farm gig, grim-faced MacPherson himself at the reins, the footman on the back, straddling the slewing wood. When the decanter was empty, and close objects required a lamp for clarification, Invernevis decided to make another attempt to see Alexander's widow. It was not only for condolence. He was quite drunk, and her refusal to see anyone that morning rankled as a personal insult, for she must have known that he would come.

This time he took Inverness cape and cromach, his bitterness against her increasing with every step down the avenue. He stopped on Wade's Bridge, resting his lantern on the parapet to look over into the Yellow Pool, where Laura had waded, wrestling with life before war and death divided them. But the water was cold and grey, quickening and discolouring through rain from the corries above, the camouflage of spawning.

He walked over unsettled soil to the new house by the river, his fist raised to newly varnished wood, then hesitating as he drew a deep breath, the walk having sobered him slightly. Suppose she had won her battle for the body? No, he couldn't bear to.

But when she opened the door, he knew it was not there.

'It was kind of you to come,' she said, leading him into the sitting-room. She set the lamp down on a scarred table and prodded the log with iron.

'It's so very tragic,' he began, his anger modified by her welcome, and the simple dignity of her features in the climbing flame.

'If it hadn't been last night, it would have been another night. And I thought it was going to be different when we got in here.'

While the log let the shadows grow again, he sat on drinking his brother's whisky.

'I never understood him. I thought he was just out for a good time.'

She raised her head in surprise. 'Oh, there was nothing complicated about Sandy. He wasn't really interested in a good time.'

'Then why desert his own house?' he asked bitterly.

'But I thought you understood. It was the land that he loved. He used to say: what's the point in looking out over all that land if you can't work it yourself? That's why he came to the Home Farm in the first place. Up at the big house he was expected to dress and talk properly, not get his hands dirty, but he didn't want it that way: he wanted to feel he belonged to the land, to be able to *touch* it. And your father encouraged him by leaving him all that money, because your father wasn't happy up at the big house, after the freedom he'd had in India. That's why he went drinking and shooting with the folks in the village, the folks that understood him, or *said* they did, like my own father.'

'You sound as though you approved,' he said, his anger rising.

'I understood, but I didn't approve. I kept telling Sandy that it wasn't that simple.' She leaned forward into firelight. 'Look at it this way. I'm different from the tinkers, and you're different from me. That's the way it is, the way it'll always be, the way it should be. Your father might have got drunk with his tenants, but he always went back across the river, to the big house, because he knew that that was where he belonged, and they respected him for it. But Sandy made the mistake of staying on this side of the river all the time, of mixing with them as if he was one of them. That's why I didn't want to marry him, for *his* sake, even though I was expecting to him, but he kept on and on. And one night up at the standing stones he ate a fist of earth to prove to me how much he loved the place and wanted to work it with his own hands. I'm not saying that he didn't love the place, only that he couldn't love it, the way he wanted to, with his hands, because he didn't belong in the fields. His family might have owned them, but he didn't belong in them. I wanted him to go home, make it up with his own family, marry someone from his own class, but he wouldn't listen.'

'So he was doomed from the start,' Invernevis said, frightened.

'You could put it like that. Putting on ploughman's clothes doesn't make you a ploughman, and drinking in the Arms doesn't make you a local. Sandy's trouble was that he was too innocent and trusting. He thought it was so easy to cross the river, to take off his breeding as though it was a jacket. I never told him, but my father said that the loonies in the hay loft could do better with the plough.

'Your brother caused a lot of trouble for himself and others by crossing to the Home Farm. It set my eldest brother Archie against my father because he thought my father preferred Sandy, and was going to arrange for him to get the lease of the farm. And it caused me a lot of trouble, because there wouldn't have been such trouble if I'd married a local. But you see, Sandy got encouragement from my father, because my father saw him as a good catch, for himself as well as me.'

Watching her face in firelight as he listened, Invernevis was beginning to realise how much he had misjudged her, but there were still some details he was puzzled about.

'Did you know that he had a weak heart, and shouldn't have been doing heavy work?'

Her head turned. 'He never told us that. He was always boasting he could hold his own, in the fields or in a fight.'

'But he didn't want to go to the war, though he was in the volunteer company with my father.'

'He wanted to, all right, but thought you would think he was trying to do your eye out. It would have been better for himself had he gone, and not come back.'

'Did you know he disinherited himself?' he had to ask.

'Yes, and I was thankful, because he wouldn't have been any good for this place. And how could I have fitted in? No, I was grateful to God when you came home safe from the war. This house was his idea, not mine: I would have preferred one in the village, but he didn't want to lose touch with you. That was why I was so sorry and ashamed about what happened at the christening. But he was too proud to go and apologise.'

'He can go beside our father,' he said hoarsely.

She shook her head. 'No. On the night we were married he made me promise that if anything happened, he would be put into the village cemetery, where he felt he belonged. He was wrong, but I did promise.'

'And you're not to worry about money.'

She laughed bitterly. 'Oh there's a lot left because my father took charge of it.'

Then the little girl started crying in another room, and she went to comfort it. Invernevis was preparing to take his leave when her father came in. He stood in the doorway, towering, terrible in his black rage, the gold watch-chain running like fire across his waistcoat.

'You bloody nincompoop. Didn't I warn you the night of the moor fire that something like this would happen, unless you closed down the quarry? You sat on your arse by the fire in your big house because you couldn't bear to lose the rent, otherwise your fancy bloody wife would have to go short of dresses. Instead of behaving like the man your father was, you had to get the ghillie's daughter away to Edinburgh and give her money for what you were after. And because the footman saw you up to your dirty bloody tricks, you threw him out without a penny.' His finger was wagging. 'Well, I warn you; everywhere you turn, from now on, you're going to find me, in your way. I've a bloody good mind to —'

But his daughter came behind him, to drag down his fist.

'In God's name, haven't you done enough damage? And where is his body? He's my husband, not your son.'

Invernevis's shaky hand shaved him the next morning, and he dressed in the same garb he had worn for Laura's funeral, kilt, dark jacket and waistcoat, black ribbon dangling from his balmoral. He walked down the avenue, cromach giving security to his game leg and a body weakened by alcohol and grief. The autumn morning was grey and silent, without the usual flurry of pigeons overhead at the footsteps of man. Already the trees were being stripped, shrivelled leaves crunching under his brogues. The incision of his own and Laura's initials was green on a trunk twisting its branches skyward. On the August afternoon before South Africa, when he had walked that avenue with his bare-footed sister, the beating of his heart had been part of the landscape, like the wood pigeon's throbbing breast glimpsed between foliage, a bluebell swinging. Now it was as if his spirit had leaked away among the treacherous exposed stones, as if he was being supported on either side by two ghosts, girl and boy.

Instead of climbing to the Home Farm, he waited by the gate, among the crofters who had escorted Alexander home from the Arms nightly, sharing their tongue as he shared his whisky. They looked sympathetically at the laird, and he stood, leaning on his cromach, looking at his brogues until the cart bearing the coffin began its difficult descent, steadied on either side by the two loonies from the hay loft, laughing as they scrambled over shining wood and hauled at brass.

There was no piper as there had been for Laura, only a silent procession wending towards the village, being augmented at every house, MacPherson in a new bowler and mirrored boots walking behind the cart, Invernevis among the crofters. By the time it reached the railway bridge it was the biggest funeral that the village had ever seen, far bigger than his father's, joined now by gigs and traps from outlying farms, jamming the narrow track up to the hillside cemetery. MacPherson stood on a knoll, taking the cord cards from his waistcoat pocket, splaying them in his grained fist, the head one to the brother, not letting their eyes meet as he handed it down, but taking the one at the foot himself. The others went to local worthies, drinking companions of the dead man, and the two loonies were to share one cord, a decision that brought gasps of surprise and angry audible Gaelic.

Silhouetted against the mountain, the wind flicking his gilded Missal, Father Macdonald made the sign, and the red cords lowered, earth ringing on the brass plate:

ALEXANDER MACDONALD OF INVERNEVIS
1877 - 1905
R.I.P.

Only Invernevis and the two loonies were holding the cords when the coffin was at rest, the three refusing to let go, the loonies laughing and tugging at the tassel, MacPherson slapping down their unco-ordinated hands, then having to jerk the cord from the stiff fingers of the brother straddling the *cruive* in which the line ran out, without hope of extrication.

He refused numerous lifts and walked home, down the steep brae, past the big Welsh slates of the disused iron furnace glittering with frost, its pyre of spent charcoal one source of funds for his father's fornications. Opposite was the Macdonald croft, tenanted by another family now, where the big house gig with himself aboard had picked up Maggie's brother, the piper Donald, on their way to war six years before. How long ago it all seemed. How weary of death he was.

The circular scar of the granite quarry was coming into view, looming beyond the wooded chapel where Laura lay under suspended stone. The solution had come too late, like so many things in his life. To the left the river, hoarse with frost; *Linne Cruibeag*, the Summer House Pool where a ghost in lilac stepped zig-zagging stones; *Poll Criadha*, the Clay Pool where Laura had seen water-ouzels walking on the bottom and cried for them to be saved; *Linne na Craoibh Daraich*, the Oak Tree Pool from which his father had hauled the record fish; *Casan Dubh*, the Black Gorge through which his uncle had gone to the other side; *Poll Dubh* , the Black Pool, his dead brother's house on the bank; and, under the arched stone of Wade's Bridge where he leaned, *Linne Bhuidhe*, the Yellow Pool, where a girl's ghost raised living silver to a brighter sky.

Once between the white pillars his brogues slowed, and not only because of the fatigue of his game leg. What was there to hurry home to, but a door locked against him, and a silence like death itself? He passed the tree with his own and Laura's initials within the crude shield, or was it a heart? Frost had made it a glistening wound.

Approaching the blind bend, he stopped, having to lean on his cromach, certain that he was seeing an apparition, for Mary Rose was coming round it, waving in greeting, her other hand hugging the fur stole, the fox's head with the glass eyes swinging, her hair welcome flames in the winter landscape.

'I wanted to show you I'm not afraid of the bend any more,' she said, hugging him. 'It wasn't a warning to me, but to poor Alexander. Now you *must* allow me to go down and see his wife later. I'll walk - by myself.'

They linked arms, her cold cheek close to his, her voice hoarse with excitement as she told him: 'Guess what? I had a letter. Jamie wants to come.' She gripped his arm and pulled him closer to a subtle scent.

'I think we'd better try for a little boy, don't you?'

Standing at the scullery window, waiting for water from the big brass tap, Maggie saw the Master and his lady coming arm-in-arm down the avenue. She stood staring for several seconds, torn between two emotions, tears triumphing. Her sobbing brought Mrs Livingstone shuffling through to lean and stare.

'That tap's frozen. Let's go back into the kitchen,' she advised. She eased her swollen legs under the big table and waited for Maggie to tilt the little brown pot, all the time watching her assistant's face.

'Now girl, a word of advice from an old hand. You respect them and serve them as best you can, but that's as far as you go. You put food into their bellies, but you take good care that they don't put anything into yours because they're only human. If they get the chance they'll take it, because how else have they held on to what they've got? Like father, like son. I wish I had a sovereign for every maid I had crying in here, and the damage done. Be grateful it hasn't happened to you, because they only marry their own kind. Oh yes, there was Master Alexander, but look where it's got him. You're old enough now for me to be telling you such things, and that's what your mother would have wanted. I hear the footman's leaving the Home Farm, going to work at the Arms, so you'll have to watch out, because where there's drink there's mischief. I've got something to show you.' She went to a cupboard and with a flourish lifted down a brown paper bag, tilting the contents on to the big white table, the sovereigns clattering and rolling. 'Do you know how I got these back? Mad Betsy brought them to the back door this morning. Apparently the girl hid them in the byre. Well

Betsy gave her an awful thrashing and came all the way up here with them herself because she said the old laird never passed her in the village without giving her a sovereign, and that it was a sin to steal from the big house. Which shows you there's still some good left in the world.

'Anyway, girl, my feet won't see me through another year, so I'll go in the early summer. You're young and you've got a lot to learn, but I'm going to put in a good word for you. But these two through there can't live on love, so you'd better see what's in the larder for tonight. That's what we're here for.'

END OF THIS CHRONICLE

LEE COUNTY LIBRARY
107 HAWKINS AVE.
SANFORD, N. C. 27330

Macintyre
The blind bend

A

LEE COUNTY LIBRARY
107 HAWKINS AVE.
SANFORD, N. C. 27330